1. Mrs. Alex. Bruce, died 1885, aged 94. 2. Andrew Grey, died 1874, aged 91. 3. Peter Murray, died 1873, aged 97. 4. Mrs. Alex. MacKay, age 93. 5. Nelson B. Edward, age 94. 6. Mrs. David Ross, died 1885, aged 92. 7. Mrs. A. MacKay, age 94. 8. John Carroll, died 1855, aged 102. 9. John Gilchrist, died 1871, aged 105. 10. John McLean, died 1889, aged 102. 11. Mrs. Hacket Macdonald, age 94. 12. Mrs. John McPherson, died 1898, aged 93. 13. Wm. Murray, died 1894, aged 94. 14. Roderick Ross, died 1890, aged 92. 15. Mrs. Hugh Gordon, age 95. 16. Mrs. Alex. Murray, died 1897, aged 95. 17. John McIntosh, died 1891, aged 92. 18. Robt. McIntosh, died 1891, aged 92.

PIONEER LIFE IN ZORRA

BY

REV. W. A. MacKAY, B.A., D.D.

WITH INTRODUCTION BY

HON. G. W. ROSS, LL.D., M.P.P.

Minister of Education for Ontario

"The faithful delineation of human feelings, in all their strength and weakness, will serve as a mirror to every mind capable of self-examination."
—CARLYLE

WITH PORTRAITS AND ILLUSTRATIONS

TORONTO
WILLIAM BRIGGS
1899

Entered according to Act of the Parliament of Canada, in the year one thousand eight hundred and ninety-nine, by WILLIAM BRIGGS, at the Department of Agriculture.

To My Mother

ONE OF THE EARLY ZORRA PIONEERS,

WHO HAS GIVEN FIVE SONS TO THE CHRISTIAN MINISTRY;
AND WHO NOW,
IN THE EIGHTY-SIXTH YEAR OF HER AGE,
IS ENJOYING
THE CALM EVENING OF A BEAUTIFUL CHRISTIAN LIFE,
THIS BOOK IS AFFECTIONATELY INSCRIBED

BY THE AUTHOR

CONTENTS

Chapter		Page
	Introduction	7
I.	Zorra in the Thirties	21
II.	The Home Life of the Pioneer	37
III.	The Pioneer and the Sabbath	52
IV.	Gangin' tae the Kirk	64
V.	The Men's Day	78
VI.	An Old Communion Sabbath	101
VII.	The Old Communion Sabbath—" Doing the Word "	114
VIII.	The Catechising	127
IX.	Pioneer Politics	140
X.	Zorra and the Rebellion of '37	154
XI.	Logging Bees and Dancing Sprees	166
XII.	Pioneer Songs	183
XIII.	A Funeral Among the Pioneers	198
XIV.	Ghosts, Witches, and Goblins	211
XV.	Pioneer Schools and Schoolmasters	235

CONTENTS

Chapter		Page
XVI.	Rev. Donald Mackenzie, the Pioneer Preacher of Zorra	254
XVII.	Rev. Lachlan McPherson of Williams	272
XVIII.	John Ross of Brucefield	284
XIX.	Rev. Daniel Allan of North Easthope	308
XX.	Rev. John Fraser, M.A., of Thamesford	325
XXI.	Rev. William Meldrum of Harrington	340
XXII.	Rev. Daniel Gordon	352
XXIII.	Pioneer Methodism in Zorra	370
XXIV.	Zorra's Famous Missionary	384
XXV.	What Shall the Harvest Be?	398

LIST OF
PORTRAITS AND ILLUSTRATIONS

	PAGE
Zorra Pioneers—	
Honor List (Ages from 90 to 105)	*Frontispiece*
Mrs. Marion MacKay (Age 86)	*Dedication*
Exterior View of a Pioneer's House	21
Interior View of a Pioneer's House	32
Pioneers, (Ages from 82 to 91)	37
Pioneers, (Ages from 80 to 84)	52
Pioneers, (Ages from 77 to 89)	64
Zorra's Old Log Church	78
Pioneers, (Ages from 76 to 79)	101
Pioneers, (Ages from 54 to 78)	114
Zorra's Tug of War Team	166
Pioneers, (Ages from 65 to 76)	198
Pioneer Preachers—	
Rev. Donald Mackenzie of Zorra	254
Rev. Lachlan McPherson of Williams	272
Rev. John Ross of Brucefield	284
Rev. Daniel Allan of North Easthope	308
Rev. John Fraser, M.A., of Thamesford	325
Rev. William Meldrum of Harrington	340
Rev. Daniel Gordon and Mrs. Gordon of Harrington	352
Rev. G. L. Mackay, D.D. (Zorra's Famous Missionary)	384

INTRODUCTION

To the early settlers of Western Canada a volume on pioneer life requires no introduction. We paint in glowing language the courage of the soldier who made long marches and endured hardships to maintain the honor of his country, or to advance her interests either for conquest or defence; and yet we forget that similar qualities were exercised, even under less favorable circumstances, by the pioneers who entered the forests of Ontario within the present century. The soldier had the stimulus of his companions, the flaunting of flags, the beating of drums, the example of his officers, and all that sentiment could do to urge him forward even at the peril of his life. The pioneer had no such stimulus. He often went single-handed into the deep forest; he had to separate himself from friends and neighbors, to endure perils by night and by day, to live on the scantiest fare and in the most depressing isolation; and yet in spite of all these disadvantages he never relaxed in his determination to make himself self-sustaining, or even more, if a kindly Providence would only so favor him.

The early settler was no knight-errant, no speculator in margins, no waiter upon Providence, but, as a rule, a man of indomitable energy, courage, physical endurance, and with confidence that seed-time and harvest would in due time bring him reasonable prosperity. No better stuff stood beside Nelson on board the *Victory*. No better stuff climbed the heights of Alma, or charged the dervishes at Khartoum.

The Ontario pioneers (and I am speaking now particularly of those who settled the western counties) left the old home as a matter of choice, except perhaps a few who might have been evicted because their landlords wanted the paddocks they occupied for other purposes. The great majority of them, however, felt that in the land of their fathers their sphere was circumscribed, and if their position was to be improved at all, and provision made for their families, they must seek homes abroad. This was particularly the case with the settlers from Scotland. True, they may not have expected the hardships they subsequently endured; but what were hardships to them so long as they had a free home, their families around them, and the prospect of independence within their reach? In the old land they were tenants; in the land of their adoption they were landlords—owners in fee simple of the soil they tilled. It was theirs to improve; it was theirs to bequeath to their children after them; and this one fact was a silver lining to the darkest cloud that hung over them.

Notwithstanding this, it is almost impossible to over-estimate the hardships endured by the early pioneers. There is a great deal of romance cast around the log house of the settler, with its open, glowing fire-place, generous hospitality, and its unsophisticated simplicity of manners. The novelist likes to speak of the hollyhocks that nodded lazily beneath the window, as if to remind one that hope still blossomed within; of the wild rose or honeysuckle that climbed over the unhewn walls, as if to show the sympathy of nature with the plainness of the architecture. That is the romantic view of the pioneer's first home. But to those who know some of the realities of pioneer life, the log house too often furnished but scant shelter from the pitiless rains of autumn or the tempests of winter. Its hospitality was frequently taxed far beyond the comforts of its owner, and its open fire-place was too often insufficient for the fullest enjoyment of life, either by night or by day.

Sixty years ago a thousand or more such homes could have been seen amid the forests of the west. How came it about that the same district is now dotted with homes—one might almost call them mansions, so beautiful are they in design and so attractive in appearance? How came it about that the forest path over which the settler carried supplies to his family on his back, is now an easy highway for the traveller and pleasure-seeker? How came it

INTRODUCTION

about that the ploughshare and the reaping machine now move freely where once stood the giants of the forest? How came it about that happy villages occupy the camping ground of the Indian? Is it not because the pioneer stretched forth his strong arms against the natural obstacles of those early times, and with a stout heart resolved to bring them under the influence of intelligence and civilization? And can it be possible that we, who see the changes wrought at such tremendous cost of energy and toil, can forget the sturdy qualities of those by whom these changes were brought about?

It is said that the Pilgrim Fathers of New England were the sifted wheat of the early colonists, and that to them the United States owes the vigor of its national character. In many senses of the term the pioneers of Ontario were chosen men—sifted wheat. As a rule, they were men with a fair education; but even where this was denied them, they had a high sense of the value of education as a preparation for the duties of life. Accordingly, we find that wherever there was a settlement, were it ever so small, there was a school house; and although the school master of those days would not rate very high, judged by the standards of modern education, he was honored because of his calling and the responsibilities of his office. Being obliged to accept the hospitality of his patrons in lieu of the full wages to which he was entitled, he had the opportunity of carrying the torch of learning, flickering though its light may have been, from house to house, and no doubt often stimulated the pioneer to a greater interest in the education of his children. Though books were few in number they were eagerly read, and when a newspaper found its way, by a weekly mail, to the homes of those who could afford such a luxury, the work of of the school master was still further strengthened and the interest of the pioneer quickened. As years went by, some member of the family would venture out into the world to seek a professional career. His example became the object of admiration far and near, and so the native ambition, sometimes of many fathers, but more frequently of the mothers, was aroused to see that the honor of the family was similarly maintained. In many a home luxurious ease and ordinary comforts were abandoned that the nascent genius of some embryonic Mansfield, or Candlish, or Simpson, might be developed.

The religious character of the pioneer was also an important factor in strengthening his arm as he grappled with the difficulties of early settlement. He had not left his own land because he mistrusted Providence, but because he believed Providence was specially directing him as to his future course. The God that watched over him and his fathers in the land of his birth, he believed was present in the forests of Canada ; and so with an unbounded faith he entered upon his daily labors. Until he was able to erect a church for public worship, he placed his humble dwelling at the disposal of his neighbors, and by his daily life and his devotion showed that he believed religion had its obligations as well as its comforts.

In maintaining his religious life, the pioneer

was greatly aided (and I only speak of the Presbyterians) by the character of the early Presbyterian missionaries. With nearly all the ministers mentioned in this volume I was personally acquainted. I have heard them preach, sometimes in the forest, where parallel ranges of logs were the only pews, and the overshadowing trees the only shelter from the sun; sometimes in a barn, when no church was available; sometimes in a log church as primitive as the log house of the pioneer. I have heard some of them conduct an English service and others a Gaelic service. It is but natural, having regard to the emotional character of one's early life, that I should recall with more than ordinary enthusiasm the personality of the men and the vigor of their discourses. Even making due allowance for this, I think I am safe in saying that some of them were endowed with apostolic fervor, and with more than the usual gifts of eloquence. I fancy I can now hear the Rev. John Ross, in his peculiar penetrating voice, depict the future terrors of the unregenerate, till the blood was chilled with horror; and then in tones soft and soothing as a zephyr plead for the acceptance of the story of the cross. To hear him was to feel that he had lived near the Master, and that no life was worth living unless permeated with a sense of the great hereafter.

The Rev. Donald Mackenzie, of Zorra, was one whose personality I can also recall most vividly. I remember distinctly a sermon preached by him—it must have been in the early fifties—from that sublime passage in Isaiah: "They that wait upon the Lord shall renew their strength," etc., and I think I can still hear the tumultuous eloquence with which he set forth the glory of that strength and the overwhelming power it gave to those who possessed it. Mr. Mackenzie's delivery had one peculiarity. While in his exordium he was argumentative—speaking quietly and apparently hesitatingly—as he proceeded he gained strength as a river does in the multitude of waters that are poured into it. Step by step the volume became stronger as he approached the peroration—a peroration that was sometimes almost terrific in its earnestness and elocutionary force. When he reached the climax he suddenly ceased, as a Roman candle seems to explode when it has reached its maximum height, and then, in the quietest tones, as if exhausted nature could do no more, he uttered a short prayer.

The Rev. Lachlan McPherson was for many years minister of the congregation at which my father and family worshipped. He received the greater part of his education in Canada, and was, I think, licensed to preach by a Canadian Presbytery. Mr. McPherson was usually of a very calm temperament. He wore a sadly sobered look, and had the expression of one who gave himself much to meditation of a very solemn character. His disposition was by no means morose, however, for he enjoyed a joke and could tell a good story; but his manner was ordinarily reserved and serious. He was, moreover, a good Gaelic scholar, and as Gaelic was his mother-tongue, he had special aptitude as a preacher in the Gaelic language. His delivery was often characterized by those undulating cadences peculiar to the Gaelic and Welsh languages, and when he fell into this rapturous oratory he was very impressive. He was, however, in many respects more of a theologian than a pastor, and had a special affection for the doctrines of John Calvin and his disciples. Predestination and the formulæ of the Shorter Catechism were frequently his theme, and, as a consequence, he touched the hearts of his people less than he otherwise might. Nevertheless his sermons were stimulating and did much to keep alive the intellectual life of the people whom he served.

Of the others mentioned in this volume I need not speak in detail, though all partook more or less of the character of the men to whom I have already referred. Several of them served as superintendents of public schools as well as ministers of the gospel. All of them commanded the deepest respect of those to whom they ministered, and left on the generation they served the impress of their own religious constancy and earnestness. But they, too, like the pioneers among whom they labored, endured hardships, travelling on foot through the deep forests, and accepting, without a murmur, the scanty comforts of the pioneer's home. Their labors may not be recorded in large biographies, as is the work of such men as Guthrie and Chalmers and Wesley and Spurgeon; but their work is recorded in the lives they have comforted, the churches they have founded, and the example they gave to the community in which they lived. Well will it be for the religious character of future generations if they have many disciples.

In view, therefore, of the character of the pioneers whose early lives Dr. MacKay has here so vividly depicted, and particularly in view of the character of the missionary pioneers whose work like a golden thread runs throughout the narrative, I would commend this book to the people of Canada.

"Prominence is not necessary to true greatness." The pioneer had no prominence—he had, nevertheless, the elements of true greatness. The qualities which enabled him to establish a home for himself and his family, in the face of so many difficulties, are the qualities by which nations are built, good government established, and prosperity and peace made possible. To follow in his footsteps is a guarantee that Canada will grow in influence and power as one generation follows another.

GEO. W. ROSS.

TORONTO, *August 2nd, 1899.*

EXTERIOR VIEW OF A PIONEER'S HOUSE

PIONEER LIFE IN ZORRA

CHAPTER I

ZORRA IN THE THIRTIES

" Oft did the harvest to their sickle yield,
  Their furrow oft the stubborn glebe has broke;
How jocund did they drive their teams a-field!
  How bowed the woods beneath their sturdy
    stroke!" —GRAY.

THE traveller going through Oxford to-day and viewing its large towns, its busy factories, its elegant churches, its commodious schoolhouses, its comfortable homes, and its fertile fields, finds it hard to realize that within the memory of some of us the whole district was an unbroken forest, where the wild Indian roved and the bear and wolf prowled. This wonderful change speaks to us of difficulties overcome, of trials patiently endured, of earnest purpose and indomitable perseverance. The men and women who were chiefly instrumental in bringing about the change have strong claims upon their descendants, and the memory of their holy faith and heroic deeds ought not to be allowed lightly to perish. The following pen pictures, though sketched with a feeble hand, are conceived with a loving heart; and they are placed as a few sprigs of heather upon the graves of ancestors who deserve our highest gratitude.

Away back in the thirties Zorra was settled by a race of sturdy Highlanders from the north of Scotland, chiefly from Sutherlandshire. As early, indeed, as 1820, two brothers, Angus and William MacKay, settled in the district—some of their descendants are still living there in comfort. After braving the hardships of the forest for nine years, Angus MacKay returned to Scotland, but in the following year returned, bringing with him his aged mother and a shipload of Sutherlanders.

These people left their native land, not as a matter of choice, but from necessity forced upon them by the covetousness of Highland landlords. Aristocratic proprietors formed the plan of driving away the peasantry in order to turn their little farms into sheep pastures and sporting grounds. The result was that men who never flinched in battle for the defence of their country—the descendants of those who drew their swords at Bannockburn, Sheriffmuir and Killicrankie—the children and nearest relations of those who had sustained the honor of the British name in many a bloody field—the heroes of Egypt, Corunna, Toulouse, Salamanca, and Waterloo—the men of whom General Havelock exclaimed at the close of one of the most fiercely-fought battles of modern times, "Well done, brave Highlanders!"—these noble men, who deserved so well of their country, were robbed and trampled upon; and, as they would not be enslaved, they were compelled to seek an asylum across the Atlantic.

With sad hearts and tearful eyes they bade farewell to their heath-clad hills, and the homes they loved so dearly, faced an ocean voyage of twelve weeks in an old emigrant ship, endured all the hardships of a two weeks' journey up the St. Lawrence in open boats towed by oxen, penetrated the unbroken fastnesses of the forest; and, in spite of bears, wolves, and mosquitos, laid the foundation of the prosperity we see on every side of us to-day.

The question has been sometimes sneeringly asked : "Why should our fathers have been so, intensely attached to their native soil?" That attachment had piety as well as patriotism in it. The houses from which our pioneer fathers and mothers were driven were not only the homes which they and their forefathers had occupied from time immemorial, but they were spots hallowed by the most sacred associations —spots not a few in which individuals had in their hearts "built a pillar and anointed a stone," and worshipped their God and the God of their fathers. A forcible separation from such homes was felt as none but members of the household of faith can feel.

But enough said on a dark subject. The memory of these men and women ought to be revered by their descendants. We owe them a great deal—our pleasant surroundings, the blood that flows in our veins, our energy and solidity of character, and, in as far as spiritual things can be inherited, the hope that cheers in life and sustains in death.

That the Highlanders of to-day have lost none of the " martial fires that thrilled their sires," the Dargai Heights abundantly testify; but, alas! the Gordon Highlanders can no longer be recruited from the land of their forefathers. A story is told that, after a large number of the Highland tenantry had been evicted and their places filled with sheep, a recruiting officer happened to come into the neighborhood, but the only response received by him to his request for volunteers for the army was, " Baa, baa," thus indicating that as sheep had been substituted for men, the recruiting officer might look to the sheep for his soldiers.

"A bold peasantry, their country's pride,
When once destroyed can never be supplied."

When these expatriated men and women came to Zorra there were no roads—only a blazed path here and there to guide the traveller. Such a path led in a "bee line" from Woodstock to where Embro is now situated. A large part of the county was at that time swamp, and in the spring and fall of the year the swamps would be full of water. The waters contained myriads of frogs, which kept up an incessant croaking all day and night.

There is a story told of a famous "frog-scare." In the fall of 183– several families settled in the south and eastern part of the township. Very early one morning, next spring, the whole district was suddenly awakened by unearthly sounds on every side. The terrified ones quickly got out of bed and made what preparations they could to meet the foe. Some thought the dreaded Indians were upon them, others vowed that the voices were those of witches or devils flying through the air. Windows were fastened, doors bolted, and prayers offered. For a couple of hours before dawn the greatest panic prevailed.

With the first grey streaks in the east, a party of men armed with axes, clubs, and such other weapons as were available, climbed the hill to the eastward to see if the Indians were indeed coming; but seeing no enemy, they soon returned to allay the fears of their friends. It was not long before some of the older inhabitants explained to the people that the sounds proceeded from the thousands of frogs which, frozen in during the winter, and suddenly let loose by the advent of spring, were expressing their joy in very hearty though very unmusical notes.

The dismal howling of the wolves, together with the "mony eldritch screeches" of the frogs outside, and the crickets inside the houses, were a torment to the new settlers till their ears got accustomed to the disagreeable sounds. The woods were full of wild beasts, such as the deer, bear, wolf, fox, hedge-hog, wild-cat and squirrel, also many snakes and other reptiles. Many stories are told of bears appropriating, Rob Roy-like, the lamb, the calf, or the pig of the settler. Such birds as the crow, hawk, robin, woodpecker and bluejay made the forest vocal with their notes in spring.

Besides the really dangerous bear and wolf, there was another source of fear, as great or even greater. These were the ghosts, the existence of which was most certainly believed in by these Scotch settlers. Many a time have the chills run up and down my back as I have listened to the weird, uncanny tales told at the "ingleside" by the light of the old back-log, and evidently believed by the narrator as well as his hearers, who gathered closer to the fire and to one another after each blood-curdling story was told.

Mr. L——, one of these pioneers, had a new blue denim pair of trousers, and one day, after being in Woodstock and partaking of a " wee drappie," he returned home at night. The night was wet, and every time one leg passed the other while walking, the trousers, in rubbing, gave forth a peculiar squeaking noise. It was a ghost, sure! Mr. L—— ran for life in the direction of the nearest house, but the ghost ran too, and kept up the terrifying sounds till, over bogs, through swamps and brushwood, out of breath, the fleet-footed Highlandman at last found safety in the nearest shanty.

On another occasion, this same pioneer returned from the county town in a wretched plight. He had imbibed freely during the day, and coming home at night lost his way. It was in the spring-time, and the swamps and streams were full of water. In his wanderings he crossed and re-crossed some of the streams several times, until he arrived at home scarcely recognizable. "O my poor man," exclaimed his wife on seeing him, "where have you been?"

"Och, woman," replied the drouthy and drenched Hielanman, "she's cam' from Egypt, and she pe crossing the Red Sea of'en, of'en."

When some unfortunate went astray in the woods and did not return in the evening, his friends would commence hallooing or blowing a horn, neighbors would take up the call, and in a short time the whole country round would be hallooing or blowing horns. These sounds could be heard a great distance, and never failed to bring the wanderer back.

It is related of one of the settlers that, having

gone astray several times, his friends advised him to procure and use a compass. He did so; but the next time he went from home he lost his way as usual.

"Why did you not steer by the compass?" said a friend to him afterwards. "Because," was the prompt reply, "I could not get the gude-for-naethin' thing to point right."

These settlers lost no time whimpering over the cruelties of the past or the hardships of the present; but, with brave hearts and stout arms, they at once went to work, and from dawn till dark the forests resounded with the strokes of the axe, and the crashing of the falling trees.

Soon little clearances, like so many breathing spots, could be found scattered over the whole township; but nowhere could one clearance be seen from another. This rendered unusual the "flying visit" of to-day. The visitor was expected to remain two or three hours at least, and if the visit was cut short, the visitor would likely be asked, "Have you come for fire?" a query which requires a little explanation. The hearth fire, like that in some ancient temples, was not allowed to die out; and the last act of the "gude" man or his wife before retiring to rest was to cover the bright embers over with ashes, which, when raked off the next morning, disclosed the nucleus of a new fire. Occasionally, however, the fire would go out, and an aged pioneer mother relates how, on one such occasion, she had to travel nearly two miles by a path through the woods to the nearest neighbor for a kindling-brand. Such a visit was necessarily very brief, hence the popular taunt to a hurried visitor, "Have you come for fire?"

Every farmer had a bell on one of his cattle, so that when they wandered they could be more easily found. Old settlers often remark what great distances sound could be heard through the woods as compared with the present day, when the land is cleared. The stroke of an axe, it is said, could easily be heard a mile away, while a falling tree could be heard at a distance of three miles. Sheep were folded every night as a protection from wolves. Hearing the wolves howling, one would think they were very near, while perhaps they were a mile away. The wolf has an instinctive dread of fire, and if a man was benighted in the woods he was safe if he could only light a fire. A settler put a wager that tobacco smoking had saved his life, and that he could clearly prove it. The explanation was that, being one night lost in the woods, he lighted a fire, and thus saved himself from the wolves; "but," said he, "I would not have had the wherewithal to make that fire had I not been a smoker." This plea for the pipe is, to say the least, far-fetched, and cannot be used to-day, for the wolves are all gone.

The first cabins were 12 x 18 feet, perhaps 9 or 10 feet high, and, of course, built of logs. The roof was constructed of basswood logs, hollowed out, and laid alongside each other, with the hollow side up. Then other logs, similarly hollowed, were laid on these, with the hollow side down, and so as to overlap those underneath. Such a roof was waterproof, but not always proof against the driven snow. The inside of the cabin was divided into two rooms,

INTERIOR VIEW OF A PIONEER'S HOUSE

with a loft above. In this loft the children usually slept, and they mounted to it by means of pegs driven into the wall. The openings between the logs were filled with moss obtained from the trees, and the moss was daubed with soft clay. There was a big fireplace constructed of stones, wood and clay. Such families as could afford it had a couple of andirons in the fireplace, upon which the sticks were carefully laid; others used a couple of flat stones for this purpose. From the top of the chimney was suspended a chain with a hook at the lower end, capable of being raised or lowered, so as to adjust the pot to the fire. By and bye this chain gave place to a "crane,"—a movable bar of iron, attached by hinges to one side of the chimney, and placed horizontally over the fire. Upon this could be suspended two pots, one for the porridge and the other for the soup. The bread was baked at first in a kind of flat-bottomed pot, called the bake-kettle, which stood upon three legs about three inches in length. This pot had an iron lid with a broad rim and a loop handle to lift it by. The raised dough was put into this pot, which was placed upon the hearth and covered all over with coals. Soon the loaf issued, well raised and baked, sweet and wholesome as any to-day from the best of modern ovens. In the course of time the pot gave way to the "reflectors"; and they, in turn, to the black, cheerless modern stove. The table was bare, but always scrupulously clean. Two bedsteads, a few stools, some rude chairs and a big Sutherlandshire chest constituted the furniture. The chairs or stools—for there was not much difference—consisted of rough slabs of wood, in which holes were bored, and legs fitted in. There was usually one window, consisting of four panes of glass, 6 x 8 inches each. Most of the dishes were of pewter, and taken from the old country. The spoons were made of horn, and the knives and forks were horn-handled. The fare was "hamely" but wholesome, "porridge and milk" with oaten cake being the staple.

These pioneer homes were undoubtedly rude, and in many respects uncomfortable, but they

THE PATIENT HOUSEKEEPER

sheltered many a happy family, illustrating the sentiment of Scotland's poet:

> "What though on hamely fare we dine,
> Wear hoddin' grey and a' that,
> Gie fools their silks and knaves their wine;
> The man's the gowd for a' that."

The fire blazing in the big chimney at night cast many a weird figure in the corners of the shanty; and often, while gazing into the glowing coals, has my fancy conjured up Scottish castles, bloody battles, martyr scenes, and forms of beasts, birds, etc.

We usually had to burn "green wood." This was not so bad if the fire kept up well; but, alas for the poor shivering ones when the night was cold and the fire burned low! It seemed impossible to get it up again. A pioneer once remarked, in the presence of a neighbor, that he did not believe anything could ruffle his wife's temper. "I can tell you something that will, if you'll consent to try it," replied the neighbor. "Agreed," said the pioneer. "Just bring home and cut up a load of the crookedest green sticks you can find," proposed this disturber of the peace, "and if that don't worry her I don't know what will." The plan was complied with, but there was no change in things around the pioneer's home; in fact, everything seemed to be more agreeable than before. At last our friend said: "Wife, how do you like the wood I brought you last?" "First rate," said the wife. "These crooked sticks fit right round my kettle, and make it boil in half the time."

The good wife had learned the important lesson that things which "can't be cured must be endured." A difficulty which would have evoked bad temper in another, in her only developed patience, one of the noblest Christian graces. Let the housekeepers of to-day take a note!

ZORRA PIONEERS—(Ages from 82 to 91).

1. Capt. Wm. Fraser, age 84. 2. Mrs. Fraser, died 1876, aged 84. 3. John MacKay, died 1885, aged 91. 4. Mrs. Pet. MacKay, died 1891, aged 81. 5. Hugh Ross, died 1876, aged 82. 6. Mrs. Hugh Ross, died 1888, aged 85. 7. Mrs. Wm. MacKay, died 1894, aged 84. 8. Mrs. Geo. Ferguson, age 85. 9. Mr. Geo. MacKay (Miss'y), died 1885, aged 84. 10. Mrs. Geo. MacKay, died 1885, aged 84. 11. Mrs. Catharine MacKay, age 89. 12. John Macdonald and wife, died 1890, aged 87; wife died 1899, aged 86. 13. Mrs. James MacKay, age 82. 14. John MacKay, age 87. 15. James MacKay, age 83. 16. Mrs. A. Rose, age 83.

CHAPTER II

THE HOME LIFE OF THE PIONEER

"By the soft green light in the woody glade,
On the banks of moss, where thy children played;
By the gathering round the winter hearth,
When the twilight call'd unto household mirth;
By the quiet hour when hearts unite
In the parting prayer and the kind 'Good-night';
By the smiling eye and the loving tone,
Over thy life has the spell been thrown,
And bless that gift, it hath gentle might,
A guarding power and a guiding light!"

WE have endeavored to describe the humble cabin in the woods, with its rude furniture and meagre fare. But every log in that cabin was put in its place with a grateful heart to God; and however scant the furniture, there never lacked the family altar, around which parents assembled, morning and evening, for the worship of the Most High; and however meagre the fare, it was never partaken of until the blessing of God was asked upon it. Again at the close of the meal, all eyes were closed and hands folded, while every head bowed in reverent thanks to God for his bounty in providing for the wants of his unworthy creatures. Reference has been made to the *ceilidh*, or the friendly visit of one neighbor to the house of another. But even in this apparently trivial event God was recognized. When any one, old or young, came to a neighbor's house, he first knocked at the door. At once from within came the clear, ringing invitation, "Come in." The party without opened the door, uncovered his head, and standing still for a moment, invoked a blessing, "*Beannaich so*," (bless this place). Quickly the response came from the head of the house, "*Gum beannaich e sibhfein*" (may he bless yourself). So also on rising to leave the house the visitor said, "*Beannachd leibh*" (blessing with you), to which the response came as before, "*Beannachd leibh fein*" (blessing with yourself).

But the most important event in the daily

religious life of the pioneer was undoubtedly family worship. Come with me on a quiet summer morning or evening to one of these homes. In a small clearing in the dense forest stands the little log cabin. A blue curl of smoke rises from the wooden chimney; it is a symbol of the incense that is being offered up within. We will not disturb the solemnity of the worship, but we will take our place near by. Listen to the sweet strains as they slowly and solemnly ascend on the still air. They are singing the Shepherd's Psalm. Father and mother, far away from the home of early days, unite with those whom God has given them, in the overflow of soul in song, and amid such primitive surroundings their hearts go out in the words :

> " The Lord's my Shepherd, I'll not want,
> He makes me down to lie
> In pastures green ; he leadeth me
> The quiet waters by."

After this a chapter is read slowly and solemnly, with occasional observations by the high priest of the family. At the close of the reading the children are expected to tell something of what they have heard. Then "the books" are closed, the spectacles laid on top of them, and the face of the father clothes itself with grave, dignified solemnity, and a strange, unwonted, tremulous depth comes into his voice as he says, "Let us pray." The prayer is certainly not an "oration," nor is it, from a literary point of view, a gem; but it is earnest and emotional, nothing stilted, formal, or frigid in it, and uttered by one who feels the presence of God. We are near enough to hear some of the words, and hearing them we cannot easily forget them:

"O God, our Father, we bow before Thee. We are not worthy of this privilege, but we come in the name of Thy dear Son. Hear us for His sake. Thou art great beyond our understanding, but Thou art infinitely good. Thou didst give us our being, and Thou hast cared for us all our life long, leading us by the still waters and through the green pastures of Thy grace. Thou hast brought us to this good land, and hast given us a house to dwell in. Thou dost spread our table morning, noon, and night; and Thy presence cheers us, so that we need fear no evil. We thank thee for Jesus

Christ, Thy Son, and for redemption through His precious blood. Assure our hearts of an interest in the great atonement. Guilt is ours, grace is Thine. O Father, help us this day. Give us strength and courage and peace. Carry us in Thine arms, and keep us near Thy heart. Hear us, O God of our fathers, for our children. We have given them to Thee in solemn covenant. Write Thy law upon their hearts, so that they may never depart from Thee, but may live holy, happy, useful lives. The Lord hear us for Jesus' sake."

The church was always prayed for, and especially on Saturday night was the divine blessing invoked on the services of the following day. Usually mention was made of "the country in which we dwell" and "the dear land from which we have come." I pity the man who can ridicule, or speak lightly of, such a scene. Richard Baxter tells us of a time when the power of the Gospel was so felt in Kidderminster, that in every house on many a long street, family worship was devoutly observed. The writer can recall a time when in every house on many a long concession line in Zorra God was worshipped morning and evening. Who can estimate the value of such worship in the formation of character? It promotes order and regularity in a home, and diffuses a sympathy among the members. It calls off the mind from the deadening effects of worldly affairs. It says to every member of the family "There is a God; there is a spiritual world; there is a life to come." It fixes the idea of responsibility in the mind of a child. It develops, as neither pulpit nor Bible class nor Sabbath School can do, a sense of duty to God and man. Blessed is the home that is thus devoutly consecrated to God. Whatever uncertainties hang, to human view, over its future history; whether predominates there the voice of health and gladness, or the wail of sorrow and pain; whether its larder be filled with plenty, or made lean by poverty; how oft soever its windows may be darkened by calamity and death,—one thing is sure, it is the abiding place of the Most High; the Angel of the Covenant is there, and in the deepest night of grief that home has light and hope and peace. What has given Scotland the proud position she occupies today among the nations of the earth? Is it her insular position, the wisdom of her rulers, the valor of her soldiers, or the genius of her poets? No, not at all. Her greatness and her power are to be explained in the honor in which God has been held in her families. It is Christianity among her people that is the grand secret of all her prosperity and her greatness. And this Christianity is fed and nourished chiefly at the family altar, amid such scenes as Robert Burns photographs in his "Cottar's Saturday Night."

> "From scenes like these old Scotia's grandeur springs
> That makes her loved at home, revered abroad.
> Princes and lords are but the breath of kings,
> An honest man's the noblest work of God."

Here is the secret of Scotland's greatness. It lies not in her ironclads and her Armstrong guns, but it rests on something far mightier than armies and navies—the Christianity of her people, a Christianity that begins and is carried on at the family altar. This is the righteousness that has exalted that nation, and this righteousness, far more than the richest products of our mines, fields, and forests, will make this Dominion truly great and happy. Talk of colleges! The best college from which the professional men of Zorra ever graduated, that which has left the most lasting and beneficial influence upon their minds and hearts, was the college of a Christian home. These men to-day are scattered far and wide, and they belong, some to the medical, some to the legal some to the theological, and many to the teaching profession; but they look back with fond recollection to the days when with father and mother, brothers and sisters, they reverently knelt in prayer on the rude floor of the little log cabin.

How tender the memory of that last home-leaving, when the boy was going far away to enter college, or engage in business, or to learn a trade. For weeks past kind hands have been preparing such little articles of clothing as will be useful to him when away from mother and sisters: and now the little trunk is packed and the morning of separation has come. There are but few words spoken, and feeling is wonderfully suppressed, but

"Kneeling down to heaven's eternal King,
　　The saint, the father and the husband prays ;
Hope springs exulting on triumphant wings,
　　That thus they all shall meet in future days."

Many years have since passed by, bringing with them many and varied experiences, but the influence of that solemn hour is with us still, and will abide with us while memory lasts.

Ours is a day of competition, hurry, excitement, when business is war, and anything is fair. Home life is largely broken up, and the conditions are not favorable to the cultivation of kindness, quietness, and a tender regard for the happiness of others. Some men are nowhere greater strangers than in their own homes, and they know but little of the beautiful domestic life of our fathers.

And it was a busy life. In the winter season all day long the axes rang incessantly, and the trees crashed and fell. Then in the spring and summer there were " the ploughing and sowing, reaping and mowing" from dewy morn till dusky eve. It was a Zorra lad who, being told that he was too short for his age, replied, " Father keeps me so busy I haint time to grow."

Roderick C—— was noted far and near for his early rising—in winter time never later than four a.m., and during the summer months even earlier than that. Of course, at the rousing call of the head of the house every member of the family was obliged to rub his sleepy eyes and scramble out of bed. Because of this, old Rod found it hard to keep hired help. Three different men, it is said, in as many weeks, had tried and failed. At length the supply of men and boys seemed to be exhausted, and old Rod found himself at the beginning of the harvest season with no help, and with no prospect of procuring any. Just at this juncture a young Highlander, a stranger in Zorra, appeared upon the scene, and announced his willingness to work for Rod. Many were the warnings which he received, and many the wagers made as to how long young Donald would remain in Rod's employ. But Donald persisted in turning a deaf ear to all warnings, and soon his bundle of clothes was reposing in the loft of Rod's shanty, and he himself installed as a member of the household. His sleep that night was sound and dreamless, so far as it went; but scarcely, as he afterwards declared, had his head touched the pillow, before he was awakened by a terrible commotion. The dog was barking and the children howling, while a strong smell of fried pork from the kitchen below floated to his nostrils. Presently he heard old Rod climbing the ladder, and stumbling in the darkness towards his room. "Wake up, wake up, m' man," cried old Rod, opening the door noisily. But young Donald was equal to the occasion. "Thank y', sur," he replied, "but she will not eat so late at nicht." Then as Rod's retreating footsteps grew fainter, Donald sank again into well-earned repose.

A few nights afterwards, however, Donald did by some mistake respond to the four a.m. call of the head of the house. The first thing after coming down was family prayer, in which Rod thanked the Lord for the "licht of anither day." "Toot, toot, mon," said Donald, "it will no be licht for twa hours yet; why thank the Lord?"

As might be anticipated, the social life of the settlers was very strong. Common difficulties drew them closer together. A good woman, we are told, entered a grocery store to purchase some lozenges. But the store was damp, and the lozenges were adhering too closely together to suit the purchaser. "What kind of peppermints are these?" The grocer being somewhat of a wag, and knowing the woman's nationality, replied, "These are Scotch peppermints." "Ou, aye," was the ready reply, "is that the reason they stick sae closely t'gither?"

There were no club-rooms or bar-rooms in those days, but the woodsman spent his evenings where every husband and father should do, in his own home and in the bosom of his own family. The time was occasionally improved in sharpening his axe, or making a handle for it, or mending an old pair of shoes, or putting a patch on his trousers. Sometimes a neighbor would drop in, or perhaps two or three, and the conversation would turn on the weather, the crops, the taxes, last Sunday's sermon, the next Communion, or the time and place of the next catechizing. The friends in Scotland would be remembered, the records of this and that family traced, and the hope expressed of such a person or family coming to Zorra. Newspapers were scarce, but such as came to hand were eagerly read and the contents discussed.

Stories of olden time were told, some of these of an historical character, some religious, but many of the humorous sort. Old and young greatly enjoyed such a meeting for an hour or two at the close of the day's work.

> "Talk not of joys, indeed, till thou
> Hast seen the smile of age;
> Or of the laughter in the which
> The 'hoary' ones engage.
> When it is theirs in fellowship
> To stories tell, galore,
> And to portray, time and again,
> The scenes of days of yore."

The library was small, but it always contained a Gaelic Bible, a metrical version of the Psalms in Gaelic, and the Shorter Catechism. Besides these, there could usually be found in it one or more of the following books: a Gaelic version of Boston's "Fourfold State," Bunyan's "Pilgrim's Progress," "Edwards on the Affections," Allaine's "Alarm," Baxter's "Call to the

Unconverted," Doddridge's "Rise and Progress of Religion in the Soul," and a number of songs or Gaelic poems by such Highland ministers and laymen as Macdonald, Kennedy, Aird, Peter Grant, and Dugald Buchanan. All these were read and re-read, over and over again; and I have no hesitation in ascribing much of the vigor of intellect, liveliness of imagination, and spiritual discernment which so strikingly characterized many of the fathers, to their thorough knowledge of the Bible and of these theological and poetical works. Of very many of the fathers it may truly be said that in at least three books they were deeply read; two without—the Bible and God's Providence; the other within—the human heart. The first two filled their minds with lofty and elevating thought; the other gave them that knowledge of themselves which, however important, schools or colleges cannot impart.

There is no greater delusion than that intelligence increases in proportion to the number of books read. The reverse is frequently the case. Reading should be a means to develop thinking. A book should never read simply because it is interesting. If one's reading decreases the respect for moral purity, or reverence for God, if it gilds vice and ridicules goodness, if it exalts political party above moral principle, or dollars above duty, if it makes a criminal into a hero, or in any way weakens the sense of responsibility to God and man, it is worse than no reading at all, and the mind should no more feed upon such reading than the body upon foul carrion. The Bible is the grandest book in the world. It will develop the intellect, strengthen the will, and purify the life as any or all other books cannot do. It was read and studied by our fathers; and it cheered them in life and supported them in death. This I know, that the fathers in Zorra "who knew and only knew their Bible true," could discourse on the laws of mind and matter, the relationships of society, and the responsibilities of manhood and womanhood, as the wholesale devourers of sensational newspapers and the "penny-dreadfuls" of our day cannot even conceive of. It is better to deeply read than to be widely read.

CHAPTER III

THE PIONEER AND THE SABBATH

" I am now in my 87th year, and I ascribe my physical and mental activity largely to my strict observance of the Sabbath."—HON. W. E. GLADSTONE.

AT the present day it has become popular in certain quarters to characterize the fathers as narrow and bigoted, and especially to charge them with Puritanical strictness in their observance of the Sabbath. Herein we have powerful, though unconscious testimony to their loyalty to the truth. In a day when avarice combines with licentiousness and infidelity in trampling under foot the most sacred truths, and especially the Sabbath law, it is refreshing to call to mind the integrity, the fearlessness, the adherence to principle exhibited by our fathers. They felt that there was a vital and eternal

ZORRA PIONEERS—(Ages 80 to 84).

1. Mrs. A. Macleod, died 1889, aged 81. 2. John McDonald, age 81. 3. Wm. Bruce, age 83. 4. Mrs. W. Bruce, age 81. 5. John Forbes, died 1893, aged 82. 6. Capt. A. Gordon, age 80. 7. David Ross, died 1895, aged 82. 8. Mervin Cody, age 83. 9. Alex. Ross, died 1877, aged 83. 10. John Anderson, died 1871, aged 83. Mrs. Robt. Ross. 11. Mrs. Janet Nasmyth, died 1871, aged 84. 12. Alex. Murray, died 1882, aged 84. 13. Mrs. Alex. Murray, died 1889, aged 83. 14. Donald Urquhart, died 1880, aged 81. 15. Alex. MacKay, died 1893, aged 83.

A SABBATH WELL SPENT

difference between truth and error, and as they believed so they lived.

Some of the fathers may have erred on the side of literalism, but their error has been greatly magnified by scoffers. The following beautiful description of a home in Scotland, with its reverent and happy Sabbath, will call up in the mind of many a Zorra man and woman to-day equally happy scenes in years gone by :

" We had special Bible readings on the Lord's day evening, mother and children and visitors reading in turns, with fresh and interesting question, answer, and explanation, all tending to impress us with the infinite grace of a God of love and mercy in the great gift of His dear Son Jesus, our Saviour.

" I can remember those happy Sabbath evenings ; no blinds drawn and shutters up to keep out the sun from us, as some scandalously affirm, but a holy, happy, entirely human day for a Christian father, mother, and children to spend. How my father would parade across and across our flag floor, telling over the substance of the day's sermons to our dear mother! How he would entice us to help him recall some idea or other, rewarding us when we got the length of 'taking notes,' and reading them over on our return ; how he would turn the talk ever so naturally to some Bible story or some martyr reminiscence, or some happy allusion to the Pilgrim's Progress!

"And then it was quite a contest which of us would get reading aloud, while all the rest listened, and father added here and there a happy thought, or illustration, or anecdote. There were eleven of us brought up in a home like that; and never one of the eleven, boy or girl, man or woman, has been heard or ever will be heard saying that Sabbath was a dull or wearisome one for us, or suggesting that we have heard or seen any way more likely than that for making the day of the Lord bright and blessed alike for parents and for children."

Oh, for an honest love of the truth, and a readiness to contend for it at all hazard! Three distributors of church charity in Toronto, last winter, fearing that they were imposed upon by all assisting the same persons, determined to compare notes. One of these distributors was a Roman Catholic, another a Methodist, and the third a Presbyterian. They soon found a woman whom they had all been assisting on the ground that she belonged to each of their churches. This woman had her babe baptized, (1) by the Priest, (2) by the Methodist minister, and (3) by the Presbyterian; and she was only

A FALSE CHARITY

waiting till her child got a little bigger, to show that she had no prejudice whatever against the Baptist Church. This woman was no bigot, and she is a fair representative of multitudes who in our day boast of their religious liberality, and whose godliness is only a matter of gain. Liberality to error is treason to the truth. Some people are so "charitable" that they have no controversy with sin or Satan. The pioneers of Oxford were Bible-reading, God-fearing, Christ-loving men and women, who believed something, and lived as they believed. To them truth was the Saviour's crown-jewels, and they would as soon think of loving a king and trampling on his crown, as pretend to love Christ, and then trample on his law.

Who will deny that the devout observance of the day of rest developed in the fathers a vigorous and Christian manhood and womanhood, and made them strong physically, mentally, morally? France, with her infidelity and her reckless desecration of the Sabbath, stands to-day face to face with the solemn problem of national extinction. When the Parisian

Sabbath has produced better men and women than the Puritan Sabbath has done, it will be time enough to sneer at the fathers. Many of us have heard of the great Breckenridge family of the United States. There were three brothers of them, and all stood in the very front rank of able men in the Presbyterian Church of that country. One day, Dr. John Breckenridge thus accosted his aged mother: "Mother, don't you think you might have been a little less severe on us boys?" "John," replied the good woman, "when you have raised three such sons as I have done, you may undertake to reprove your mother for her methods." The application of this to the Parisian and Puritan Sabbath needs no comment.

Girard, the infidel millionaire of Philadelphia, one Saturday ordered all his clerks to come on the morrow to his wharf and help unload a newly arrived ship. One young man replied quietly:

"Mr. Girard, I can't work on Sundays."

"You know our rules."

A MORAL HERO

"Yes, I know. I have a mother to support, but I can't work on Sundays.

"Well, step up to the desk and the cashier will settle with you."

For three weeks the young man could find no work; but one day a banker came to Girard to ask if he could recommend a man for a cashier in a new bank. This discharged young man was at once named as a suitable person.

"But," said the banker, "you dismissed him."

"Yes, because he would not work on Sundays. A man who would lose his place for conscience' sake would make a trustworthy cashier." And he was appointed.

Even if men had no immortal souls to be cared for, their brains and their bodies require a day of rest. If we are to make the most of ourselves even in this life, we must take one day in seven for a quiet rest from physical toil and mental excitement. It is one of the cunning devices of the devil to destroy men, by tempting them to turn God's appointed day of rest into a day of work or pleasure. Hon. W. E. Gladstone is only one of many who ascribe their physical strength and mental activity in extreme old age to a devout observance of the Sabbath.

The following incident will illustrate the loyalty of our ancestors to the Sabbath, and the quaint, original manner in which some of them could enforce their views of the holy day. A good elder one day came upon a number of young lads who were grossly profaning the Lord's day. In gentle tones, and without the slightest sign of anger, the old man said: "Boys, let me tell you a story. There was a rich man, and he owned seven fine cows. He had a neighbor who was very poor, and possessed nothing at all. But the rich man was so generous that he gave the poor man, free, without any price, six of his fine cows. And now what think you the poor man did?" "Well," said one of the boys, "he would be very grateful to the rich man." "I would think," said another, "he ought to show his gratitude by doing what he could to please and honor the man who treated him so kindly." "No, my boys," said the old man, "you will be surprised when I tell you that he was neither grateful nor respectful to his benefactor; but, on the contrary, he used to come and steal the milk from the only cow the good man kept for himself."

Is that story true?" said one boy. "Who is that man?" cried another. "Why, that man's too mean to live," shouted a third. "Stop, my dear boys, and I will explain. I have told you a story to teach you a moral. God in His infinite goodness has given us six days in the week for our own use, but the Sabbath He has retained to Himself. But, boys, you seem not to be satisfied with six days, for you are robbing God of His day. Is this right? Is this manly?" "You've got us this time," said one of the boys. "He gave us a lump of sugar with a pill inside," said another; but there was no more desecration of the Sabbath for them that day.

All the pioneer fathers were not equally successful in their endeavors to preserve the sanctity of the Sabbath, as the following will show: A good man was one day going through the woods on his way to the church. Suddenly he espied two young fellows a short distance off, one with a club holding guard over a hole in the ground, and the other farther away fishing. Going up to the nearest who, it may, be explained, was a little dull intellectually, the man remonstrated with him.

"My boy, do you know what you are doing?"

"Ou, aye, she pe waiting till the beastie comes out."

"But this is the devil's work you are doing to-day!"

"Toot, toot, it's na the deevil; its a groundhog—I saw it going in, wi' my ain eyes!"

"But do you know what day this is?" queried the good man.

Here followed a long shrill whistle from the half-witted boy, and a call to his companion, "Come here, Tam; here's a feller that disna ken what day it is!"

A story is told of a farmer in the southern part of the township who had a pond on his farm, and who also owned a ram sheep that was great with his head. On Sabbath afternoon the boys would occasionally have lots of fun with this pugnacious animal. A young fellow would take his place close up to the pond, and then keep bowing his head, as if daring the ram to fight. Instantly the ram, gathering up his strength, would rush forward to battle; but when he came near enough, the boy would nimbly leap to one side, and the ram would plunge into the water, much to the amusement of the juveniles. One Sabbath afternoon the old man caught the boys at this sport. You may be sure he gave them a sound lecturing on the sin of Sabbath desecration, and ordered them all home to study the catechism. The boys soon disappeared; but now the old man began reflecting on the sport, and the more he reflected the more he felt tempted to experiment a little himself. So just for once he would try. Taking his place beside the pond, he made certain movements to attract the attention of the ram. Nothing daunted by former experiences, the brave animal, with head and tail erect, came rushing to the encounter. But the old man, not being so nimble as the boys, failed to get out of the way in time. Result: the wrong party got into the water. Moral: practice what you preach.

The profound regard of some of the pioneers for the Sabbath appears in the following amusing incident. A good elder, one bright Sunday morning, donned his best suit of Sunday black. He had gone some distance with his wife on the way to the church, when that lady reminded him that he had forgotten to feed the calf. As it would be night before they could get back, there was but one course open for him. The calf must not be left to starve. So at once the elder retraced his steps, got a pail of milk, and carefully carried it into the field where the calf was enjoying life, after the manner of its kind. The elder's approach filled the calf with joy; and as the milk was slowly and carefully poured into a trough the infant bovine plunged its head, with an emphatic "splash," into it. Up spurted the milk in a score of streams, and the elder's black coat was black only in streaks. Then, in this time of trial appeared ample proof of the elder's respect for the day. Quickly he

THE SORELY-TRIED ELDER 63

grasped the calf's head, and as he spoke the following devout words, at each word he thumped that head against the trough. And this is what he said: If—it—no—be—the—Sawbath—and—she —no—be—breaking—the—Lord's—day—she —would—punch—her—head—through—this— trough." " If an aith wad relieve ye, dinna mind my presence," was the counsel given a Scotch minister by his " man " on a very trying occasion.

But while we may smile at the foibles of these men, let us not fail to admire their loyalty to conscience. And though we may not approve their severe literalism in the interpretation of the fourth commandment, let us freely acknowledge that the fault was less, infinitely less, than that spirit of to-day, which defiantly tramples under foot divine authority by turning the Lord's day into a day of worldliness and rioting.

> " O day most calm, most bright,
> The fruit of this, the next world's bud,
> Th' indorsement of supreme delight ;
> Writ by a friend, and with his blood ;
> The couch of time, care's balm and bay ;
> The week were dark but for thy light :
> Thy torch does show the way."

CHAPTER IV

GANGIN' TAE THE KIRK

"A pious peasantry, their country's pride."—BURNS.

To say that our forefathers were a church-going people would be greatly to understate the truth. They were devotedly attached to their church; their most hallowed memories and associations clustered around it, and to attend its services they gladly travelled on foot over a winding path in the dense forest, three, six, or even in some cases ten miles, returning the same day after the service was over.

To-day we will accompany these people, young and old, on the way to the kirk; and as we listen to their conversation we will leave each reader to commend or to condemn as his judgment and taste may direct. We give a few snap-shot photographs of things as they were.

ZORRA PIONEERS—(Ages 77 to 89).

1. Mrs. Soper MacKay, age 77. 2. John Macdonald, died 1884, aged 87. 3. Wm. Murray, died 1899, aged 86. 4. John F. Matheson, age 87. 5. Mrs. Wm. McIntosh, died 1865, aged 88. 6. John MacKay and wife, ages 84 and 79. 7. Geo. W. Reed, died 1896, aged 88. 8. Mrs. Robt. Munro, age 86. 9. Alex. Murray, died 1882, aged 84. 10. Alex. Clark, age 85. 11. Mrs. Donald Clark, died 1895, aged 87. 12. Robt. Sutherland, age 89; wife, died 1893, aged 80. 13. A. A. MacKay, age 86. 14. Mr. A. Macleod, aged 84. 15. Angus Munro, age 87. 16. Lant Youngs, age 85.

It is a beautiful day in the beginning of June, 18—. A brilliant Canadian sun is overhead, the air is laden with the fragrance of apple, plum and pear tree blossoms, and sweet clover; the wild birds, freed from the enforced silence of a long winter, make the forests vocal with their merry notes. Here comes a group of people, most of them of the younger sort, on their way to the Communion. Not that it is Sabbath, or that the holy feast will be observed to-day. It is Friday, or what is commonly known as the "Men's Day."

At this time the Communion was observed only once a year, and lasted five days. It commenced on Thursday, which was called the "Fast Day," (La Trasgaidh). Friday was the "Day of Self-examination," (La Rannsaichaidh); Saturday was the "Day of Preparation," (La Ulluchaidh); Sabbath was the "Day of Communion," (La Comunnaidh); and Monday was the "Day of Thanksgiving" (La Taingealichd). With that respect for order said always to characterize the Presbyterian Church, the various religious services of the communion occasion, such as the reading of scripture, prayers, singing, sermons, and even the personal conversation of each day, always bore upon the uniform subject of that day, as indicated by the name of the day above given.

And now we join the happy company of church-goers at a place where two roads meet, and we enter upon a four-miles' path through the woods. We soon learn the subject of conversation. One of the party has just received a letter from a friend in Dornoch, Sutherlandshire, Scotland. This letter had lain in the post office for several days, owing to the inability of Mrs. Burton, the person to whom it was addressed, to pay the postage, viz., two shillings (50 cents). However, the two young sons of Mr. N., hearing of the good woman's difficulty, and having no spare cash, took their flails and hired out for two days, threshing wheat for Mr. McAlpin, a farmer near Woodstock. For their work they received two shillings, and that night the money was handed to the widow Burton. Next morning the letter was received and eagerly read. Many of the neighbors, hearing

YOUNG PEOPLE'S CONVERSATION

of its arrival, called on Mrs. Burton, to see if there was any news about their friends "ayont the sea." The letter had, in fact, become a sort of circulating library, and the chief subject of conversation in the district. In it the information was conveyed that a number of families were just about leaving the parish of Rogart to make a home in the woods of Zorra. From this the conversation drifted to the social life of some of the settlers.

"Did you hear," said a young woman, "that another of the Mackay girls is going to get married?"

"Ou, ay," said an elderly spinster, "Angus Mackay's daughters are going fast."

"That's so," said two or three voices at once. "It's only a year since Angus Mackay settled on the seventh line with a family of eleven children, seven daughters and four sons. Four daughters and two sons were married last winter, and now the fifth is going. And all are lucky enough to be settled in Zorra."

"Marriage is a lottery, and the luck is very doubtful," said the aforesaid dame. "There is

Sandy McKinnon; losh man, he's nae Christian ava. Have ye no heard what he said tae his puir sick wife the ither day?" Upon being assured that the important information had not yet reached the company, she proceeded: "Weel, the puir woman has been unco sick for a while back, an' confined tae her bed. Noo, ye ken there's only ae cruzie in the hoose that has the creesh an' wick in't, an' the ither nicht it was slowly burnin' in Peggy's room. But in the forepairt o' the nicht some o' Sandy's cronies cam' on a ceilidh, an' they were sittin' i' the kitchen i' the dark. An' what think you Sandy did? He just took the cruzie oot o' Peggy's room and put it on the kitchen table, that he an' his cronies micht see the smoke curlin' up frae their pipes. Then Sandy gaed back tae his wife's room tae see if she wantit onything. And Peggy, glowerin', scaulded him. 'Ah, Sandy, ye'll no' gie a puir body a licht to dee wi'.' 'Dee! dee! is that what yee say, Peggy? I'll gie ye the licht'; an', runnin' tae the kitchen, he taks the cruzie in his twa hans, an' plantin' it doon wi' a bang on the wee table at the front o' Peggy's bed, said, 'There, dee, noo!'"

"That reminds me of auld Blue-bonnet and his wife," said young Peter Laird. "Ye ken Blue-bonnet is some twenty years aulder than his wife, and a short time syne he thocht he was gaein' to dee. But after a while he began ta mend, and yin day says he to his wife, 'Dod, Maggy, I think I'll pu' through this time yet.' 'Tam,' answered the partner of his bosom, 'as you are a' prepared, an' I'm quite resigned, I think it wad be just as weel if ye wad gang the noo.'"

"Weel, I could tell something in that line myself," said a young fellow, directing his remarks to the elderly dame. "Mr. M—, living on the eighth line, was once asked by a friend if he knew Mr. G—, who lived in the same parish with him in Scotland. 'He's dead lang syne,' said his friend, 'and I'll never cease regrettin' him as lang as I live.'

"'Dear me, had you sic respect for him as that?'

"'Na, na! It wasna' ony respec' I had for him masel', but I married his widow.'"

At this witticism there was considerable

laughter, until the wife of Elder Matheson interposed. "Young people," said she, "be serious. This is na' time for makin' fun—remember ye're gangin' tae the kirk."

Whatever objection may be brought against the above conversation among our pioneer juveniles, no one will accuse it of overmuch Puritanical strictness.

Our pen picture would be very defective, indeed, were we to rest here. Let us listen for a little to the conversation of the more elderly men and women, who are, this beautiful morning, on their way to the kirk. Here is Donald Campbell walking alone, and apparently absorbed in his own meditations. We will introduce ourselves: "Good morning, Mr. Campbell. You are alone to-day." The reply was gentle but prompt: "To myself it seems I am not alone," meaning, of course, that the Lord was with him.

John Gunn and Tammas Clarke are old neighbors. They left Scotland together, and together they endured for some years the hardships of pioneer life. Their common environment, however, did not shape them alike. John Gunn stood six feet high, straight as an arrow, with well developed forehead, melting blue eyes, and features betokening strength of character and kindliness of heart. He was devout with more than an ordinary education, and a worthy member of the church. Tammas was tall rather than stout, a wonderful talker on religion, could discuss theology, and was great on the "decrees."

> "He could a hair divide
> Betwixt the west and north-west side."

He was not a member of the church, but was most regular in his attendance on religious services.

"Good morning, Tammas," said John, as the two neighbors met the first time for several weeks, "I am glad to see you coming to the kirk to-day."

"Well," replied Tammas, "we are told 'not to forsake the assembling of ourselves together.'"

"You are right," said John; "these seasons come so seldom, they are so refreshing, and our Heavenly Father is so good. Ah, Tammas! it's a bonnie world we live in. It must have been at some such season as this that Solomon said:

> "The winter is past,
> The rains are over and gone,
> The flowers appear in the earth,
> The time for the singing of birds has come,
> And the voice of the turtle is heard in the land."

"Did you observe," said Alex. McNeil, "how beautiful our neighbor McAllister's orchard appears? the trees, so dead and bare durin' the winter, now clothed in their beautiful white robes."

"I see, Alex., you are quite poetical this morning, and I do not wonder," said Tammas. "All nature is poetry just now. But to tell the truth, when coming by McAllister's orchard I was thinkin' not so much of the blossoms as of the busy bees that were feedin' upon them. What a lesson of industry to us farmers."

"Ay," replied John Gunn, "and a lesson also to a' who read or hear the gospel."

"I dinna see that," frankly confessed Tammas.

"Well," responded Gunn, "some gospel readers and hearers are like butterflies, others are like bees. The butterflies flit over the flowers, and nothing comes of their flittin', but the bees dive into the heart of the flowers and emerge filled with sweetest honey. I trust this Communion will be a time when we will get into the inward meaning of scripture, and our souls feed on the sacred sweetness which the Lord has put there for the spiritual nourishment of his children."

"Ye needna fear that," said Alex. MacNeil, "if Mr. Allan is with us. Mr. Allan is so spiritual, and Mr. McPherson is aye happy in openin' up and applyin' the scripture, and our ain minister is second to nane in driving home the truth."

"Let me put a question to you learned men," said Tammas. "Why is this great forest like the Christian Church?"

"Do you mean," replied John, "that it is composed of a great variety of trees, some great and some small, some strong and some weak, just like the Church?"

"And," continued Tammas, with a shrug of his shoulder and a wink of his eye, "some straight and some crooked?"

"That," said Tammas, "is not a bad comparison, but try again."

"Well, then," replied John Gunn, "in the woods we see the strong shelterin' the weak, and each helpful to the life and growth of the whole."

"Very good again," said Tammas, "but I would like to hear what our friend Donald Macleod has to say about the forest and the Church."

Mr. Macleod was a man greatly esteemed for his moral worth, but was not forward in pushing his views. At the mention of his name several voices united in calling for his reply to the question under consideration. "Let us hear it," said a number of voices at once.

"Well, I am no preacher and cannot discourse on spiritual things like some of you, but I can see a likeness between God's work in nature and his work in grace. The Church is built up with members as this forest is replenished with trees, not so much by importation from abroad, as by growth, multiplication from within. Thus the Church of old grew from one family, and one son in that family—Isaac—to be, with few extraneous additions, a nation of many millions. By all means let us add to the Church from the heathen world, but still more," said Macleod, pointing to some very young children in the company, " let us carefully raise these tender plants within its sacred enclosure, so they may never know the bitterness of the wilderness life."

It may here be observed that, of all the men in Zorra, none so carefully looked after the " tender plants " as this same Donald Macleod.

Now the party are emerging from the woods, and are getting over the crooked rail fence by means of three steps on each side, rising one above the other. Suddenly little Gerald Gordon is heard calling out at the top of his voice, " Mamma, I have found a robin's nest, and there are three little birds in it." There was a halt in the procession. The young people especially wanted to see " the dear little things."

" See how they are all opening their bills so wide," said Willie Graham. " What is that for?"

" Ah, Willie," said his mother, " they want

their food. And our Heavenly Father says to men and women 'Open thy mouth wide and I will fill it.' I hope the lesson will not be lost on you, dear children, to-day in the church."

"I remember," said Lucy MacDonald, "a verse in our school book about little birds in their nests."

"Let's hear it," cried out several juvenile voices. Then Lucy repeated the familiar little rhyme:

> "Birds in their little nests agree,
> And 'tis a shameful sight
> When children of one family
> Fall out and chide and fight."

"Aye, aye," said Tammas, "sometimes pretty big children in one family and in one church, 'fall out, and chide, and fight.'"

"Well," said Alex. MacNeil, "the little birds should teach big and little people to live in peace with one another. The God whom we serve is a God of peace, and the Saviour whom we love is the Prince of Peace. And yet, it is, alas! only too true that, as our brother says, children of the same family, and members of the same church, quarrel. Yonder are Mr. G— and Mr. M— coming to church to-day, but they don't speak to each other. Their dispute is concerning the right place for the line fence. The strip of land claimed by each is perhaps long enough, but scarcely wide enough, to accommodate a coffin."

"And yonder is auld Maggie Reid," says one, "she'll no spak to her neighbor, Mrs. Ross, because Mrs. Ross washes the dishes on the Sabbath, a thing which Maggie Reid says is verra wrang, and which nae Christian would do."

We have now reached the kirk, and here we must leave our friends for the time.

What we have said will help the reader better to understand what "going to church" meant to both juniors and seniors in the days of old. No one complained of the distance—rather it was regarded as a providential opportunity for the interchange of thought. The young people gossiped away, much as I suppose they have done since the days of Adam and Eve, while the old people recalled scenes and events of former days, and loved to spiritualize the works of nature; and no less an authority than Ruskin assures us that "all most lovely forms of thought are directly taken from natural objects."

CHAPTER V

THE MEN'S DAY

"The king lost his head—fools may whimper and whine,
But he lost it, believe me—by judgment divine.
Our kings were the godly, the grey-plaided men,
Who preached in the forest and prayed in the glen.'
—J. S. BLACKIE.

THE old log church was not an elegant structure, but it was the best building in the township. Its dimensions were forty-eight feet by twenty-eight feet, and eighteen logs high. It was well hewed outside and inside; chinked, and plastered with lime. There was a gallery, access to which was by an outside stair. There was no spire, no cushions, no carpet, and for the first winter or two, not even a stove. The windows and furniture were of the most primitive kind. It was capable of holding about four

ZORRA'S OLD LOG CHURCH, ERECTED 1832-3

hundred persons, though on Communion occasions many more would be crowded into it.

But this first Zorra church was the religious centre of a very large district, and it had associations that made it dear to the hearts of our Scottish forefathers. Thither the tribes went up, not only from the two Zorras, but from Nissouri, Blanshard, North Easthope, East and West Williams, and other Highland settlements. There the pioneers heard those precious gospel truths, and sang those sweet Psalms so familiar to them in their native land There they dedicated their offspring to God in baptism, and often sat around the Communion Table in loving fellowship.

It is 10 a.m.; the regular service will not begin for an hour, but the church is already well filled with devout worshippers from far and near, and Sandy Matheson, in a clear, distinct voice, is reading a chapter " just to improve the time." This same Sandy Matheson was the precentor, and as he sang those majestic Psalms in the old Gaelic airs, right heartily did the whole congregation join with him, until there was a volume of sound surpassing in power, if not in harmony, anything furnished us to-day by our choirs and " kists o' whus'les."

Here it may be stated that the work of the old Gaelic precentor was not so easy as many to-day many suppose. He had not, it is almost needless to say, the help of organ or choir, and even the tuning-fork was regarded with suspicion. He was religiously required to "line" the Psalm, that is, to repeat or chant each line before singing it. This habit originated, very likely, in those days when the people were poor, Bibles scarce, and few able to read. But the habit has come down from one generation to another, and in many Gaelic congregations can still be seen. The minister announces the Psalm, and reads over the stanzas he wishes to be sung. He repeats the first two lines, and the precentor sings them, and so far all is easy. But now the precentor has to chant or repeat the next two lines, and here is where the difficulty begins. He has to keep in mind the note with which he concluded his second line, and he has also to keep in view the note with which to begin his third line, and begin and end his chant accordingly. And it was just here that many an *oganach*, or youngster who had aspirations for the precentor's chair, came to grief.

To those who did not understand the true poetic sentiment in the Highland nature, this singing may have seemed a strange combination of weird, meaningless sounds, but to the warm-hearted Highlander they were the "Songs of Zion." The swaying motion of the precentor, the movements of the hand, foot, and the Psalm book, the uplifting of the eyes to heaven, and the hearty responsiveness of the congregation, were an inspiration to preacher and people.

Now the tall, stately, familiar form of the pastor appears. He is accompanied by some neighboring ministers who have come to assist him on this occasion. I say "neighboring," although some of them lived fifty or sixty miles away. The reading instantly ceases, and there is a hush of silence pervading the congregation, as with solemn mien Mr. Mackenzie enters the pulpit and takes his seat. The service is mostly, though not exclusively, in Gaelic; but for the sake of unlearned readers we will give it, with the exception of a sentence or two, in English. The opening sentence was as follows: "Toisichmid air aoradh follaiseach an Tighearna le bhi seinn chum a chliu anns a' naothamh salm thar a cheithir fichead," which is thus rendered: "Let us begin the public worship of God by singing to His praise in the eighty-ninth Psalm." The reader who understands both the Gaelic and the English will at once see a majesty and solemnity in the Gaelic of this religious formula that is wholly lacking in the English translation. The first Gaelic word, for instance, as any reader can see, consists of no less than ten letters, and is equivalent to the first three English words, "Let us begin." And yet, let me observe, the Gaelic, so rich in words of devotion, has no profane words. When Gaelic men utter profanity they have to use the English language.

And now every heart goes forth in the words:

"Air tròcair Dhé sior-sheinnidh mi
Is ni mi oirre sgeul;
O àl gu h-àl gu maireannach
Air t'fhìrinn thig mo bheul."

("God's mercies I will ever sing;
And with my mouth I shall
Thy faithfulness make to be known
To generations all.")

After singing there was prayer; but frequently before the prayer the precentor would rise in his desk and say, "The prayers of the congregation are asked for —— on lot — concession —, upon whom the hand of God is being heavily laid." Then the congregation stood up, and with bowed heads engaged in prayer. After this a chapter was read, and another Psalm sung, and then began the distinctive work of the "Men's Day," sometimes called "The Question Day," and sometimes also "The Day for Self-examination," (La Rannsaichaidh).

It was always the Friday before Communion, and the proceedings formed a marked feature of Highland Presbyterian worship. The exercises corresponded in some respects to the Christian Endeavor meetings of to-day, but only "the men"—that is, persons of age, experience, and prominence—took part in them. Our account of the proceedings of this day is necessarily very imperfect; but it will at least show that our fathers were brainy men, close observers of nature, devoted students of the Bible, and able, in an original and quaint manner, to express their views of Bible truth. The general subject was always self-examination, or the marks of the true believer, and was always expressed in the form of a question. The minister invited some brother, in dependence on divine guidance, to propose a scripture text appropriate to the occasion. Soon there arose a venerable man, his head silvered with the frosts of more than threescore and ten years; only a few grey locks are left him, and these float over his shoulders. In slow measured cadence he read Gen. xxiv. 58, " Wilt thou go with this man? and she (Rebekah) said I will go." " These words," said the speaker, " will afford us an opportunity of inquiring into the evidences of character in those whose purpose in life is to go with the Man, Christ Jesus. A tree may be known by its leaves, a flower by its fragrance, music by its harmony, and all things by the qualities which they present to our senses. So a Christian should be known by the life he lives. Will the brethren point out some of these marks?"

The minister re-stated the question, explained its nature, indicated its application, and encouraged all to speak their minds freely. "The question proposed," said he, "is a very appropriate one. This man we will take as representing the Son of God, who became man, lived as our example, and died as our substitute. In Him are stored up all the blessings which infinite wisdom and love have appointed for sinners, both in the state of grace and the state of glory. 'I am He who liveth and was dead, and behold I am alive forevermore.' Because He lives He blesses those who 'go with Him'; and by His Spirit changes them into His own image, from glory to glory, until at last they shall be like Him, when they 'shall see Him as He is.' May there be many to-day willing to go with the man Christ Jesus. That you may know whether or not you are going through life with Him, we will consider the marks of those who go, as well as their blessedness. And as Rebekah's purpose, in going with Abraham's servant, was to enter into the marriage union with Isaac, we will consider the relation between Christ and His people under that suggestive and beautiful figure. Now, brethren, waste no time."

John Mackay was the first to respond. "Observe, my friends," said he, "that Rebekah was willing to leave her country, her relatives and friends, in order to go with this man, and receive Isaac for a husband. 'Thy people,' said she in her heart, to Isaac, 'shall be my people, and thy God my God.' Young people, you have been baptized in the name of the triune God—Father, Son, and Holy Ghost. Forsake the world, and enter into this sacred union with Christ, and you will be as Isaac and Rebekah, as Ruth and Naomi, as Jonathan and David."

"Christ's bride," said Alexander Munro, "was black and uncomely when He set His heart upon her, but she became fair and beautiful. I remember hearing a father in Dornoch tell the story of a man who owned a garden that was overrun with weeds. But in some way this man became the possessor of a foreign flower of singular vitality. He sowed a handful of the seeds of this flower in his weedy garden, and then left it to work its own sweet way. Time passed on, and the man knew not how the seed was doing, till one day he opened the garden gate, and saw a sight which astounded him. He knew that the seed would produce a beautiful flower, and he looked for it; but he little dreamed that the plant would cover the whole garden. But so it was; the flower had destroyed every weed, till, as he looked from one end of his garden to the other, he could see nothing but the fair colors of that rare plant, and smell nothing but its delicious perfume.

"Christ is that plant of renown. If you take Him into your heart He will gradually destroy every weed of sin, and over your whole nature there shall be the beauty of the Lord."

"We see," said Robert Matheson, "that Rebekah joined interests with Isaac, a man of God, one of whose characteristics was 'meditation in the field,' v. 63; and it seems to me that those who are wedded to the Lord Jesus Christ will meditate on the works of God, and hear what God has to say to them in the world around. They will see Him in the flowers, and hear Him in the winds, and behold His glory in the heavens. And thus in the house or in the barn, in the field or in the woods, they will be 'still with God.'"

The Christian Endeavor era had not yet dawned in Zorra, and it must be confessed that some of the fathers regarded with suspicion young persons aspiring to prominence in the church. "Young people," said one speaker, "should be seen, not heard. What would you think of a chicken, just out of the egg, getting on the fence and crowing? Don't you think he should wait till his feathers appeared? A colt, only a few days old, is long in his limbs, tall, erect, lively, but as yet very unfit for burden or harness. Modesty became the wife of Isaac, and modesty is a becoming grace in the young bride of Christ."

In a somewhat pessimistic strain the next speaker continued, "Our age is a superficial one—fair exterior, but hollow at heart. Last autumn, just after the first frost, I was walking in the woods, when I saw a most beautiful sight. I was fairly enraptured with the gorgeous scene. All the colors of the rainbow seemed commingled in beautiful harmony. I stood and gazed upon the sight, and lest I might never see so fine a sight again, I went up and closely examined, when alas! alas! it proved to be nothing more than a hollow stump covered with ivy. That is the religion of too many—nothing but leaves. Remember the fig-tree and what became of it."

It has been charged against the pioneers that they were contracted in their views, and took little interest in anything beyond their own bounds. No doubt the fathers lived in the same world as other Christians of their day. The spirit of missions has greatly deepened and broadened since their time. But to accuse the fathers and mothers of Zorra of meanness or selfishness, or of a lack of broad, generous sympathy, is to bear false testimony. Nobly they bore one another's burdens, and according to their opportunities did good unto all. And on these occasions selfishness was strongly denounced, and the duty of the Church to the heathen world never failed to be emphasized.

Donald Macleod was a man of blessed memory. My heart thrills with gratitude as I recall his influence upon my early Christian life. During a ministry of thirty years I have been associated with not a few earnest, effective Christian workers, but never have I known any one who did so much, and did it so unostentatiously as this man, so tender, yet so strong; so quiet, yet so aggressive! He was elder and deacon, and well did he discharge the duties of both offices. He was precentor in both the Gaelic and English services, and though receiving no fee, he was never absent from his post of duty. He was the only teacher of a Sabbath School of seventy scholars; and each winter he taught, without remuneration, a large singing school. Twice each year he travelled over a large section of country, collecting for the minister's stipend and for the missionary schemes of the church. And while fervent in spirit he was diligent in business, and was regarded as one of the best farmers in the community; there were no standing accounts against him, nor was there ever a mortgage upon his farm. He was an advanced temperance man, and declined to supply his harvesters with whiskey; but for this wholesome deprivation he allowed them extra wages. There was a poor old creature in the neighborhood without money and without friends. Donald Macleod built for her a little house near his own, and fed her from his own table till the time of her death, at the age of about one hundred years.

A Presbyterian missionary relates the following: One night in company with a young friend I was passing by this old woman's house and heard her earnestly praying aloud. Curiosity prompted us to go up to the door and listen. Her prayer was as follows: "Lord I am a poor old woman, lonely as the pelican in the wilderness, the owl in the desert, the sparrow upon the house top; but Thou hast not forsaken me. I thank Thee, Lord, for this good man, and his wife and children, who are so kind to me. Be good to them and bless them in time and eternity."

Let us hear what Donald Macleod has to say on the "Men's Day." This is how he spoke: "Unselfish devotion to the interests of her husband is a mark of a good wife. Are we unselfishly devoted to the interests of our Lord, and of one another? Alas, how selfishness abounds! How many are like the whirlpool, always taking in, and never giving out; like the marsh, keeping all it gets till it becomes stagnant, putrid, pestiferous; or like the clod, daily drinking in the light and warmth of the sun, but giving out none, remaining the same black clod still. We are all more or less selfish. There has never been but one absolutely pure, unselfish life,—that of the Lord Jesus Christ."

Spiritual life dies not, but there are times when it sinks low, like the sap in the tree during the winter, to rise again at the voice of spring. The pioneers were not strangers to such religious experience. Few of them, indeed, claimed the full assurance of salvation. "God only knows the depravity of my heart," said one. "Was there ever such a guilty wretch? I sometimes wonder if I am a child of God at all. O minister," said he, turning to the pastor, and speaking in most pathetic tones, "were I ready I would willingly depart; but alas! those doubts and fears. Still, like Rutherford, I will hold to Christ under the water, and if I must drown I will not let go my hold of Him." The speaker was one greatly beloved by the people, and many were moved to tears by his earnest words.

As he sat down, there slowly rose to his feet an old man with wintry beard falling upon his breast, but a strange glow of fire in his eyes, which told of a life within that winter could not touch. With evident but delicate reference to the last speaker, he said in a quiet, subdued voice, "We are guilty, but let us not forget the infinite ransom paid. Rebekah knew that she was Isaac's wife, and it would be no honor to Isaac to have her doubting her relationship to him. We owe ten thousand talents, and we are not able to pay one, but the husband assumes the wife's debt. The God-man has paid our debt to the uttermost farthing. We believe this, and the result is as a calm after a storm. A sweet peace fills the soul. The clouds vanish, the sun appears brighter than before, the earth puts on her robes of beauty; the flowers pour out their fragrance, the birds sing, and all is joy and peace."

"Whether I sing or whether I sigh," said Elder Rose, "the promise is true, and the Promiser is faithful. Sometimes I stand on Tabor's summit, and sometimes I am hidden in Baca's vale, but His love abideth, and His promise is, 'They go from strength to strength, every one of them in Zion appeareth before God.'"

The next to speak was George MacKay, better known as *duine Righ-lochan* (the man of Kinglochan). He was a man of strong religious character, and bore a very prominent part in the early religious life of Zorra. "It is many years," he said, "since I decided to go with this Man, and I have never found Him once unfaithful. Goodness and mercy have followed me all my life. Not one good thing hath failed of all the Lord God hath promised."

There he stood, the aged saint, tottering into the grave, but happy as happy could be.

Turning to the young people he continued, with a heavenly glow upon his countenance, "Come early into the marriage union with Christ, and you will be His happy bride as long as you live."

Such an appeal coming from a veteran Christian, covered with the scars of battle, made a powerful impression.

"It seems to me," said James Adams, "that a sure mark of being Christ's bride is to be like Christ. We sometimes see a striking resemblance developing between husband and wife— a similarity, not merely in modes of thought and in general character, but in their very appearance, their countenance. Certainly it is so with Christ and his people. You thrust a bar of cold black iron into the fire, and keep it there. By and bye the iron becomes changed into a red fiery mass. So when we come into close union with Christ, we become gradually changed into the image of Christ."

"Friends," said Alexander Wood, "do not lay too much stress upon mere internal feelings, or mere external marks. They are both liable to mislead. There may not be much peace or comfort, and the life may be imperfect, and yet there may be true faith. The most devoted wife is not always the one who speaks most about her love to her husband. Grace is a thing of the heart, and sometimes, like a spark of fire, it may be very small, but oh! blow gently upon it, fan it, and it will become a flame. Last winter I rose early one morning—a very cold, frosty morning. I found the fire was entirely out; but I took the steel and flint, and although shivering in the cold, I patiently kept striking till I espied a little spark down in the tinder. It was a very little one, but I gently blew it into a little flame, and soon the whole room was warm. And our dear Lord quenches not the feeblest spark, but by His blessed Spirit fans it into a flame that will give light and warmth to all within its reach."

Alexander Nasmyth was not a Highlander, but seemed greatly to enjoy "the Men's Day." "Rebekah," said he "was sought and found and espoused to Isaac. So with Christ and the believer. We did not seek Him till He first sought us. We are the bride to win whom He came from afar. And since we heard His sweet, clear, tender voice, it has been, as our brother has said, rest and peace and joy. The bird, resting upon the branch and pouring forth its volume of song, is a true picture of the believer resting on Jesus."

Hector Ross spoke of the blessedness of the bride of Christ, and quoted the words of the song, " My beloved is mine and I am his."

The last to testify was Donald Urquhart. " Of Rebekah," said he, " it could be said, ' The heart of her husband doth safely trust in her.' Can Christ, in like manner, safely trust us? Can He trust us with time and money and opportunities? Can He be sure that we will not purloin for ourselves what is rightfully His?"

Such were some of the men that formed the first church in Zorra, a church which for more than three-score years has been a light that has never been extinguished, guiding wandering ones, and pointing them heavenward; a fountain from which have issued refreshing streams for thirsty souls. Humble though their lot was, and rough their appearance, these men had clear heads and warm hearts ; they gave of their scanty means, made sacrifices and self-denials ; endured discomfort, sitting upon bare, hard board benches, in a cold, unwarmed building in midwinter, that they might worship God and bring up their families in the fear of the Lord. To-day we are reaping the fruit of their toil and sacrifice. They labored faithfully and we have entered into their labors.

It was now 3 p.m., and the services had continued since 11 a.m. Still there was no uneasiness or desire to break up the meeting. Rev. Mr. Mackenzie summed up the addresses, reviewing and emphasizing salient points, counselling the erring, encouraging the halting ones, and driving home the truth to saint and sinner.

"Give Christ," said he, "your heart, your life, your all. 'None but Christ, none but Christ!' This has been the martyr's cry amidst the fire ; let it be ours in life and in death!"

He then called upon Rev. Mr. Allan to close the service. Mr. Allan was eminently fitted to do so. He was a man of a broken spirit. Having felt the bitterness of sin in his own soul he knew how to deal with inquirers ; and, when he spoke, there was power in every word. On this occasion he was peculiarly tender in his pleading. " The servant," in verse 66, " telling Isaac all things that he had done," he used as a figure of the child of God telling his Master of his work in bringing anxious souls to Christ. With melting pathos he dwelt on the spiritual side of the fine picture in verse 67 : "Isaac brought her into his mother's tent, and took Rebekah, and she became his wife, and he loved her." " Here," said the preacher, " is a picture of Christ loving the church, and giving Himself for the church. ' I am married unto you, saith the Lord, I have loved thee with an everlasting love.' " Then, in the most persuasive tones, the preacher appealed to his hearers, " Will you go with this Man ? " Having put the question, he made a long and solemn pause. Then, looking from side to side of the church upon his hearers, he quietly asks, " Who says, I will go ? "

The inspired counsel to Christ's bride is then sung:

> "O daughter, take good heed,
>   Incline, and give good ear;
> Thou must forget thy kindred all,
>   And father's house most dear.
>
> "Thy beauty to the King
>   Shall then delightful be;
> And do thou humbly worship him,
>   Because thy Lord is he."
> —Ps. xlv. 10.

Rev. Lachlan McPherson led in prayer, and the people departed, feeling it was good to be there.

ZORRA PIONEERS—(Ages 76 to 79).

1. Alex. McCorquodale, died 1896, aged 78. 2. Colon Sutherland, age 76. 3. Thos. MacKay, age 78. 4. John M. Ross, age 78. 5. W. Macdonald, died 1875, aged 79. 6. J. Yool, age 77. 7. Donald Matheson, M.P., died 1884, aged 78. 8. Alex. Murray, died 1873, aged 77. 9. James Adams (and wife), died 1892, aged 78. 10. Robt. Macdonald, died 1875, aged 77. 11. Mrs. John Ross, died 1893, aged 77. 12. Mrs. Jas. Sutherland, age 78. 13. John MacKay, age 77.

CHAPTER VI

AN OLD COMMUNION SABBATH

> " There, there, on eagle wings we soar,
> And time and sense seem all no more,
> And heaven comes down our souls to greet,
> And glory crowns the mercy seat."

CHRISTOPHER NORTH speaks of the Scottish Sabbath as "a day upon which the sun rose more solemnly, yet not less sweetly, than on other days, with a profound stillness pervading both earth and skies." Such was the Communion Sabbath in Zorra, on the occasion of which we write. A brilliant Canadian sun cast a radiant light on field and forest, while above was the dark blue sky, with here and there a fleecy cloud. For hours before the time of meeting, worshippers, many of whom had travelled from five to ten miles, might be seen gathering to the log church.

It was a time of much prayer in the congregation, and it was no uncommon thing for the church-goer to see, here and there, persons emerging from the woods, where they had spent the whole morning in wrestling with God for his blessing upon the Communion services. Such prayers united the pioneers with their Maker. To-day the British people all over the world are sounding the praises of General Gordon, and doing themselves honor by erecting a monument to his name. Perhaps a braver man never breathed God's air. But whence his faith, his courage, his heroism? He was what he was because of secret prayer. During each morning of his first sojourn in the Soudan, there was one half-hour when there lay outside his tent a handkerchief, and the whole camp knew the full significance of that small token, and most religiously was it respected by all, whatever was their color, creed, or business. No foot dared to enter the tent so guarded. No message, however pressing, was carried in. Whatever it was, life or death, it had to wait till the guardian signal was removed. Everyone knew that God and Gordon were alone in there together.

In more senses than one the pioneers were strong men, because they were men of prayer. Some came to the church with ox-teams, but most on foot, and up to the time of worship they darkened the roads as they still kept coming.

And now the church is crowded from end to end with thoughtful, earnest worshippers. Perhaps the majority of those present are men, but the women are there in large numbers. They sit in families, the mother at one end of the pew, the father at the other, with the children in the order of their ages between—a happy contrast to what we too frequently see in our churches to-day—father and mother in a centre pew, the boys in the gallery, and the girls somewhere else. While, of course, the greater number are residents of the township, many are there from such places as East and West Williams, Ekfrid, Mosa, Gwillimbury, etc. Looking around the congregation you can discern almost everywhere that physical robustness and vigor, and that energy and force of character, that have always distinguished the best class of Scottish peasantry. The old women wear the white mutch with a black ribbon tied around; the young women are plainly dressed, but for neatness and good looks would compare favorably with those of any congregation to-day similarly situated.

> " A tuck, a frill, a bias fold,
> A hat curved over gypsywise,
> And beads of coral and of gold,
> And rosy cheeks and merry eyes,
> Made lassies in that long ago
> Look charming in their calico."

Regular living, plenty of sleep, fresh air, plain diet, and wholesome exercise did more for health and beauty than all the advertised nostrums of our day could have done. These men and women loved their church, and were ready to make any sacrifice to attend its ordinances. Around the pulpit and in front of it were seated the elders. We give their names: Robert Matheson, George MacKay, John MacKay, Hector Ross, Alex. Matheson, Alex. Rose, Wm. MacKay, and Alex. Munro. The preacher was the Rev. D. Mackenzie, and seldom did he preach with more fervor and power than on this occasion. The Psalm sung was the one hundred and sixteenth:

> " I love the Lord because my voice
> And prayer he did hear.
> I while I live will call on him
> Who bowed to me his ear."

It is needless to say there was no choir or organ. The singing was not artistic, but it was hearty and congregational, unlike too much of the singing of to-day, where all is done by a choir and an organ, while the congregation remains as voiceless as an asylum of mutes or a graveyard of the dead. The prayers were specific, appropriate, fervent, and unctional. The text was 2 Cor. viii. 9: "Though He was rich, yet for your sakes He became poor." Every eye was upon the preacher as he dwelt on (1) what Christ was—"He was rich"; (2) what He became—"He became poor"; (3) why this wonderful change—"for your sakes". With clearness and effectiveness the preacher described Christ as the sinner's substitute. "For your sakes He left the glory He had with the Father from all eternity; for your sakes He became man; for your sakes He lay in the manger, suffered hunger, thirst, weariness, and persecution. For your sakes He spoke wonderful words and wrought wonderful miracles. For your sakes He endured the mock trial, the scourging, the agony, and the crucifixion." Then there was an invitation given to all poor and sorrowing ones to come and, through His poverty, receive the riches of divine grace. "You are poor in the things of this world," said the preacher, "but to-day you may become millionaires in grace." A part of the twenty-sixth paraphrase was sung:

"Ho! ye that thirst, approach the spring
  Where living waters flow;
Free to that sacred fountain all
  Without a price may go."

After this there was the "fencing of the table." This was a distinctively Highland custom, and has now fallen into disuse. But whether its disuse is conducive to better church membership, or to a higher type of religion generally, is very doubtful. It is quite possible that in unskilled hands the "fencing of the table" might discourage weak believers; but it preserved the true dignity of the sacred ordinance, and made a clear distinction between the genuine and the spurious—a distinction that is certainly not too much emphasized in our churches to-day. A faithful "fencing of the table" in our day might considerably diminish the list of church members, but would it diminish the real strength and efficiency of the Church? If it diminished the quantity would it not improve the quality? "But what was this fencing?" asks one of my young readers.

At the old Communion the communicants did not, as to-day, sit in their pews while they partook of the bread and wine. There was a long table extending through the centre of the church, from one end to the other. This was covered with a snowy white linen cloth. And before the communicants were invited to surround the table, the fencing took place. First the minister warmly invited all true believers to the table. "Eat, O friends; drink, yea, abundantly, O beloved." Then unworthy communicants are solemnly warned. The holiness of

God's law is declared, and its application to the thoughts of the hearts as well as the outward life. "This is a holy ordinance, and only those who are living holy lives have a right to it. Any living in sin who approach this table are guilty, as Ananias and Sapphira were, of lying unto God. All such we solemnly debar from the table of the Lord. This bread and wine are not for you. Some of you know the sins you indulge; perhaps it is the profanation of the holy Sabbath, 'doing your own ways, finding your own pleasures, speaking your own words.' Some of you may be guilty of swearing or lying, or dishonesty, or drinking, or uncleanness. If you take your place at this table you will eat and drink unworthily; and in the name of the Lord Jesus, the great King and Head of His Church, I solemnly debar you. Remember, he that eateth and drinketh unworthily eateth and drinketh judgment to himself. But all you who truly love the Saviour, and are seeking to serve Him, come and welcome."

Slowly, one by one, the communicants leave heir pews and take their seats at the table.

Evidently the feelings in the minds of some are those of dread rather than of affection; and the minister occasionally remonstrates with them for their slowness in coming forward, reminding them that they are not coming to a place of execution, but to a feast of love. At length the table is supplied with guests, and what was called the "first table address" is delivered. This is full of encouragement and comfort to believers. Then, in solemn silence, the ordinance is observed, each partaking of the bread and wine. After this there is the "second table address" in which the communicants are reminded of the solemn vow they have taken, and are exhorted to go forth into the world living the life of Jesus.

The services are now over; yes, they are over, but not in their results. These still live, not only in the hearts of the few who enjoyed them and remain to this day, but in the hearts and lives of their children, and their children's children. In lives made purer and nobler and better throughout all time and eternity, the service of the old "Communion Sabbath" will be seen.

Much criticism has been expended on these great Zorra Communions. We are told that the ungodly of the township, as well as those of the neighboring towns and villages, took advantage of these gatherings for no good end—that they came to them only to indulge in rioting and drunkenness. This is no doubt true, and is one of the numberless instances of the abuse of a good thing. But yet, even if we had the power to prevent such persons coming to such gatherings, we would hesitate to use the power. True such persons are no help to the ordinance, but they have precious souls; and where is it more likely that the "other sheep not yet of this fold" may be gathered in, than in the "green pastures" where the Good Shepherd feedeth His flock, and where His "remembrancers" are met together in His name and by His authority?

But again, it is objected that even the Lord's people, coming in such numbers from a distance, would have been better at home; that their coming was an imposition upon the hospitality of the congregation. Such a complaint, however, never came from those who entertained them.

Such a complaint would have been quite inconsistent with the well-known hospitality of our pioneer fathers and mothers. "Come with me," said a good woman to a group of strangers standing at the church door, "there is room in my house for ten of you, and there is room in my heart for ten times ten."

It was the poet Burns who said:

> "When death's dark stream I ferry o'er,
> A time that surely shall come;
> In heaven itself I'll ask no more
> Than just a Highland welcome."

These were times of refreshing, and the greatness of the multitude added to the enthusiasm of the occasion. A big church and only a few people in it, the fathers used to say, was like a great barn with only one bundle of straw in it—the winds howl through it. A coal of fire left alone is not likely to burn brightly, but many glowing coals laid together help to keep each other alight. In the Church of God under the Old Dispensation the men of Israel did not come up to Jerusalem by twos and threes, but from all parts of Judea—north, south, east, and west—

with glad hearts they came in great companies, and their praise was a great shout, like the voice of thunder.

The pioneers, like the apostle, were "filled with the company of the brethren," These sacramental occasions were the only opportunities many of them had of knowing each other in this world, and of holding pleasant and profitable intercourse. Acquaintances sprang up between persons from different parts of the country who met at the Communion. This acquaintanceship in many cases warmed into Christian fellowship, so that ultimately one element of happiness in the Zorra Communion was the pleasure of seeing the faces of dear friends, and enjoying the sweet fellowship of kindred souls. Who can forget the heartfelt greeting that took place when a number of old friends met after an absence of a whole year; or the joy, commingled with sorrow, that filled the hearts of the Lord's people on Monday, the last day of the feast—joy, because of the spiritual and social blessings of the season, but profound sorrow that now the Communion was at its close, and that they were about to separate and return to their distant homes, many of them not expecting to meet again for another year, that is till the next Communion season? " When shall we have a Communion without a Monday ? " was an expression on the lips of many, and meant " When shall we meet to part no more ? " Nearly all of these grand old saints are now enjoying their Communion without a Monday. May we be worthy sons of noble sires !

CHAPTER VII

THE OLD COMMUNION SABBATH :—"DOING THE WORD"

"Raise ourselves above ourselves we must,
Else our lives to others are but dust."

"Is the sermon done?" was the question asked one who had returned from church sooner than expected. "No," was the prompt reply, "the sermon is preached, but it is not done. The 'doing' of it is for you and me during the week." Having seen our pioneer fathers as "hearers of the Word," let us to-day accompany a few of them on their way home from the communion, and see them as "doers of the Word." "We have heard wonderful things th' day," said Elder Munro. "Yes," observed Alexander Murray, "that was a very practical discourse. If the Lord did so much for us, ought we not

ZORRA PIONEERS—(Ages from 54 to 78.)

1. Rev. A. MacKay, D.D., age 66. 2. Joshua F. Youngs, died 1883, aged 71. 3. Mrs. Joshua F. Youngs, died 1883, aged 71. 4. D. R. McPherson, died 1878, aged 64. 5. Mrs. Jas. Sutherland. 6. Donald Macleod, died 1869, aged 67. 7. Miss Margaret MacKay, age 72. 8. Alex. Wood, died 1878, aged 78. 9. Jas. Wood, age 66. 10. Mrs. Alex. Wood, died 1854, aged 54. 11. Hugh S. Mackay, age 67.

to be ready to do something for Him and for one another?"

"I sometimes think," said Donald Urquhart, "that it was to take away our selfishness, and to make us kind and generous to one another, that the Lord placed us in Zorra. Yonder we were in Scotland, caring nothing for one another, but the Lord disturbed our nest, forced us from our homes, and placed us in this wilderness, where we are so dependent on one another's sympathy and help."

"And how easy it is to help when there's a mind to," added Mrs. George MacKay. "The other day my little girl came home from school, telling me what a dear little girl Maggie Murray was. Next day I met Maggie, and thanked her for being so good to my little girl. 'Why no!' said Maggie, 'I did nothin' for her, she was cryin' and I just cried with her.'"

"Ah," said Donald Urquhart, "there is a great deal in crying with one another. Do you know that one of the best Christians in Zorra to-day was converted by a tear? Alexander MacNeil, whom you all know and love, had for years listened to some of the grandest preachers in Scotland, including the great Dr. MacDonald himself. But the most earnest and evangelical preaching did him no good. Many others were converted, but he remained hard as ever. After coming to Zorra he often exchanged work with John Morrison, a man who had felt the power of the truth. One day, as MacNeil and Morrison were threshing wheat together in the barn, between the strokes of the flail Morrison spoke a word for Jesus; but MacNeil only laughed at him and hinted at hypocrisy. Now Morrison, as you know, is a man transparently honest and very sensitive, and his soul was filled with grief at MacNeil's banter. So in the flush of emotion a big tear, like a pearl, dropped, although he still kept on with his flail. He tried to hide the tear as well as he could, but MacNeil noticed it; and what years of preaching could not do, that tear did effectually; for MacNeil thought to himself, 'What! does John Morrison care for me, and weep for my soul? Then it is time I should care for it, and weep for it myself.' And from that day to the present Alexander MacNeil has lived a different life. He was converted by a tear and between the strokes of a flail."

Thus the conversation went on for the first mile or so of the homeward journey. Here John Gunn suggested to Tammas Clarke the propriety of both of them calling upon a poor sick girl who was wasting away in consumption. This girl had a somewhat remarkable experience, and before inviting the reader inside the humble home, we must give him a bit of her history. She and a younger sister had emigrated some years before with their parents from Sutherlandshire. They located in the eastern part of Zorra. With untiring perseverance the father worked, clearing the bush lot, until back of the little log house there was a clearance of fifteen or twenty acres. But alas! one day, chopping alone in the woods, a limb fell upon him, and mortally wounded him. For hours he lay upon the cold earth, bleeding and groaning, with no one to help. His wife was the first one to find him. She did not faint nor scream, but acted like a good, sensible woman. Her shawl she put as a pillow under her husband's head, and with part of her other clothing, she hastily bandaged the gaping, bleeding wound. Neighbors soon arrived. Two boards were procured and nailed side by side. Upon this the poor man was carried home; but he survived only a few days. His last words were, "Oh, Jean, I'm unco' sorry to leave yersel' and our twa bonnie bairns, but the Lord will tak' care o' you an' them."

With a noble spirit Jean faced her now heavy task, trying to do the work of both husband and wife; but the task was too much for her. Sorrow, want of proper nourishment, overwork, and exposure, constituted a burden too heavy to bear; and in a few months a naturally frail constitution succumbed, and Jean followed her "gude man" to the land o' the leal.

And now the two girls were left without father or mother, in a strange land, with no one to counsel or to provide. For a time they fought bravely the battle of life. Mary, the elder, had learned to sew, and her mother had also taught her until she had a fairly good education. Being left destitute, she gathered around her a number of the neighboring children, and taught them reading, writing, arithmetic, and sewing. Then, after her scholars were dismissed, with busy needle, under the midnight lamp, she toiled for herself and sister, and the prospect seemed to be brightening. But alas! the delicate frame had been overtasked. The hectic flush and the hacking cough soon revealed the fires consuming within. And now, in that humble home, she sat a patient sufferer by day, a weary watcher by night, unable to lie down for fear of suffocation, kept awake all night by the incessant cough, dependent largely upon the charity of neighbors, her only prospect that of early descent to the grave.

"Poor girl!" I hear the reader say, "could any lot be harder?" But along with our two friends let us enter the little log shanty and hear what she has to say. With kind but manly bearing, John Gunn walks forward to the invalid and, taking her thin wax-like hand in his, asks:

"Mary, how are you to-day?"

A bright smile plays over her face and lightens every feature, as she answers, "Thank you. I am very well." By this she means, not that her health is good, but that she has no complaint to make against Him who doeth all things well. John draws up a chair, sits down beside the invalid, still holding her hand in his. In sympathetic tones he asks:

"Are you suffering much to-day?"

Another sunny smile. "Yes, a great deal to-day; but it is all right."

Will the reader tell us what enables this poor child of sickness, sorrow, and want, to know that it is all right with her? Has human philosophy ever taught so profound a truth? Listen again:

"Do you not," says John, "get very tired sitting day and night in this chair without change of posture?"

"Of course it would rest me very much if I could lie down sometimes, but my Heavenly Father has been so good to me since I have been in this chair, that, if it were His will I could sit here forever."

Again let the reader reflect. Who is this Heavenly Father? How has He been good to her? What gives her contentment in that chair of suffering? Another question the good man asks:

"Are you not very lonely in the dead hours of night, when your cough keeps you awake and your sister is asleep?"

"Oh, no! When my cough is not too distressing, the night is my happiest time; for when my sister, at my entreaty, has gone to sleep, and the fire burns low, and everything is still in the house, then my Heavenly Father is nearest, and my Saviour is right by my side, and I am so happy that I can hardly keep from awakening my sister to tell her how happy I am."

"Well," replies John, "I am so glad that Jesus is with you and sustaining you."

"Oh, yes," says Mary, and taking a little Bible from the table beside her, she reads, "Yea though I walk through the valley of the shadow of death I will fear no evil, for Thou art with me." Turning to Isaiah xxvi, she says, "Here is a passage that is sweet to my soul," and then reads, "Thou wilt keep him in perfect peace whose mind is stayed on Thee: because he trusteth in Thee."

Four verses of the grand old Covenanters Psalm were sung:

> "God is our refuge and our strength,
> In straits a present aid;
> Therefore, although the earth remove,
> We will not be afraid."

Then all engaged in a few words of earnest prayer:

"O thou Eternal Father, infinitely great, and good, and tender! hear us, we beseech Thee. Clouds and darkness often encompass Thee, but justice and truth go before Thy face. Thou hast a right to do with Thy own what seemeth good to Thee, and Thou dost never love them more than when they are in the furnace. O Father! look in pity upon this poor child of sickness and trouble; reveal to her Thy grace, and enable her calmly to rest in Thy love. Sustain her faith, brighten her hope, and cause her to triumph to the end. Amen."

As again John Gunn and Tammas Clarke took the road, the latter said,

"Well, John, I never saw nor heard the like o' that afore. I dinna understan' it."

"Ah!" said John, "the secret of the Lord is

with them that fear Him. This experience he imparts to His beloved. Take Christ as your Saviour, Friend, and Brother, and then you will know what sustains this dying girl, and what makes her so contented and happy amid all her sufferings."

"I never before," said Tammas, "felt as I now do, that there is something real in religion. Why, the sermon this morning, and the sight of the sacred emblems, did not impress me like the testimony of that poor girl."

Not a word was spoken while they travelled the next two or three miles along the narrow path through the woods, the one man following the other, as we say, in Indian file. It was evident that there was a fierce conflict going on in Tammas's mind. The testimony he had just heard was a revelation to him. He had never heard anything like it since, in Dornoch, his dying mother took him by the hands and told him to meet her in heaven. John was quick to discern Tammas's mental condition, and thought it prudent to leave him to his own meditations.

Coming to the place of parting, John said, "You'll be at the meeting to-night, Tammas."

"Ou, aye," said Tammas, scarcely realizing the nature of the question.

It may here be stated that on each of the five evenings of the Communion, ten or twelve prayer meetings were held in the different sections of the township. These meetings were attended by the families in the locality, the young and the aged. This evening the prayer meeting was not held inside the house, but in the cool shade of a spreading beech tree near by. Tammas was there in good time, and, contrary to his usual custom, did not seek a back seat, but sat near the little table on which rested the Bible and the Psalter.

John Gunn conducted the service. It had been a warm afternoon, but now a heavy dew was falling and the evening was getting chilly. The first to lead in prayer was Elder Rose. He was in his shirt sleeves, his coat lying on the back of his chair. Just as he was rising to pray, a friend sitting by him, perceiving the lowering temperature, and apprehending the danger of catching cold, suggested to the elder the propriety of putting on his coat before engaging in prayer. Suiting the action to the word, he helped to put it on. Then began a prayer that will never be forgotten by those present. The power of the Spirit was there. Taking his idea from the putting on of his coat, the elder supplicated God :

" O Lord, put on us Thine own robe, the glorious garment of Thy righteousness (Oh Thighearna cuir umainn culaidh uat fein eadhon trusgan glortmhor t' fhireantachd); we need it ; it is a cold world this, and we cannot live without Thy robe. It is of infinite value, and has cost Thee a great price, even Thy dear Son, His life and death ; but Thou wilt give it to us without money and without price. Oh that each one here to-night would accept this beautiful robe ; then would Thy comforts fill his soul, and his peace flow as a river."

" I understan' it a' noo," said Tammas to John Gunn, when the meeting was over.

" Understand what ? was Gunn's query, put just to draw out his friend.

" Understan' what it is to become a Christian," said Tammas.

" Well, let me hear you explain it."

"It's juist to tak' Christ as Elder Rose took the coat. It is as simple as can be. I saw it while the elder was praying about the robe, its cost, its beauty, its comfort, its freeness. I see now how poor dying Mary is so patient and cheerful in her trouble. It a' comes from taking Christ without questionin'."

"Yes," said John, "that's it. Keep that always in your mind, Tammas. It will dispel every doubt and fill you with peace and comfort."

Thus came to a close an old Communion Sabbath in Zorra—a day, on the part of God's people, full of good words and works. That old Sabbath in many of its forms is now an institution of the past, but its fruits still remain. The Lord was in the midst of His people, and His presence made the Communion seasons times of refreshing, so that the Sacrament became throughout the township the great event of the year, from which all other events were dated. Ask a pioneer, "When did you begin haying last year?" and his reply would be that it was three or four weeks (as the case might be) after the Sacrament.

CHAPTER VIII
THE CATECHISING

"All that I have taught of art, everything that I have written, every greatness that there has been in any thought of mine, whatever I have done in my life, has simply been due to the fact that when I was a child my mother daily read with me a part of the Bible, and daily made me learn a part of it by heart."—RUSKIN.

"THE Lord willing, we will have a meeting for catechising in the house of Donald Ross, —— line, on a week from first Tuesday, at 3 o'clock p.m." Such was the pulpit intimation which set the whole district referred to astir during the following week.

"Eh, my!" said Mrs. MacTaggart to her neighbor, as they walked home from church, "will yon not put Kirsty Ross all in a flutter? Ye ken she is no verra strong, and she is afeard o' the minister."

"And I doot," said the neighbor, "if she kens the Catechism very well."

Great was the overhauling of things at the

house of Mrs. Ross, in preparation for the catechising. One of the three beds was removed to make room for the occasion. There were the usual whitewashing, scrubbing, dusting, and rearranging of furniture, commonly known as house-cleaning. The few simple decorations on the wall were rearranged so as to show to the best advantage; and the broken corner of the looking-glass was ingeniously concealed by a drape. All this work Mrs. Ross did unaided, for her husband, though a kind-hearted man, was occupied from dawn till dark, either threshing in the barn or chopping in the woods. The evenings were occupied by Mr. and Mrs. Ross renewing their acquaintance with the Catechism and the metrical Psalms. The two eldest children, Robbie and Maggie, were also drilled on the "questions" as far as the commandments, but the other three, Donald, Jennie, and Roddie, were taught only the creed and the Lord's Prayer, or a part of it. Similar preparation was made during the week throughout the whole district, and the candle or the rush light was kept burning in many homes

COULDN'T PASS EXAMINATION

till a much later hour than usual. Even the programme of studies in the public school was arranged with a view to the catechising.

The day announced has come, and for fully one hour before the time appointed the people can be seen coming from all directions to the place of meeting. The children accompany their parents, for there is no school to-day.

These catechisings were not all public; some of them were in private. If a man who was not in the full membership of the Church desired baptism for his child, he was required to undergo special examination as to his religious knowledge and character. And the examination was not always satisfactory. One, whom we shall call Donald, went to the minister for such examination, but failed to pass. On his way home he met another going to the minister on the same errand.

"Ah!" said Donald, "the minister was hard on me th' day. She canna get no baptism."

"And what for no?" said his neighbor. "What did he ask you?"

"Why, he axed me how mony commandments there are."

"And why did ye no say ten?"

"Ten! ten!" cried Donald, "She tried him with a hun'r (hundred), and he was no satisfied. Ye needna try him wi' ten."

Unconsciously beautiful, however, was the answer of a poor woman. Being asked a number of questions, none of which she was able to answer, she made this reply: "Minister, I canna speak weel for my Saviour, but I can live for Him, and I think I could dee for Him."

In order to understand the interest attaching to the catechising, it must be remembered that no person in the world is prouder of his nationality than the Highlander. It was a Highlander who said of the Queen, when her daughter was married to a clansman, "She'll be a prood woman noo." The typical Highlander is also intensely self-conscious, and wishes to stand well in the esteem of his neighbors for his religious intelligence. Hence the close, patient study of the Catechism before a public examination, and the chagrin when a question was asked which he could not answer, and the many expedients resorted to in order to avoid committing himself when in doubt as to the correct answer. Back seats and concealed corners of the room were at a premium. Persons well posted were in good demand as prompters. "You sit beside me, Johnnie, and gie me a word when the minister speirs me the question, for you see my memory is no sae gude as aince it was."

"Now," said the minister, "John McDonald, we'll begin with you, as you are the man of the house."

"Oh, minister, please don't; ask Peggy, my wife here, for she has more scripture nor me."

On another occasion a somewhat difficult question was asked a woman. Contrary to expectations she answered correctly. Then a still more difficult one was put. Again the reply was quite correct. And so question after question followed, each more difficult than the preceding, and every time came the correct answer. At length it dawned upon the minister that there must be in the neighborhood of his catechumen some unusually clever prompter. Quietly, and without the slightest sign of surprise or disapproval, he asks, "Am Veil Eachann Ros na shuidhe an sin?" ("Is Hector Ross sitting there?") Of course Hector Ross, an intelligent and sympathetic elder, was sitting there, and, concealed from the minister, was assisting the poor woman in her theological examination.

"Don't be bothering me," said a short, stout, middle-aged man to those around him, when the question was put to him. "If I go wrang will the minister himsel' no tell me?" This was said as "a blind"; the man did not know the question, and as a matter of fact there was no one prompting him; but he wished to convey the idea to his examiner that his failure was owing, not to ignorance, but to the too great eagerness of those around him to assist. The trick worked well, for the minister at once said, "That's right, John, depend on yourself; here's the question," and with this the good man repeated nearly the whole answer for John, while a grim smile played over John's countenance, and his eye twinkled at the thought of how he had cheated the minister.

Sometimes the answer to a question was exceedingly though unconsciously droll, causing ill-concealed amusement among the younger portion of the audience, while the old people looked more than ordinarily grave. A boy, who had been specially trained by his mother in good manners, was being examined on the following passage:

"We have all sinned."

"Now, my boy," said the minister, "does that mean that every one of us has sinned?" putting the emphasis on "every one."

The boy hesitated, fearing an affirmative answer, lest he might cast a reflection on the character of his pastor. But, upon a repetition of the question, the lad replied:

"Every one has sinned except yoursel' and the elders." He saved his manners at the expense of his theology.

It may here be explained that while the minister presided at these meetings, putting such questions and making such remarks as he saw fit, the questions were usually asked, not by the minister, but by one of the elders. There was tact and wisdom in this. The elder selected on this occasion was one who could not read, but who was, nevertheless, thoroughly conversant with the Catechism and with his Bible, and a man of intellectual power and native eloquence.

"Johnnie Dougall," said the elder, "give us, the twenty-third Psalm."

The Psalm is repeated from beginning to end without a slip:

> "The Lord's my shepherd, I'll not want.
> He makes me down to lie
> In pastures green: he leadeth me
> The quiet waters by."

"Now," said the minister, addressing himself to the father of the young man who had just recited, "your son has done well. I trust the words he has repeated are the testimony of his heart concerning the Lord's goodness. But you are a man of experience; you can look back upon a life of many ups and downs. Can you give us this beautiful Psalm, changing the time of it from the present to the past?" With some kind help from his minister, and an occasional word from young Willie Saunders, the father repeated as follows:

> "The Lord has been my shepherd, and I have not been in want.
> He hath made me to lie down in green pastures; he hath led me the quiet waters by.
>
> "My soul he hath restored again,
> And he hath made me to walk
> In the paths of righteousness,
> Even for his own name's sake."

The change in the tense of the Psalm conveyed an entirely new idea. The minds of the aged men and women present went across the ocean to the heather hills of Scotland and the old kirk, to the parting with friends, and the long sea voyage, and the journey into the unbroken forest, and the varied experiences of years. And, as they thought of these things, tears came to the eyes of some while the testimony was borne, "The Lord has been (not 'is') my shepherd."

"Well," said the minister, "if Jehovah has been your Shepherd in the past He is your

Shepherd to-day, and He will continue to care for you unto the end, and you will dwell in His house for evermore."

Among the Shorter Catechism questions, of course, "effectual calling" was not overlooked.

"Catherine MacIntosh," said the elder, "will you tell us what is effectual calling?"

At once, in a clear, sweet voice, that could be heard distinctly by everyone in the house, came the answer:

"Effectual calling is the work of God's Spirit, whereby, convincing us of our sin and misery, enlightening our minds in the knowledge of Christ, and renewing our wills, He doth persuade and enable us to embrace Jesus Christ, freely offered to us in the Gospel."

"This," said the minister, "is a great question, and contains a complete account of the scheme of human redemption." Then in a plain, simple way he comments upon each clause of the question. "And now let us see how many here can bear personal testimony to these blessed truths. Let us use the singular number and the past tense, instead of the plural number and the present tense, as in the Catechism. Who can repeat the question with these changes, and thus make it the expression of their own experience?" The pastor's idea was a little further explained, and then it was quickly apprehended. One head after another was bowed in humility. Still none ventured to respond. Again the question was asked:

"Is there no one who can bear clear personal testimony to the truth of his effectual calling?"

Slowly a young man rose from his seat. His frame shook with emotion.. His voice trembled, and tears filled his eyes, while he repeated the question with the change suggested.

"Effectual calling is the work of God's Spirit, whereby He hath convinced *me* of *my* sin and misery, enlightened *my* mind in the knowledge of Christ, and renewed *my* will and persuaded and enabled *me* to embrace Jesus Christ freely offered to *me* in the Gospel."

While the young man was speaking there was a solemn silence, and as he sat down there was an audible sigh of praise, with here and there an expression of "Thank God." A profound impression was produced, for all present knew the lad as one of noble Christian character. He had a genuine spiritual experience, and he told it. "Go home to thy friends," said Christ to the man healed, "and tell them what great things the Lord hath done for thee, and hath had compassion on thee."

And now the benediction was pronounced. There was much handshaking, and many were the inquiries as to the welfare of the children away from home, and "friends ayont the sea." The minister, one or two elders, and a few of the more intimate friends of the family, remained and partook of the "hamely" but hospitable meal.

These occasions are gone, and few of those who took part in them are now with us, but the good effects are still to be seen. We have occasionally heard Mr. Mackenzie charged with remissness in looking after the young of his congregation. This is a great injustice to the memory of a good man. Mr. Mackenzie carefully sought the godly upbringing of the young, and that he sought it not in vain the history of the congregation amply testifies. But he secured this end, not so much through the Sabbath school, as by taking pains, in private and in public catechising, to teach parents and children their duties to God and each other.

The men from Zorra who have become missionaries, ministers, lawyers, doctors, and Christian workers of all kinds, received their early religious education, not so much in the Sabbath school as at the fireside, and from their parents, God's own specially appointed teachers. It is quite possible to abuse a good thing, and there is reason to fear that we are at the present day allowing the Sabbath school to supersede parental effort.

Dr. Guthrie ascribes the mental vigor and business tact of the Scottish people largely to their familiarity with the Book of Proverbs. And so we hesitate not to ascribe a large measure of the material, mental, and moral worth of Zorra to the faithful training of their children by the pioneers, an important part of which was connected with the catechising, so faithfully attended to by the Rev. Donald Mackenzie.

CHAPTER IX

PIONEER POLITICS

"Party is the madness of the many for the gain of the few."—SIR JOHN A. MACDONALD.

FOR some years after the first settlement, the Zorra pioneers took little interest in politics. What with clearing the forest, "ploughing, sowing, reaping and mowing," they had hard work to provide food and clothes for themselves and their children. In Parliament there scarcely existed what we now call partyism. The politicians, acting upon the principle that the "State belongs to the Statesman," were occupied in gobbling up as much of the land as possible at a shilling an acre.

There was but one voting place for the whole county. This was at an hotel called "Martin's old stand," near Beachville. It was open voting; the election lasted for five days, and feeling ran high. During the election, free meals and liquor were supplied by each candidate to his friends. Barrels of whiskey were placed near the polling booth; pails, dippers, and little tin cups were supplied in abundance, and as may be easily imagined, the consequent scenes were far from edifying. The wonder is that under such circumstances the consequences were not even more serious. But the typical Highlander, although never chargeable with lack of courage, is not disposed to fisticuffs. This is too small game for him, and if he fight at all, he aims at killing "twa at a blow."

A Highlander and an Irishman fell out and began to quarrel. Instantly the Irishman's coat was off. "Tut! tut!" said Donald. "Pe quate, and we will jaw it for a while."

But while personal encounters were not so frequent as under the circumstances might be expected, the poverty and degradation caused by strong drink were very great. In Britain's battles, from the days of old down to Dargai Heights, the Highlander has taken his full share of fighting and honors, and he has proved himself able to hold his own "man tae man the world o er;" but alas, there is one enemy that has time and again, in Zorra and elsewhere, proved more than a match for him—the enemy that gurgles out of the neck of a black bottle.

Cheap as whiskey was in those pioneer days it was frequently hard to get, for the money was not there. A poor old woman, who was very fond of a dram, sent her daughter round to Sandy's bar for a gill. As she sent no money, but only a promise to pay next morning, the girl came back without the whiskey, and reported that the tavern keeper would not give it to her without the cash. The woman had no money, but she told the girl to give the family Bible as security till the next morning. Even that was refused. When this was reported to the old lady she exclaimed, "What will I do when he'll neither tak my word nor the Word of God for a gill of whiskey?"

"Bring out Jeroboam," said the head of a house when a friend called, meaning a jug of whiskey. But why was the whiskey jug called

"Jeroboam"? Because it was "Jeroboam, the son of Nebat, who made Israel to sin." Thus the Highlander, with a native religious instinct, confessed his fault while he indulged the sin.

It was in the thirties. Mr. Ayers was driving a flourishing hotel business in Embro. The political contest was between Peter Carroll and Robert Rollo Hunter. Mr. Ayers each day drove a four-horse sleigh, loaded with voters, to "Martin's old stand," the place of voting. There was always a piper on board, who skirled away the music that never fails to inspire the Highland heart. They had cast their votes, and were "na fou, but juist had plenty." The four-horse team had been left standing for hours in the shelter of a log house. In this domicile lived two bachelors, who, for various reasons, were notoriously unpopular. Indeed it was whispered that these men did not distinguish between their neighbors' hen roosts and their own. On this occasion a wag played a cruel practical joke on the bachelor brothers.

While the sleigh stood beside the house, an enemy found a couple of logging chains, fastened them securely together, then attached one end very carefully to both cross beams of the sleigh; then the other end was attached to the top log and roof of the shanty. The chain was carefully concealed with snow. Well, the time came for the Zorra boys to start for home. They had the *Deoch an doras* (drink of the door, that is, the last drink). "All aboard!" There was a rush, and soon all found a place, in various postures, in the long sleigh-box. "Hurrah! Whip! Crack! Get up!" With a bound the horses dashed forward, but in an instant came to a standstill. The driver, knowing nothing of his attachment, struck up again with more vigor, and in less time than it takes me to write it, the topmost log of the shanty, accompanied by the roof, lay on the ground.

When, with bunting flying, pipes screaming, and twenty free and independent electors shouting, the sleigh reached Embro, there was a hot time in the old village that night. Every man, woman and child turned out, and long and loud was the cheering when it was announced that Hunter (Embro's favorite) was ahead. But next night the news came that Carroll was ahead. The third night Hunter's majority was seventy, and he kept the lead to the end, much to the satisfaction of the Zorra men.

The first Parliament of Upper Canada was elected in 1792, and was held at Niagara. I can find no trace of any representative of Oxford in the first or second Parliament, but in the third Parliament, 1800-1804, Oxford, along with Norfolk and Middlesex, was represented by Hon. D. W. Smith.

From 1804 to 1812 Oxford and Middlesex were represented by one man—Benaiah Malory.

From 1812 to 1820 by Mahlon Burwell.

From 1820 to 1840 the elections resulted as follows: 1820, Thos. Horner; 1824, Thos. Horner and Chas. Ingersoll; 1828, Horner and Malcolm; in 1830, Chas. Ingersoll and Chas. Duncombe; in 1835, Chas. Duncombe and Robt. Alway.

Duncombe having left the country, there was a contest, as we have seen, for his seat, between Robert Rollo Hunter a ndPeter Carroll, resulting in the election of the former.

After the union of Upper and Lower Canada, in 1840, Oxford was represented by Francis Hincks, afterwards Sir Francis Hincks.

In 1844 Mr. Robert Riddell was elected, and in 1848 Peter Carroll and Hon. F. Hincks.

In 1849 Lord Elgin was egged, and the parliament building in Montreal burned. There was great excitement throughout the country.

In 1851 Hon. F. Hincks was elected; after which the county was divided into two ridings —North and South Oxford.

In 1854 the north riding was represented by D. Matheson, Esq., of Embro, and the south riding by Hon. F. Hincks.

In 1858 Hon. Geo. Brown, of Toronto, was elected for the north riding, and also for Toronto, and decided to sit for Toronto. Then the constituency was represented by Wm. McDougall.

In 1861 the north riding re-elected Wm. McDougall, and the south riding Dr. Connor; and on the demise of Dr. Connor, Hon. Geo. Brown became representative for South Oxford.

In 1863 the north riding was represented by

Hope F. McKenzie, of Sarnia, and the south riding by Hon. Geo. Brown.

In 1867 the north riding elected Thos. Oliver, of Woodstock, as its representative.

In 1872 Thos. Oliver was again returned for North Oxford by acclamation, and E. V. Bodwell for South Oxford.

In 1874 Thos. Oliver was returned a third time for North Oxford, and Col. Jas. A. Skinner for South Oxford.

In 1880, on the death of the late Thos. Oliver, the present member, James Sutherland, became member for North Oxford. Since then Mr. Sutherland has been elected four times, and each time by an increased majority.

The election of Hon. (afterwards Sir) Francis Hincks, in 1851, was perhaps one of the most exciting contests ever witnessed in the county. The "Clergy Reserve" question and the "Separate School" question were up, and a great deal of religious feeling was aroused. The writer has now before him one of the campaign sheets of the time. It is a large poster, eighteen inches by twelve. The head-lines are in very large letters, and the whole get-up quite sensational. For clear ringing denunciation of a political opponent this electioneering document would be hard to beat. Here it is as far as it can be exhibited on our small page:

"ATTENTION!

" REFORMERS!!

"Hincks, the traitor to Reform Principles, and his Office-hunting friends have reported that Scatcherd will resign. This is false!
"Scatcherd cannot resign!

"400

"Free and Independent Electors have signed his Requisition, and he is pledged to go to the polls. He is opposed to tax the people $800,000 a year to pay the 'Interest' on money for a railroad from Quebec to Halifax, for the benefit of Lower Canada.
"Electors of Oxford!—Can you vote for Hincks, who has falsified every promise, and betrayed your dearest interests?
"Who voted against the Marriage Bill? Hincks.
"Who voted against the Rectory Bill? Hincks.

"Who voted against the Clergy Reserves Bill? Hincks.

"Who is patron of the fifty-seven Rectories? Hincks.

"Who said you persecuted the English Church? Hincks.

"Who turned Merrit and Malcolm Cameron out of the Executive Council? Hincks.

"Who supports Sectarian Schools? Hincks.

"Who said Upper Canada Reformers were a set of Pharisaical Brawlers? Dr. Taché, one of the new Ministry.

"Who got $7,000 to pay for dinners given in Montreal, and called it 'extra services'? Hincks.

"Who voted $80,000 of your money to repair the Governor's residence in Quebec? Hincks.

"Who spent $350,000 to remove the seat of Government? Hincks.

"Who voted $300,000 last year to pay for the Administration of Justice? Hincks.

"Who divided the County? Hincks.

"REFORMERS!—AWAKE.

"Record your votes for Scatcherd, for his Election must be secured. Read his Address. He is a Farmer, and a resident of your county. His Interest is yours.

"Mr. Hincks has received a Requisition from the County of Kent, to run in opposition to Mr. George Brown, and has accepted it.

"November 18, 1851."

Strange that after such a fusilade Hincks was triumphantly elected!

A Zorra man who is still living, speaking of the excitement of this election, says: "They axed me how I was going to vote. I said I would vote for ——; and as soon as the word was out of my mouth the blood was out of my nose." This was voting solid!

How did the early elections compare with those of to-day? As we have already clearly shown, they were not ideal. We wish we could say:

"Then none were for the party, then all were
 for the state;
Then the great man helped the poor, and the
 poor man loved the great;
Then spoils were fairly portioned, then lands
 were fairly sold,
And the Romans were like brothers in the brave
 days of old."

In the olden times, as to-day, whiskey was the foe of everything pure and good. The fact also of there being only one polling place in the county, and the open voting, helped greatly to increase the excitement.

But notwithstanding the excitement and excesses of the early elections, they were conducted in a manner immeasurably more pure and honorable than some similar campaigns in our time. Are not our politics rapidly degenerating into a very cesspool of corruption? The boodling and bribery, the frauds and corruption which have characterized many recent elections, are enough to bring the blush of shame to the cheek of every honest Canadian. Occasionally we have an election trial, and then, although only a corner of the covering is raised, we see something of the seething mass of corruption underneath. And yet how seldom do we hear the ring of genuine, honest indignation against political corruption, except when it hurts "our party" or "our man."

What is the remedy? The remedy lies largely with the Church. Unless the Church throws off her indifference, arouses herself to cry aloud and spare not, the cancer will spread. Legislation can do something; and by all means let good laws be sought—laws that will make it as easy as possible to do right, and as difficult as possible to do wrong. But legislation can deal only with environment. The Divine Spirit alone, working upon the hearts of men, can create and foster a love of righteousness, and a hatred of iniquity.

We may change the tariff, reform the finances, prohibit the liquor traffic, obtain better Sunday laws, enact severest laws against bribery, kill off the monopolies, and shake off the bosses, but unless the electors enthrone Jesus Christ in the politics of the land, there will soon be as much oppression, dishonesty, intemperance, and corruption as ever. Radical and lasting reform must begin in the heart. "Let Glasgow flourish by the preaching of the Word," said John Knox. So we say of Zorra, Oxford, Canada. Men of God, arise!

> "Perish policy and cunning!
> Perish all that fears the light
> Whether losing, whether winning,
> 'Trust in God and do the right.'
>
> "Trust no party, sect, or faction;
> Trust no leaders in the fight;
> But in every word and action
> 'Trust in God and do the right.'"

As soil, shower, and sunshine can make more

flowers and fragrance than all the chemists, so God's Word and Spirit can effect more in moral reforms and human regeneration than all human legislation. Let every Christian patriot therefore proclaim the glorious truth that Christianity is not a mere sentiment, or a system of cold abstractions, but a power that shows itself grandly in the domestic, the social, the political life of a people. It ennobles every department of life, making the polling booth as sacred as the prayer meeting, and the act of voting an act of worship.

CHAPTER X

ZORRA AND THE REBELLION OF '37

"Dulce et decorum est pro patria mori."—HORACE.
("It is sweet and noble to die for one's country.")

THE first settlers in Zorra were not from Scotland, but represented various nationalities; some of them were United Empire Loyalists, or more or less remotely connected with them. Among these early settlers were the Hodgkinsons, Codys, Karns, Youngs, Coukes, Burdicks, Reeds, Galloways, Wilkersons, Aldridges, and Tafts. Many of these names are still familiar, and those bearing them regarded as among the most intelligent and progressive in the district. One of them, Marvin Cody, writes to me from Sarnia, as follows: "I came to Zorra in March, 1824. When in my seventeenth year, under a deep sense of my lost condition as a sinner, I went out one evening into the field by the fenceside and cried for mercy, and mercy was given me. There and then I became a new creature. The peace, the love, the joy which followed made me very happy; I united with the Baptist Church. And now, in my eighty-fourth year, I must be nearing the great solemnities of eternity; but I have a confident hope in my dear Saviour, who has stood by me these many years; and the prospect of going to be with Him in heaven through eternity is very delightful."

The war between the United States and Canada began in 1812 and lasted about three years, and was the cause of much bloodshed and hardship to the Canadian people; which, however, only intensified their loyalty to Great Britain.

Soon after this began the political struggle that ended in the rebellion of 1837-9. In this struggle we find on the one hand, a number of patriotic men fighting for popular rights, and on the other hand, what is well known as the "Family Compact." The Family Compact was a small but compact body of men, most of them Loyalists, combined together for the purpose of securing and retaining all the government offices for themselves or their relatives. There was at this time no responsible government as now understood; that is, the Governor and his cabinet were not responsible in any way to the people. The Governor was sent out by England, and he had the power to choose his own cabinet to suit himself. He did choose, not according to the wishes of the representatives of the people, but according to the dictates of the Family Compact, who had wormed themselves into power, and were determined to stay there regardless of the wishes of the people. For some twenty-five years the struggle for responsible government continued to be the burning question of the day, the particular matter in dispute during the latter part of the period being the "Clergy Reserves." A word of explanation may be in place:

The Clergy Reserves had their origin in what is known as the "Constitutional Act of 1791." By the thirty-sixth clause of that Act provision was made for reserving out of all grants of public lands in Upper and Lower Canada, past as well as future, an allotment for the support of a "Protestant Clergy." This allotment was to be equal in value to the seventh part of the lands so granted. By the next section, it was provided that the rents, profits, and emoluments, arising from the lands so appropriated, were applicable solely to the maintenance and support of a "Protestant Clergy." These provisions were in their result most unfortunate for both Ontario and Quebec. Especially so for the former province. They sowed the seeds of sectarian and political strife, retarded the growth of the country, divided the people, called into existence bitter feelings, which have hardly yet subsided, and were the immediate cause of the rebellion of 1837. As the holders of public offices were chiefly members of the Church of England, that body obtained, under the Family Compact system, then in force, fully eleven-twelfths of all the reserves. According to a return made to the House of Assembly of lands set apart as glebes in Upper Canada during the forty-six years from 1787 to 1833, it appears that 22,345 acres were so set apart for the clergy of the Church of England, 1,160 acres for ministers of the Kirk of Scotland, 400 for Roman Catholics, and none for any other denomination.

Besides which the lands of the Clergy Reserves, instead of being set apart in blocks, were interspersed with the grants made to settlers, thus giving the Church the benefit of the increased value of the neighboring land caused by improvements made by settlers; while the Church lands were left unappropriated and wild, thus increasing the difficulties of road-making and causing other inconveniences. The grievance was first felt by the settlers in their private capacity, and the first protest made against the reservations on purely secular grounds. In 1836 great indignation was caused by the discovery that Governor Colborne had, on January 15th, while sitting in Council, created forty-four rectories of the Church of England, and endowed them with extensive and valuable glebe lands, out of the Clergy Reserves; thus creating practically an Established Church. This was done in a clandestine manner, without the knowledge and in opposition to the declared policy of the Imperial Government, and also in opposition to the resolutions of the Legislative Assembly of Upper Canada. This act of the Governor-in-Council was regarded as a breach of public faith and a violation of the rights of the people, and led to open rebellion a few months after.

At last, under the leadership of William Lyon Mackenzie, things came to a crisis. Perhaps unwisely, recourse was had to arms, but desperate diseases require desperate remedies. Blood was shed, and a number of executions followed, but the result was the inestimable blessing of popular government as we have it in Canada to-day.

W. Lyon Mackenzie has been stigmatized by a certain class of writers, as an agitator, a firebrand—injudicious and reckless. This, however, has always been the fate of patriots and true reformers. To him more perhaps than to any other man we owe the popular, civil, and political rights we enjoy to-day. The Family Compact was a strong and unscrupulous party and it took a man of dauntless courage and indomitable perseverance to fight it. Such a man was W. L. Mackenzie. Several times he was expelled from Parliament, and as often re-elected by his loyal constituency in York. Once he had his type thrown into the lake by a mob headed by the chief men in Toronto. But against tremendous odds he persevered in his struggle for the rights of the people; nor did he struggle in vain. The rebellion brought the misgovernment of the country, for a quarter of a century by the Family Compact, prominently before the British people, and woke them up to a sense of their duty, and the necessity of giving to Canada the right to govern herself according to the wishes of the majority, expressed through the representatives in parliament. This is what we now call responsible government, which we largely owe to W. L. Mackenzie, and for which we cannot be too thankful. We hope to see the day when Canada will erect a monument to the memory of Mr. Mackenzie and honor him for his patriotic readiness to shed his blood, rather than see his country enslaved by an unprincipled and wicked oligarchy.

In 1854 the Canadian Parliament, authorized by the Imperial Government, alienated the Clergy Reserves from religious to secular purposes, having due regard to the life-interests of all beneficiaries, whose stipends were not to be reduced.

The money was divided among the municipalities, and each municipality decided for itself what use to make of it. Many apportioned it to public roads, but Zorra, we think greatly to her credit, set it apart for the permanent benefit of her public schools.

But what part did Zorra take in the rebellion?

> "I hae but ae son, my brave young Donald,
> But gin I had ten they would follow Prince Charlie."

When the news of the uprising came, great indeed was the excitement. No question was asked as to the justice or injustice of the cause. The Highlanders, as well as their neighbors, the

United Empire Loyalists, were prepared to do or die in defence of the Crown, right or wrong.

> " To doubt would be disloyalty,
> To falter would be sin."

A call was made for volunteers, and promptly two hundred stalwart men presented themselves in Embro ready for drill. Crittendom's distillery was extemporized for a drill-shed. The vats were filled with snow well packed in, so that the floor was all of one uniform level. There were not guns enough, but Cooper Welsh's hoop-poles were used instead. The drill-master was Mr. Nasmyth. After about a week's practice, word came that the rebels were marching on to Woodstock. At once the Embro company, reinforced by another company from the country, headed by their respective pipers, and carrying guns, clubs, poles, etc., set out on the march to meet the enemy.

It was at the time of the Fenian raid, many years after, that an old lady in Zorra is reported as having declared with much vehemence, " They may tak Montreal, and they may tak Toronto, and they may tak Woodstock, but they'll never tak Z-o-r-r-a." This was certainly the spirit of the Highlanders in 1837. Having reached Woodstock, they found no enemy anywhere in the neighborhood; and, after remaining under arms for a few days, they were permitted to return home.

The homeward journey from Woodstock to Embro was made on foot through the woods. The night was very frosty. When the volunteers were about two miles east of the village, suddenly they heard the loud cracking of the trees because of the frost, resembling the reports of rifles. The brave boys instantly concluded that Mackenzie's rebels were after them. They became panic-stricken, and took helter-skelter to their heels, hiding behind trees, logs, and brushes, until, after some difficulty, they were persuaded that there was no real cause for alarm. But the boys never liked to be reminded of this exhibition of weakness. It is related that some years ago, when there were no railroads in Scotland, an Englishman and a Scotchman were riding together on the top of a coach running between Stirling and Dumblane. The Englishman inquired of his neighbor the name of a certain place. With feigned surprise, the Scotchman replied, "Dinna ye ken whaur ye were weel lickit?" In this way the Englishman was given to understand that he was unconsciously passing over the field of Bannockburn. So it is said the Zorra people would, for years after, point out to the volunteer boys the famous woods, reminding them, "that's whaur ye were lickit by the rebels."

However, the volunteers stood high in the estimation of their countrymen, and at a gathering given in their honor great was the praise bestowed upon them. It is said that in the gathering there was an old woman who, observing some young men not cheering as lustily as she thought they should do, remonstrated with them, saying, "Why you no cheer? These are the men who fought and dee'd for ye."

I have before me as I write a very interesting document. It is dated July 5th, 1838, and is very much the worse of the wear of three-score years, although still quite legible. It is the pay-sheet of the Zorra volunteers, and the heading reads as follows: "We, the undersigned officers, non-commissioned piper, and privates of the detachment of the 3rd Oxford Regiment, under the command of Captain Wm. Mackay, serving from the 30th of June to the 5th July, 1838, acknowledge to have received our pay for that period, for which we annex our names."

Then follow sixty-four names, nearly all written by the persons themselves, and the greater number of them written in a good round hand, speaking well for the literary training of these pioneers.

Among the names are Macdonalds, Murrays, Munros, Mathesons, Macleods, Sutherlands, Campbells, and Mackays—the latter, of course, predominating. Not one of those whose names are on this document is now living. Peace to their ashes.

CHAPTER XI

LOGGING BEES AND DANCING SPREES

"If you want knowledge, you must toil for it; if food, you must toil for it; and if pleasure, you must toil for it. Toil is the law. Pleasure comes through toil, and not by self-indulgence and indolence. When one gets to love work, his life is a happy one."—RUSKIN.

THERE may be no logical connection between logging bees and dancing sprees, but they were intimately associated in the experience of the Highland pioneers of Zorra. And their union illustrates the truth of Ruskin's statement, that "toil is a condition of enjoyment." It also shows that the pioneers were not a set of dullards, whose life consisted only in a weary round of hard, irksome duties. They were a hardy people, full of energy and vivacity. If they endured much, they enjoyed much.

There were three ways by which the first

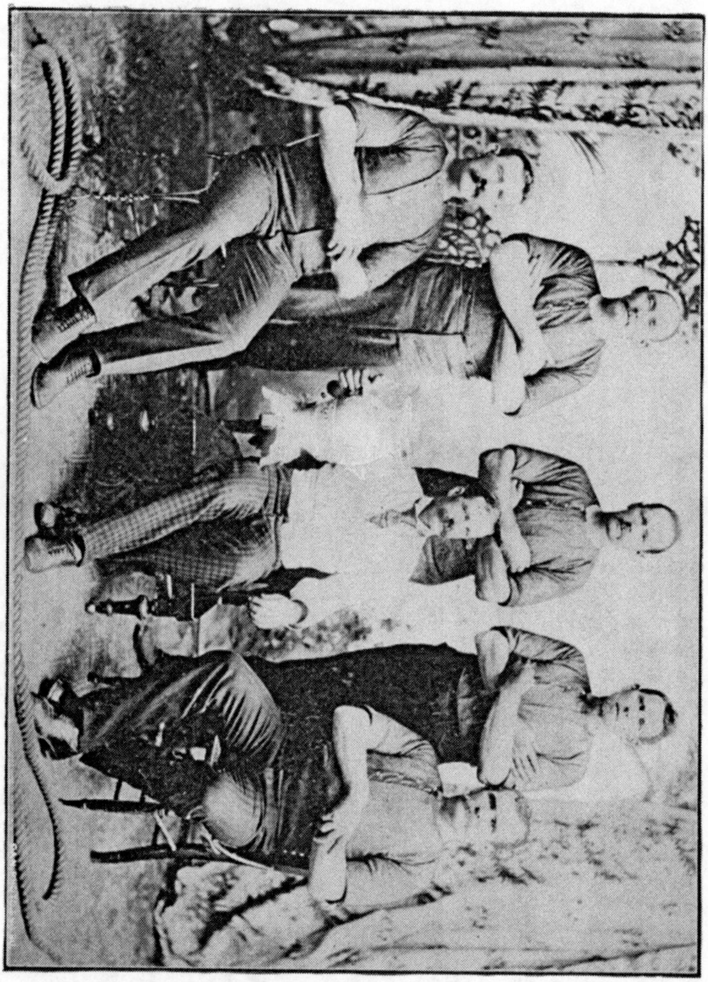

settlers cleared the land. The first was called "slashing." The farmer slashed the trees down in winnows, and let them thus lie on the ground for three or four years. Then in dry weather he would set fire to the winnows, and soon the whole slashing of ten or twelve acres would be a great mass of smoke and flame. The brush and smaller timber would be burnt up; but the great logs, the beeches, elms, oaks, and maples, would still remain. It was necessary, therefore, to cut them up, so that they could be piled into heaps to be burnt. This was done not altogether with the axe, but largely by means of what were called "niggers," which consisted of fire placed on top of the logs at intervals of twenty or thirty feet, and by means of small dry timber laid across, kept burning until the big log was burnt through, and thus divided into several short sections, such as the oxen could haul.

It was a Zorra man who wrote a letter to his friends in Sutherlandshire, Scotland, declaring that he had a hundred "niggers" working for him. He mentioned that there were very dark people in America called "niggers." He then went on to give a minute description of his farm—so many acres cleared, such good crops from year to year, and how well off he was now, compared with what he was in Scotland. "Even to-day," said he, "I have no less than one hundred niggers working for me to clear my farm." Of course, he meant the fire used on the tree for cutting it instead of the axe; but he kept the explanation to himself. It is said the whole parish in Scotland was agog with excitement over the Zorra man's wonderful wealth in controlling the services of no less than one hundred negroes.

In the same spirit another pioneer informed his friends in Scotland that in Zorra men received five shillings ($1.25) for rocking a cradle. The "cradle" meant was that used in the harvest field, though a different one was suggested to the man in Scotland.

Another way to clear the bush was by "girdling." This consisted in hacking the tree all around, so that in the course of six or seven years it would decay and fall. This method of clearing was, however, found very dangerous for the cattle, and whenever the wind would blow limbs would be falling, and many a farmer had his ox or cow killed. It was wonderful, however, the instinct of danger which the animals acquired, so that as soon as they perceived the wind rising, they would rush terrified from the girdling. Another objection to this method of clearing was that, while the big trees were decaying, the underbrush would grow up to be small trees difficult to destroy. A man could girdle two acres a day.

The third way was the most laborious, but considered by far the quickest and best. It was to cut down the trees and make them into logs from fourteen to eighteen feet long, then pile the brush, and cut the underbrush. A good chopper would thus cut down an acre in about seven days.

When these people came to Zorra they knew nothing about chopping, most of them having never seen a chopping-axe, or its handle; everything had to be learned. All the more credit to them for their brave and successful fight with the forest.

These pioneers carried their religion into all the affairs of life. I have heard one of them state that before tackling a giant of the forest, he invariably knelt down and prayed for strength and protection. He evidently feared only the large trees, and was willing to take chances on the small ones, though, as a matter of fact, the small ones were the most dangerous. Notwithstanding all precautions, however, many a broken leg, cut foot, and crushed arm testified to the dangers incurred by our uninitiated forefathers in hewing out for themselves homes in the forest.

The first thing done on coming to the township was to choose a spot for a house. The spot selected was usually the highest hill or elevation that could be found on the farm. The next thing was to cut down all the trees that in falling might reach the building. Some instances, however, occurred in which through miscalculation, some tall tree was left, which in a storm fell upon the shanty, seldom, however, doing more damage than frightening the inmates, for the big logs of the shanty were strong enough to hold up the heaviest weight.

The immigrants usually arrived in August, and, having built the shanty, the next few weeks were given to underbrushing. Then all winter the forest resounded with the woodman's axe. In early spring there was the sugar-making. Not infrequently would the sugar-makers remain in the woods most of the night boiling down the sap.

It is related of a pioneer that one night he continued boiling down till two o'clock in the morning. He then started for home; but, leaving the bright blaze of the fire, and entering the dark woods, he got bewildered and lost his way. He travelled about for an hour, and then made up his mind that he had better remain where he was until daylight. With the first streak of dawn he descried in the distance a small shanty. He hastened towards it, and knocked loudly at the door. A small boy, *déshabille*, opened. Mr. W. inquired if anyone here knew where Mr. W.'s house was. The little fellow quickly ran back to another room, excitedly crying, "Mither, mither, faither has come hame, but he has gone daft." In his bewildered state Mr. W. failed to recognize his own house, or his boy.

The time for logging has come, and there is to be a great "bee" on the farm. Farmer Murray has six acres to log of heavy timber, and he will need six yoke of oxen and thirty men. So he goes round the district and invites all to his "bee." Those who have oxen are to bring them. Their wives and daughters are also invited to come and help prepare the dinner and supper, and also to make a quilt. Young farmer A. is told to bring along his bagpipes, and B. is to bring his fiddle. C. is to come to make handspikes, and D. is appointed butler.

In many cases, however, the handspikes were prepared previously to the day of the "bee." They were made mostly of ironwood, and were the shape of the well-known iron crowbar of to-day. Many kept them from year to year, until they got smooth from constant use, and light by seasoning.

Well, the day for the "bee" has come, and a beautiful, sunshiny day it is. By six o'clock in the morning the men and oxen are ready for work. The first thing done is to divide the field to be logged into strips of equal width, and running from one end to the other. Then a yoke of oxen, attended by five men, is put in charge of each strip. After each man has taken his "horn," or glass of whiskey, the work of the day begins in real earnest.

I was at that "bee," a very young boy, but the scene is vividly before me just now. Each driver has a long blue beech switch, specially prepared by twisting one end until it was quite limber, which he flourishes around the heads of the oxen. The men wear moleskin pants, and a belt around the waist. The shirt sleeves are rolled all the way up. The butler, or boss of the work, gives all necessary directions. The strength of the oxen is astonishing, and so is their instinct for the work. The stumps are so thick that it is hard to get room to build a heap. The chain is attached with a roll, so that the log, when moved, will turn partly over. This prevents the snags, which, of course, have not been cut away from the under part of the log, catching the ground and increasing the resistance. Then the log is pulled among the stumps to where the heap is to be built, and after the first log or two is placed, the oxen seem to know instinctively just where to go each time.

Here is a big oak tree, three feet through, and fifty-six feet long, hard to burn, stumps thick all around it. Farmer George is foreman for this gang. He has worked in France at a sawmill, and knows, or is supposed to know, how to handle logs. He claims also to be able to speak French, and he is not slow in parading his knowledge among the Zorra men. On he goes to build this heap. He says: "We'll give that cherry log a roll, swing her around beside this oak, and we'll draw them basswood and maple ones and put them in the bottom, and we'll put that rock-elm fellow on top."

Here are some of the cries constantly heard

that day, as the log-heaps were being built: "Hip!" "Roll up!" "Up she goes!" "Skade!" "Hold that catch now!" "Now boys, push!" "Can you hold on?" "I'll try. No, I can't!" "Come here, driver, quick!" Driver runs, and, putting his breast against the log, pushes with all his might. "Yes, we can hold it." "You catch under!" "Now, get ready! He-ho-he!" The strength of five stalwart Highlanders is tested. Up goes the log, but the men are out of breath. Each removes the old straw hat from his head, and the red handkerchief is taken out to wipe the great beads of perspiration from the face.

The heap is completed. Foreman George puts in his French: "Bien! eh, bien, messieurs! That heap of logs would be worth thirty pounds in France." The butler now goes his round with the black bottle and glass. Thus the work goes on, until the call to dinner is heard. There are no horns to blow in these days, the distance from the house not being sufficient to make them necessary.

"We boys" were set to watch the oxen

while feeding on the edge of the woods with the yoke on. There was no hay, but that did not matter much; the tall, rich grass afforded ample pasturage. I cannot report fidelity to duty on this occasion. We spent a considerable part of the dinner hour in trying to get the oxen to fight; but hard-working oxen, like hard-working men, are not disposed to fight, and no serious results followed.

After dinner, the work went on as before. There was whiskey galore, and as evening approached the butler was in greater demand, and the evil effects of the black bottle were becoming more manifest. The race was keen as to who should first reach the end of their strip.

Thus was Zorra cleared of its forests. Sometimes, with a blazing sun in the heavens, and log-heaps burning on every side, the heat was simply terrible and the smoke suffocating. What with the smoke-drawn tears running down the cheeks in streams, and the dust and ashes adhering, the men were scarcely recognizable.

PAT AT A LOGGING-BEE

The story is told of an Irishman who came to Zorra at this time. Shortly after arriving he one day lost himself in the woods. Hearing the shouting and noise of men who were logging, he turned his footsteps in that direction. The day was very hot, and the men very black. The Irishman soon found himself in the midst of a scene such as he had never before witnessed.

"Well, Pat, do you know where you are?"

"Faith!" was the reply, "joodging from the hate of the climate, and the coolur of the people, it must be perdition, sure!"

As I write the story of the difficulties encountered and overcome by these brave toilers of the forest, my heart thrills with admiration. How hard they wrought! How patiently they endured! How cheerfully they persevered! It matters little to me how humble their work was, the spirit in which they did it is everything. Their invincible courage, industry, determination, should put strength into the hearts of their descendants, if ever in the discharge of duty we feel disposed to yield to difficulties. Many men owe the grandeur of their lives to their tremendous difficulties.

It is now 7 o'clock p.m. The oxen are sent home, the workmen make good use of home-made soap and water, supplied them in a great oaken tub; soon hands and faces are washed, and the men are as clean and spruce as if they had never been near a log heap.

The young women of the neighborhood are gathered in or around the house, some quilting, and others attending to the cooking and serving necessary at a large gathering. Of course the tables were usually spread outside the house, and under the shade of a spreading beech or maple.

Farmer Murray had a big log house, with two windows in front, one in the back, and one in the end, and one in the top gable. After supper everything is prepared for the dance. All unnecessary furniture is put aside, boards with props underneath are put round the walls for seats, and the floor is cleared. A chair is put on top of a chest for the piper and fiddler, who are alternately to supply the music.

The piper takes the chair first, not however, till after he receives inspiration from the black bottle. And now for the dance. B. takes C.'s wife, and C. takes B.'s wife as partners in the first round. After this the floor was free to all. There were no round dances in those days.

> "But hornpipes, jigs, strathspeys and reels
> Put life and mettle in their heels."

As the evening wears on the dancing becomes more lively. The butler becomes more liberal with his bottle. The piper becomes more enthusiastic.

> "He screwed his pipes, and gart them skirl
> Till roof and rafters a' did dirl."

At intervals songs are sung and stories told. Farmer Ross sits beside the ladder, telling a crowd of eagerly listening young people how William Wallace slaughtered the Englishmen, and of all Wallace's brave deeds for Scotland. Another tells of Samuel Macdonald, the Highland giant, who took hold of the hind axle-tree of the mail coach and held back four horses; how he raised a sixty-gallon barrel of whiskey between the palms of his hands, and took a drink out of the bung-hole. Another relates the adventures of a Highlandman in running away with the laird's daughter. He tells an admiring circle of young men and maidens how the pursued lover fled with his bride:—

"He set her on a coal-black steed,
  Himsel' lap on behind her,
And he's awa' to the Hieland hills,
  Where her frien's they canna find her."

Farmers M. and G. sat on the crockery side of the chimney, trying who could repeat and sing the most songs out of Robert Brown's song book, with a laughing, applauding crowd around them. M. beat G. at repeating the most, but G. was voted the best singer.

Every now and again the butler came round and treated.

The fiddler's turn came next to supply the music, and after a deep potation, he mounted the elevated chair. The butler calls for a Highland fling. D. takes M.'s wife, and M. takes D.'s wife for partners. All take their places and the music begins. The dancers hop and reel round, toes up and heels down, and turn to the right and left on one foot, and clap their hands, and snap their fingers, and whoop, with ever-increasing heartiness. The fiddler gets inspired, plays faster and faster, his foot keeping time on the big chest, making a loud hollow sound. The boys get around him, and every time he rises from the chair they move it a little nearer the edge of the chest. At last the excitement is at its height; up goes a whoop, and down comes the chair, fiddler and all, landing on Farmer M.'s head, and the heads of two or three others, bringing them to the floor in a heap. Soon order is restored, the fiddle starts again, and the fun grows fast and furious.

By-and-bye the grey streaks are seen in the east, the blue bonnet reel is danced, *deoch-an-dorrus* is taken, and all start for home. Some of those present had two, three, or even four miles to go, mostly through unbroken woods. There were of course no buggies or bicycles, but that did not in the least detract from the pleasure of the occasion. Every laddie took his lassie, and conveyed her safely to her home. On these journeys often were the tender words of love spoken, and vows of constancy given.

Sometimes, too, one of the young people "had a crow to pick" with the other for devoting too much attention to some one else during the evening. But the spirit of manly chivalry actuated the great majority of the young men of the early days, while honest womanhood was the character of the women.

Occasionally, however, two jealous rivals would proceed to fisticuffs, while even among the women there were not wanting instances of something else than sisterly love.

The story is told of a belle of those days, commonly known as "the flower of the forest," being detained from a dance through the trick of a jealous rival. The beautiful maiden was suffering from a slight cold. Her rival called on her the day before that on which the dance was to take place, and, feigning much sympathy with her, assured her that a sure and speedy cure for a cold was too keep the feet for a couple of hours in a foot bath of hot water and mustard. The unsuspecting beauty at once complied. Result, blistered feet, no dance, and alienation of rival beauties.

CHAPTER XII

PIONEER SONGS

"My mither's sangs, my mither's sangs, I think I hear them still;
Sweet memories o' my childhood! my very soul they thrill;
They bring me back my youthfu' days, and I feel young once more,
As I lilt the auld Scotch sangs again, my mither sang before,
As I lilt the auld Scotch sangs again, my mither sang before." —JOHN IMRIE.

SOMEONE has said, "Let me make the songs of a people, and I care not who makes their laws." Doubtless the songs of a people both indicate their character and help to develop that character. And the days of the bard are not yet passed away. The present is an age of materialism and utilitarianism, but never was the world more controlled by poetry than to-day.

A short time ago Rudyard Kipling lay on what was feared to be his death-bed. Around that bed there stood, in anxiety and tears, the whole civilized world. And why? Emperor William expressed the heart of Christendom when he telegraphed his sympathy to him as the poet who had "sung about the deeds of our great common race." Kipling's "Recessional" will perhaps do more than anything else written during the present century to ameliorate the condition of the laboring man.

No country in the world can boast of a grander race of poets than Scotland ; and no people in the world have shown more of the poetic temperament than the Higlanders of that far-famed isle.

In the breasts of our Scottish pioneers there burned a poetic fire which hard work and "hamely fare" could not quench. Amid what many would consider unfavorable environments, their lives were happy and joyous. They brought with them many of the songs of the old land, and they were not without "minor bards" of their own, who, according to their gifts, sang of church and state, love and adventure.

> "The songs I used to sing,
> 'Mong Scotland's heathery hills
> Lose not their charm with age—
> Their melody still thrills;
> And echoing from each crag and fell,
> Still hold my soul in love's sweet spell."

The object of this chapter is to present some of these songs, sacred and secular, to the reader. Of the sacred songs or hymns sung by the pioneers, none outside the Psalms and paraphrases were so popular as the religious poems or songs of Dugald Buchanan and Peter Grant. These songs were called *oranan*, a Gaelic word no doubt of common origin with the Greek word *oranos*, heaven.

These *oranan* show little poetic fire, but they are, nevertheless, charming verses in which evangelical truth is presented in clear, effective language.

Buchanan, instead of selecting a variety of subjects, muses on the general subject of religion, after the manner of Tennyson in "In Memoriam."

Here are some of Peter Grant's subjects: "The Love of My Redeemer," "The Blood of the Lamb," "Calvary," "Eternal Home," "Everlasting Misery," "The State of Nature," "The Joy of the Righteous," "The Cry of the Martyrs," "The Judgment Day," "The Song of the Missionaries," "The Bible," "The Complaint of the Highlander," "Counsel to the Young."

We give the following from Grant:

URNUIGH (Prayer).

"O Thighearn is a Dhia na gloir
An t-Ard-Righ mor os cionn gach sluaigh
Cia danadh ni air t-ainm ro mhor
Le bilidh neoghlan bhi ag luaidh.

"Na h-aingle 's airde rinneadh leat
Cia lag an neart ! 's cia dall an iul !
Cia aineolach air t-oibre mor !
'S cia goird air do ghloir an clin !

"Am beachd do shuile fiorghlan fein
Cha'n 'eil na reulta 's airde glan
'S cha 'n 'eil na h-aingle 's naomha 'n gloir
Ann lathar do Mhorachdsa, gun smal," etc.

Translated thus:

O Lord the God of glory, the Supreme King over all people. How bold to celebrate thy name so great, with unclean lips.

"THE HEATHER HILLS"

The greatest angels by Thee created, how weak their strength! How obscure their vision!
How ignorant of thy vast works! How short of thy glory, their praise!

In view of thy pure eyes, the loftiest stars are unclean. The holiest angels in glory are not in the presence of thy greatness, without stain.

Here are is a sample of the patriotic songs that were favorites at one time in Zorra. It is entitled

"THE HEATHER HILLS.

" How gladsome is the sea
    Wi' its heaving tide !
How bonnie are the plains
    In their summer pride!
But the sea wi' its tide,
And the plains wi' their rills,
Are no half so dear as my heather hills.
I contentless muse on the flowery lea,
I can heedless look on the siller sea,
But my heart wi' its nameless rapture thrills
As I gaze on the steeps of my heather hills.

Chorus :—

" Then, Hurrah ! Hurrah for my heather hills !
Where the bonnie thistles wave to the sweet bluebells ;
    Where the wild mountain flood
    Heaves his crest to the cloud,
Syne foams down the steeps of my heather hills."

Here are a few verses of a martial song, once very popular:

> "Charge, ye noble-hearted heroes,
>   Make the tyrants backward reel;
> On, as did your dauntless fathers,
>   With their trusted Highland steel!

> "Charge, for Scotland's stainless honor;
>   Round her deathless laurels twine;
> Make her golden page of glory
>   With unfading lustre shine!

> "Yours the straths of purple heather,
>   Yours the mountain and the glen;
> By your valor let despots know
>   That these nurse but gallant men.

> "To the pibroch proudly sounding
>   On they bound with hardy pride;
> In the van the claymore flashes,
>   Foemen fall on every side."

After each verse there was usually sung the following chorus:

> "Charge, ye Scottish braves, in triumph,
>   Burst the proud oppressor's chains!
> Like your own immortal Wallace,
>   Noble blood rolls through your veins."

The question has been asked, "Why do

Highlandmen wear kilts?" Various answers have been given. This is certain, the Highlander's admiration for his native costume is both poetical and powerful. A few years ago a missionary from one of the Pacific isles was describing, before a congregation in London, Ontario, the costume of the natives. He spoke of it as being scanty, even more so than the kilts of the Highlanders. At the close of his address an aged Gaelic mother came up, warmly shook the missionary's hand, asking, "Did ye say that the people wore kilts?." "Well, yes, ma'am, it is something like that!" The good woman closed her eyes, folded her hands, and devoutly exclaimed: "The Lord be thankit the Gospel is makin' sic progress!"

The following characteristic incident is related of the late Sir John A. Macdonald. The Premier, talking once with a friend on the peculiar customs of different people, stated that on a visit to the West a reception was given him, at which a Bishop from Belgium was present. As the party were being escorted by a body of men in Highland costume, the foreign Bishop, seeing the bare legs and kilts, asked why the men were without trousers.

"It's just a local custom," gravely replied Sir John. "In some places people take off their hats as a mark of honor to distinguished guests; here they take off their trousers."

The cynic has sometimes charged that Highlanders wore kilts only because, having on one occasion fled from the enemy, to punish them their mothers, wives, and sweethearts took away their trousers. To redeem their character and to regain their clothing they have ever since fought bravely.

Other evil disposed persons claim that Highlanders wear kilts simply on the ground of economy. One thing is sure, the Highlander is devotedly attached to his native costume.

A good many years ago there was in some quarters an agitation to change the military costume of the Highlanders for the common colors of the British soldier. The agitation aroused the keenest opposition on the part of the whole Celtic world, as the following song will indicate :—

THE TARTAN.

" Come, Scottish men an' Scottish maids,
  Put on your tartan, kilts an' plaids,
  An' dock yoursel's wi' braw cockades,
    An' stand up for the tartan.

" Let foreign birkies gape an' stare
  At Scotland's sons in garb sae rare,
  We still will laugh at them an' wear
    Our ain world-famous tartan.

" It is the garb our fathers wore
  Wi' patriot pride in days o' yore,
  An' won on mony a foreign shore
    Bright honors in the tartan.

" Upon the field o' Waterloo,
  When bullets thick as hailstones flew,
  Our plaided pipers loudly blew
    Tae cheer the lads in tartan.

" An' when the cavalry o' France
  In floods o' valor did advance,
  In vain their fiery steeds did prance
    Around our squares o' tartan.

" The Scottish lads in close array
  Stood man tae man upon that day,
  An' thick as leaves the Frenchmen lay
    Around our squares o' tartan.

" Thrice glorious, garb o' Scotland brave
  Forever let the tartan wave !
  'Tis Freedom's flag, for ne'er a slave
    E'er wore the bonnie tartan.

> "Come rally then frae Tweed tae Spey,
> Ye Scottish lads an' lassies gay,
> An' wi' one voice declare for aye
> Tae still preserve the tartan."

I subjoin what was once well-known in Zorra as "The Hielan'man's Toast":

> "Here's to the hills, the heath, and the heather,
> The bonnet, the plaidie, the kilt, and the feather;
> Here's to the heroes that Scotland can boast,
> May their names never dee—that's a Hielan'man's toast."

A good deal has been said about the pioneer's fondness for drink. This is no doubt true of some, but that the general community realized the evils of over-indulgence is evident from the popularity of a song, the first verse of which I here give:

> "Chan e uisge-beatha ach uisge-bas
> An t-uisge chradh mo chridhe 's mo chom
> An t-uisge a dh'fhag mo cheanna liath
> An t-uisge a dh'fhag na ceudan lom."

Which may be thus freely translated:

> "The water of life! no, not at all!
> The water of death, 'twere better to call
> That which so oft has racked my head,
> That which leaves thousands lacking bread."

THE MEDLEY

Love songs were, among the young people, the most popular. Some of these took the medley form, being part English and part Gaelic. Here is a sample:

> "As sure as I'm a sinner, I never propose
> To have you decoyed no t-fhagail fo bhron
> Oir ni mi do phosadh gun mhearachd gun gho
> 'S-gur cinnteach thu do chaidreamh o'n chailin donn og."

Gaelic in second line—"nor leave you in sorrow."
Third line—"I will marry you without mistake or deceit."
Fourth line—"Fellowship from the young brown-haired damsel is to you a certainty."

To the medley belongs the following well-known verse:

> "When Eve, in all her loveliness,
>   Appeared to Adam's view,
> The first word that he said to her
>   Was "Cia mar tha sibh an diugh."

The experience of a rollicking lover, before and after marriage, was thus expressed in an old pioneer song; before marriage he gaily sings:

> "My name is Dick Thompson, the cobbler,
>   I served my time at Percant,
> I know I'm an old depredator,
>   But I am resolved to repent.

. . . . . .

"Twenty long years I've been roving,
  I've spent the prime of my life;
But now I'm resolved to gie over
  And cuttle myself to a wife."

. . . . .

Well, he gets married, and after a while what a change! Here is how he expresses himself:

"My wife she is ugly, she's lazy,
  She's dirty, she's towsie, she's black,
She's the de'il for brawling and scolding,
  Her tongue is forever click-clack.

"And now we'll be parted forever;
  This morning before it is light,
I doused her three times in the river,
  I cursed her, and bade her good-night."

One of the finest love songs I have come across, either in Gaelic or in any other language, is called "Handsome Mary." The song is ascribed to J. McDonald, a Gaelic bard of the last century, in Ross-shire. It is too long to insert the original, but I give an excellent English translation of three verses of it by the late Evan MacColl. The references to the lark thrush, cuckoo, sea-gull, and to the beautiful in nature, are exquisitely happy. Only those who

A LOVE-SONG

know the difficulty of translating poetry from one language to another, can fully appreciate the original, or sufficiently admire the translator's success.

"Her's are teeth whose whiteness
  Snow alone can peer;
Her's the breath all fragrance,
  Voice of loving cheer;
Cheeks of cherry ripeness,
  Eyelids looking down,
'Neath a forehead never
  Shadowed by a frown.

"Out on royal splendors!
  Love best makes his bed
'Mong the leaves and grasses
  Of the sylvan shade;
Where the blissful breezes
  Tell of bloom and balm,
And health-giving streamlets
  Sing their ceaseless psalm.

"No mere music, art-born,
  There our pleasures crowned;
Music far more cheering
  Nature for us found—
Larks in air, and thrushes
  On each flow'ring thorn,
And the cuckoo hailing
  Summer's gay return."

Very different from the above was the

experience of Johnny Sands, as related in a song popular sixty years ago.

" A man, whose name was Johnny Sands,
   Had married Bella Haige ;
And, though she brought him gold and lands,
   She proved a terrible plague."

Mrs. Sands was a "scolding wife," a very termagant, and so Johnny, wearied of life, agreed with his spouse that he should put an end to his existence. And this was the plan proposed : he was to stand on the brink of the deep river, and his wife was to come rushing down the hill and throw him in. And to make success certain the virago tied the poor man's hands behind his back. Let the poet tell the story :

" For, oh, she was a scolding wife,
   Full of caprice and whim ;
He said that he was tired of life,
   And she was tired of him.

" Says he, 'Then I will drown myself,
   The river runs below' ;
Says she, 'Pray do, you silly elf,
   I've wished it long ago.'

THE MORAL

" 'You tie my hands behind my back,
 And when securely done,
I'll stand upon the brink,' he said,
 'While you prepare to run.'

" All down the hill his loving wife
 Now came with all her force
To push him in ; he slipped aside,
 And she fell in, of course.

" Now splashing, dashing, like a fish,
 'Oh, save me, Johnny Sands!'
'I can't, my love, though much I wish,
 For you have tied my hands.' "

MORAL.—The wicked fall into the pit they have digged for others.

CHAPTER XIII

A FUNERAL AMONG THE PIONEERS

"There is a reaper whose name is death,
And with his sickle keen,
He reaps the bearded grain at a breath,
And the flowers that grow between."

WHEN death invaded the home of the pioneer, every mark of respect was shown to the deceased. The body was washed and laid out on a long table or board, until the coffin could be made; then the windows were darkened, pictures turned to face the wall, a white sheet thrown over the cupboard, the clock stopped, the candles lighted, everyone stepped softly, and a solemn silence prevailed. Still, there was great restraint of feeling, little shedding of tears, and seldom would a sob be heard, though there was a good deal of sighing and subdued moaning. The coffin was always home-made

ZORRA PIONEERS—(Ages from 65 to 76.)

1. Wm. K. Stewart, age 65. 2. Mrs. J. M. Ross, died 1888, aged 75. 3. Angus MacKay, died 1898, aged 74. 4. Donald Sutherland, age 71. 5. Donald Clarke, died ——, aged 70. 6. John McPherson, died 1870, aged 70. 7. Alex. Munro, died 1872, aged 70. 8. Hugh Sutherland, age 75. 9. Alex. Rose, died 1871, aged 73. 10. Alex. Murray, died 1897, aged 76. 11. Geo. Gordon, age 70. 12. Mrs. Wm. Murray (Abley). 13. Wm. MacKay, died 1869, aged 75.

by some carpenter, and was very plain, having no handles or ornament of any kind. Lamp black mixed with the white of eggs served to color the outside of it.

When the coffin was ready it was brought to the house of the dead, a white linen sheet was spread cornerwise over it; then the body, plainly dressed in a white shroud, was put in and the linen drawn over as a winding sheet.

The face was covered with a small piece of embroidered muslin, which was removed only when some one wished to view the corpse. The hands were crossed upon the breast, giving the idea of a person resting in sleep. A saucer two-thirds filled with salt, was placed on the breast, and a copper placed over each eye, which was supposed necessary to keep the eyes closed. The severest thing that could be said of any man was that he was mean enough to steal the coppers off a dead man's eyes.

After this, preparation was made for the "wake." The coffin containing the corpse was placed next the wall. A table stood in the middle of the room with the Bible and Psalter upon it. The chairs being few, boards or planks were utilized. If it was winter time, a large "back-log" was put into the fireplace, and sufficient wood brought in to last all night.

Towards evening, neighbors and friends, old and young, begin to assemble. A special messenger had gone from house to house in the afternoon, announcing the death, and it was regarded a matter of civility for at least some member of each family to attend the wake.

At first, there was but little conversation, and that little was carried on in an undertone, but, as the bread, biscuits, and cheese, went round, accompanied by whiskey, the company looked less solemn, and the conversation became decidedly more lively.

Here let us guard against doing injustice to the old pioneers. I have read of Irish and Scotch "wakes," where there was excessive drinking, and the usual accompaniments— unseemly anywhere, but especially so at a funeral. But I am bound to say that I never witnessed drunkenness at a Zorra "wake," nor have I met with any who ever did. Scenes of intemperance, alas! were only too common on mere social occasions, but the early settlers put a restraint upon themselves in presence of the dead.

A clergyman was not expected to be present, but there was no lack of men capable of conducting a religious service. In the earlier years of the settlement there were such men as John MacKay, Hector Ross, Alex. Rose, D. Urquhart, Alex. Wood, George MacKay, and Donald Macleod, who could always lead the people with acceptance in the various acts of worship, such as reading and expounding the scriptures, prayer, and praise.

Three or four times during the night, several verses of a Psalm would be sung, a chapter read, and a plain but practical talk given on some appropriate passage of scripture.

The intervals between worship were occupied with conversation, more or less edifying, frequently the latter. Some would draw useful lessons from the life of the deceased; but it must be admitted, the conversation chiefly turned upon the occult, such as apparitions, and ghosts, and death-signs of a terrifying nature.

Donald C. tells of the trials of the departed one, first in the old country where he knew him well, "and his father and his gradfather before him"; and then his trials after coming to Zorra. "Och, och!" would perhaps be the conclusion, "it's often the black ox has trampled upon his toes. Poor fellow, there's na mair trouble for him noo."

From this the conversation naturally glided into a talk on the troubles of life. "The fact is," said an aged pioneer, "there is something in every life to embitter it. Here is a story I heard in Sutherlandshire:

"A wealthy laird was travelling through the Highlands when one day about noon he came where a large flock of sheep was feeding. The shepherd was sitting by the roadside preparing to eat his dinner. The following conversation ensued between the laird and the shepherd: 'Well, shepherd, you look happy and contented, and I expect you have very few cares to vex you. I am the owner of large properties, but I am not happy, and I look at such men as you are with a good deal of envy.'

"'Well sir,' replied the shepherd, 'I have not troubles like yours, and I would be happy enough if it were not for that black ewe that you see yonder amongst my flock. I have often begged my master to kill or sell her; but he won't, though she is the plague of my life, for no sooner do I sit down to read my book, or eat my dinner, but away she sets off over the hills, and the rest follow her; so that I have many a weary step after them. There, you see, she's off, and they are all after her! I must go!'

"'Ah, friend,' said the laird to the shepherd, before he started, 'I see every man has a black ewe in his flock to plague his life.'"

A common opinion among the Zorra pioneers was that the subject sanctified the conversation. Any conversation, however gossipy or scandalous, was regarded as proper enough if the subject of it was a religious person, place, or thing. If on the Sabbath you spoke of the beautiful fields around you, a prompt reply would perhaps be, "This is na day to be speaking anent sic things"; but if you spoke of the minister, the church, or the service, you might say about anything you please without incurring risk of reproof. Hence the following story related at the "wake":

A certain minister was reputed to be a man of great nerve. Nothing, it was said, could daunt him, not even a ghost. So some of the boys decided to test him. It was known that on a certain day he would be in a distant part of his congregation visiting, and would pass through the cemetery as he returned home late at night. The winds wailed among the tombstones, the moon cast weird beams of light and shadow, and the clouds rushing across the heavens, kept the shadows constantly flitting. It was just a night for ghosts to be abroad. So two of the boys wrapped themselves in the necessary white sheets, and kept moving with certain antique motions among the stones.

By and bye the minister, footsore and weary, came along. He espies the supposed ghosts, looked at them for a little while, then coolly inquired, " Is there going to be a general resurrection, or are there just a couple of you out for a gambol?"

Such narratives, it will be readily admitted, did not powerfully tend to impress upon the minds of those present, a profound sense of the solemnity of the occasion; but told with much gravity, and interspersed with devotional exercises, they left an impression of awe upon the minds of the younger and more timid of the company which, unto the end of life they will never be able entirely to shake off.

There is little doubt that the old, and now obsolete custom of sitting up and watching by the dead, has its origin in the belief (and who can deny its truth) that the dead is still with us. They have passed beyond our ken, but we are not beyond theirs. Do our departed loved ones take no interest in us? Have they nothing to do with those strange, subtle, inexplicable influences that sometimes come over us? If our eyes were opened, who knows but that we could see those who have gone from us, and yet have not gone from us?

> " One family we dwell in Him,
> One Church above, beneath,
> Tho' now divided by the stream,
> The narrow stream of death."

Gentle reader despise not these humble toilers of the forest. Theirs not rank, wealth, or learning; but they knew their Bible, and lived according to their light; they cherished true love to God and a genuine sympathy for one another. In few things does their nobility of character shine forth more splendidly than in their tender, practical sympathy for one another in time of bereavement. The dead usually remained unburied for three days, and during this time the family was relieved of all care, not milking their own cows, feeding their cattle, or even cooking their own meals. All this was done for them by kind neighbors in turn. If severe sickness or death occurred in spring-time or harvest, I have known as many as a dozen neighbors arrange to help, and kindly give a day with the plow or the cradle, so that as little loss as possible might be experienced by those who had for a time, through the dispensation of Providence, been withdrawn from their work.

When the day of funeral came, there was in the morning a service of more than ordinary solemnity. A suitable portion of scripture was read; the twenty-third Psalm was sung; not unfrequently we sang the words of the fifty-third paraphrase:—

> "Take comfort, Christians, when your friends
> In Jesus fall asleep;
> Their better being never ends;
> Why then dejected weep?
>
> "Why unconsolable, as those
> To whom no hope is given?
> Death is the messenger of peace,
> And calls the soul to heaven.
>
> * * * *
>
> "A few short years of evil past,
> We reach the happy shore,
> Where death-divided friends at last
> Shall meet to part no more."

After solemn prayer the usual refreshments were passed around.

"The lifting" followed. The coffin containing the corpse was brought out, carried by the nearest friends, and placed on two chairs outside the door. Then the coffin was placed upon the bier and covered with the *mortecloth*. This cloth was of black silk velvet, with a white silk border, and was the common property of the district.

When all was ready six men stepped forward, shouldered the bier, and started with their burden. Frequently they had four or five miles to go, mostly by a path through the woods, involving many a sharp turn, and much caution against tripping upon projecting roots or stones. The pall-bearers were of course relieved at short distances by others. Thus tenderly upon the shoulders of neighbors and relatives were many of the pioneers borne to their last resting place, in what is now known as the "old log church cemetery."

In later years, the coffin was carried in a lumber wagon. I can well remember when a spring carriage was an unknown luxury in Zorra; but those that had a team of horses and a wagon of any kind gathered for miles round at a funeral, and the solemn procession rattled over the rough roads, with eight or ten people in each wagon. Occasionally, a front team, for some reason, would suddenly stop, and the drivers behind would not notice till the tongue of perhaps each wagon in the long procession would strike the tailboard of the wagon in front, causing one loud blow ofter another, like the firing in succession in a line of infantry.

By and bye the spring democrat appeared. The first few of these did duty as hearses for a large number of years, as they were at the service of the people for miles around.

The coming of the age of wagons gave the death blow to the ghost epoch; probably, as it was thought, because the spooks did not like the rattle of the newfangled machine.

Before the advent of the wagon, the wise and graver men of the township were said to have often seen weird, uncanny lights moving solemnly along the road after nightfall, the sure precursor of a funeral. Some of these seers were even said to have been so gifted as to hear the words of the leader of the funeral cortege, as, with military precision, he halted and gave the order, "Relief!" They could, it was affirmed, even make out the figures of those bearing the coffin.

Many stories of this kind were related at the wakes we attended in early youth; and, after hearing them, we preferred to have company on the way home at three or four o'clock in the morning.

When the funeral procession reached the grave, and all was ready, the coffin was lowered by the nearest relatives. Then, for a minute or so, all heads were uncovered and bowed in silent prayer. After this, the filling in of the grave was done, not as now by the grave-digger, but by the company in turn.

The grave being filled in, and the last sod laid upon it, all took their departure, leaving their friend's body in God's acre, and in His keeping till the resurrection day. Then, as now, the burial was with the feet to the east, doubtless with reference to the direction from which our Lord is expected to come a second time. "As the lightning cometh out of the east and shineth unto the west, so shall also the coming of the Son of Man be."

CHAPTER XIV

GHOSTS, WITCHES, AND GOBLINS

> "Unquiet souls,
> Risen from the grave to ease the heavy guilt
> Of deeds in life concealed." —AKENSIDE.

EVERY traveller knows that much of the charm of Scottish scenery is derived from the legends and myths which tradition has associated with Scottish castles, churches, graveyards, glens, caves, and waterfalls. The Scottish pioneers of Zorra carried with them the traditions of their fatherland, and were strong believers in the occult and the dreadful. With Hamlet they declared:

> "There are more things in heaven and earth, Horatio,
> Than are dreamt of in your philosophy."

Often have we sat by the old ingleside, and with mouth and eyes open, knees trembling, and the cold chills creeping along the spine, listened to weird tales told by our grandparents and others, concerning dismal sounds, ghostly appearances, and the sorceries of horrid witches. These uncanny tales made a deep impression upon our youthful minds, and we can remember occasions when, while passing through the dark woods, suddenly the hooting of the owl, or the far-away lonely cry of the nighthawk, or the rustling of the leaves by a squirrel or raccoon, broke the solemn stillness, and imagining some ghost or bogie or evil spirit approaching us, we took to our heels and ran like frightened deer. Zorra is perhaps not yet old enough to have developed a legendary era of its own, and the present matter-of-fact business age is not favorable to such a growth. Yet Zorra is by no means devoid of folk-lore. The characters, incidents, adventures, and experiences of pioneer days present as good material for the poet, the painter, the dramatist, and the legend builder as did Scotland to Scott and Miller, or the New England States and New York to Hawthorne and Irving. There is danger that the weird stories, myths, and legends of the early days may soon disappear, unless they are changed from the oral into the written form; and I feel like Selkirk on his island, when the rich fruits of autumn were dropping around him, that if I myself do not preserve some of them, they must perish.

Leaving it to others to enter fully into the subject, I shall, in this chapter, open the door just a little in order that the reader may have a glimpse at a few out of the multitude of shadowy forms that flit to and fro in the mists of Zorra legends.

Many years ago there lived in the township a family whom we shall call Gourlay. It consisted of four brothers, all unmarried. Naturally, these brothers were kind and generous enough, but, alas! they were all victims of strong drink, and when under the influence of the liquor-fiend they were, even beyond the ordinary drunkards, a disgrace to themselves and a terror to their neighbors. They would fight each other savagely, and often made night hideous by their yells, screams, and horrid profanity.

Still they scrupulously observed the outward forms of religion. Being bad during the week was to the Gourlay brothers an additional reason why they should be as good as they could on Sunday. Regularly they drove to the village church, a distance of five miles, and with a stolid stare, broken only by snuff-taking, they sat through the service. They had had, of course, a couple of drinks in the village tavern before entering the kirk, but oh, they were very, very dry before the long service was over, and glad were they to return to their favorite resort. Their reckless driving and boisterous behavior on the way home from church were a sore scandal to those who feared God and regarded His day. On Communion Sabbaths, when the roads were filled with people, men and women, old and young, the Gourlay brothers were more than ordinarily reckless.

It is 4 p. m. Hundreds of people are on the road wending their way homeward. There is a blazing sun overhead and the road is very dusty. Suddenly shouts are heard, "Clear the way!" The people pause, look back, and about half a mile behind, they see a thick cloud of dust. It's a runaway! No, it is the Gourlay brothers. Quickly the people divide, some going to each side of the road, and not a few timid ones geting over the fence, or seeking shelter behind the biggest stumps or trees near them.

With a whoop and hurrah, the four brothers, seated in their big heavy waggon, slashing the horses and waving their blue bonnets, fly past. The people utter a sigh of relief and pray the Lord to have mercy on the miserable drunkards.

Shortly after this, late one summer night, three of the brothers are returning from the village, drunk and noisy as usual. Two of them sit in the front seat of the waggon, and the third, whose name was Robert, sits by himself in the back. Coming along the sideroad through a marshy place where the road was very rough and dark, Robert takes out his black bottle, and is in the act of drinking, when suddenly the waggon gave a jolt, and the wretched drunken man falls out backward. He was a heavy man, and falling upon a projecting root, he broke his neck. Death was instantaneous. The brothers, too drunk to perceive what has happened, drive home and go to bed as usual. Next morning some neighbors find Robert Gourlay dead, his hand still clutching the neck of the black bottle, the lower part having been broken off in the fall.

For years after this, it was alleged, a strange form was seen from time to time moving to and fro along this side-road. The figure was not more than four feet high, very stout, and with little or no neck, the head set closely upon the shoulders and drooping forward upon the breast. The eyes glared like two balls of fire; the mouth was partly open and the tongue projected. It certainly presented a gruesome appearance. The voice was low and sepulchral, resembling somewhat the gurgling of a distant streamlet. Whenever the ghost appeared the dogs in the neighborhood, it was said, howled piteously, while the cattle and horses snorted and took to their heels.

The spectre uttered many groans and moans and uncanny sounds that stirred the hair of listeners on their scalps, but the only sound that could be understood was the one word—*deoch* (Gaelic for drink), uttered with a hoarse, gurgling tone. Whether this word was meant to indicate the cause of ruin, or the present thirst of the spirit, was never ascertained. But for years men, returning from the village about the same time of night that the killing took place, would see the awful form moving backwards and forwards, holding in its right hand the neck and part of a black bottle, and amid the hollow moans and sullen groans uttering ruefully the ominous word—*deoch*.

At length one dark stormy night, as an elder of the Church was passing along the side-road, the ghost appeared. The good man at once took out his Bible, and, opening it, held it right between himself and the ghost. Then for the first time the ghost found full and distinct utterance. It related with deep contrition the history of the past, and added: "This is the last time I shall ever appear on earth, for to-night I would have died had I not been killed twenty years ago on this spot through—*deoch*."

And from that day to this the "gaist of Rob Gourlay" was never more seen.

* * * * * * * * *

In an old log shanty, situated on the edge of a great marsh, usually known as the "big swamp," lived Jean Gordon. Her only companion was a black cat, which was said to be an evil spirit incarnate. Jean was an old beldam, wizened and toothless, and nearly bent double; she had apparently not troubled comb or washbasin since her infancy, which was long, long ago. She had, it was believed, the power to transform herself into a cat, dog, ape, a bat, an owl, or even a frog. She could inflict rheumatism, headache, or toothache on anyone against whom she had a grudge; she could put the cows dry and prevent the butter coming in the churn, the bread from rising and the soap from forming; indeed, the death of two calves was ascribed to her sorceries.

Andrew McCulloch's wife declared that Jean had bewitched her child, so that, while the child grew with unnatural rapidity, it sucked from her breast not milk, but blood, leaving her, the poor mother, nothing but skin and bone.

Jean spoke Gaelic, but with such rapidity of utterance that she could not be understood, and it was believed by many that she mingled with her Gaelic Hebrew or some other primitive language.

She seldom left her lonely home by day, but was often seen flitting through the shadows in the woods about the time of sunset. On dark and stormy nights she would screech and jabber down a chimney, and scream and whistle at windows, and by the dim firelight or candle-light her face might be seen peering through the panes. She was more than once seen to arise from her shanty on her broom; and, when high up, stir and push clouds before her with the broom.

On the farm of Alexander Macdonald there was a great elm tree, with branches bare and decayed, because one night Jean, going about in the form of an owl, had perched for a few moments on the topmost branch.

But, alas! one day Jean's existence came to

a sudden close. She was out in the form of a bird. A farmer, named Tom Ferguson, was hunting; he heard the rush of wings, and, looking up, saw a black bird with a long neck and with feet like scrawny hands. It uttered a cry so weird and so shrill, that it made the farmer shudder. Soon it alighted on a dead tree, and he shot at it. With a blood-curdling yell, the bird, or evil spirit, whatever it was, circled round his head. Three times he fired, with the same result. Then he concluded that it must be some uncanny thing, and he remembered that evil things could not withstand silver. (This is certainly a fact to-day.) But having no bullet of that metal on him, he took a sixpenny piece and rammed it down his gun with a piece of cloth, at the same time uttering much prayer.

At sight of this the bird screamed dreadfully with terror, and vainly tried to escape. He fired. The ugly creature dropped with the coin in its body, and fell on its right side. At that very moment, Jean Gordon, living in her shanty beside the big swamp, more than a mile away,

A GHOST WITH A FIERY HEAD

arose from her spinning wheel, gasped, and fell on her right side—dead.

* * * * * * * * *

At certain seasons of the year a ghost of most terrible appearance could be seen on a dark road east of Embro. The phantom stood about five feet high, and from the top of the head there issued a pale white light. The light was so bright that a man could see the time of night on his watch by means of it. Just below the flame there appeared two eyeballs, luminous and immovable, and a great gaping mouth. Many trustworthy witnesses there were to the existence of this ghost, and, indeed, for some time the road was deserted by the terrified people. Tradition said that in very early times a murder had been committed on this spot by the Indians, and that the pale light issued from the top of the victim's head, from which the Indians had removed the scalp.

But Sandy Dunbar was a godly man, of great courage and strength, and he determined to confront the ghost, whatever the consequences might be. So one night, taking, as his neighbors told him, his life in his hands, he went forth on his weird mission of investigation. Some half dozen brave young Highlandmen, armed with knives and sticks, accompanied him till within several hundred yards of the dreaded spot. Then the brave man proceeded alone. Sure enough, there was the ghost, and the sight of it made the sweat ooze from every pore. However, it was Sandy's boast that he had never turned his back on a foe, man or devil. So, after praying for his wife and children, and especially for himself in his present trying situation, he called to the ghost, demanding who or what he was and what he wanted. But there was no response. Coming a few yards nearer, and grasping more firmly the hickory club with which he had armed himself, he made the same demand a second time; but the same awful silence continued, and so also after a third demand. Still the ghost was there, the head blazing, the eyes glaring, and the mouth wide open.

Slowly and cautiously Sandy moved nearer and nearer the ghost, ready to defend himself to the death if necessary. At length he was so near that, with great fear and trembling, he summoned courage enough to put out his hand and touch the ghost, when, to the delight and surprise of the brave Highlander, it turned out to be the stump of a spruce tree. The light at the top was the mycelium of the fungus which, it is well known, develops on the decaying wood of the spruce and some other kinds of trees under certain climatic conditions, and shines at night with a pale soft phosphorescence. It is frequently called by the country people "fox-fire," and sometimes "wolf-fire." What appeared as mouth and eyes were only spots where the bark had fallen off, and the uncovered surface reflecting the light from above formed a crude resemblance to a human face.

This same "fox-fire," it is said, has led to many a ghost story. Trees sometimes cast their roots into a cave. These roots get injured, and consequently decay; and in the process of decay they frequently give out this phosphorescence. The light in the cave is seen at night, and a ghost story is the result.

* * * * * * * * *

A Zorra man, who is now in his eighty-fifth year, but hale and hearty, relates the following. I give the narrative in his own words: "In the year 184— myself and family were living in the southern part of Zorra. My wife's sister had come from Hamilton on a visit. Every night for several weeks, about 1 a.m., we heard the most delightful singing coming towards the house, and then suddenly ceasing at the door. The singing was in a minor key, low and soft, making a strain of rare, unearthly sweetness.

"One night my sister-in-law was sitting near the window, and, hearing the sound, looked out and saw a man approaching the house singing softly as he came. Reaching the door, he looked up to the window where she was and then passed on. She observed him particularly, and that same night gave us a minute description of his hat and clothes.

"Next day my sister-in-law, my wife, and myself were in Woodstock, and, seeing a mechanic in his ordinary every-day working clothes pass by, my sister-in-law exclaimed, 'That's the man I saw last night coming up to our house singing.' A few weeks after this the young woman was taken down with a fever, and after a few days' illness died.

At that time coffins were not kept in stock, but any ordinary carpenter made them to order. Along with a relative, I went to one carpenter after another in the neighborhood, four or five in all, but for some reason or other, none of them could make the coffin. We then came to Woodstock, went to Mr. B.'s carpenter shop, and the first man we met at once consented to make the coffin. This man was the one my sister-in-law saw approaching the house singing, and whom she afterwards identified on the streets of Woodstock."

Ghosts—what are they? Whence do they come?

> "Perhaps they are the signals loved ones send
> Who wait our coming on the other shore;
> Too spirit-full with earthly sense to blend,
> Too finely soft to fully pierce life's roar."

So, at least, says the poet; but there is another theory, not so poetical, but equally plausible, in explanation of ghostly appearances.

* * * * * * * * *

I give the following well-authenticated narrative, not as a Zorra ghost story, but because it explains a good many ghost stories in Zorra and elsewhere. The celebrated Dr. Abernethy stood at the head of the medical profession in his day. He was once applied to by a man whose terrible experience was as follows: He could neither eat nor sleep, and was wasting away day by day; and he gave as the cause of all his trouble that he was visited every night between the hours of eleven and twelve by a horrible creature, grim and ghastly, who, unbidden, would open the door of his room, walk, or rather glide in, put its skeleton arms around him, and its cold, bony face against his. The man had begged his neighbors to come and sit with him, and help him tide over the awful hour, but they were all afraid and shunned his dwelling as haunted.

He asked Dr. Abernethy if he would come

and stay with him one night. The doctor readily consented, and the man was overjoyed. The doctor came and sat with him, talked to him about his health and his habits, asked him to let him feel his arms, rolled up his sleeve, and and was apparently diagnosing the case. He then brought a basin of water, as if he was going to sponge him. As the hour of eleven drew near the patient got terribly excited, and began to shudder. Just as the clock struck the man uttered a scream. "There's the door opening, it's coming in; don't you see it?" Abernethy, with his lance, instantly bled him; but so excited was the patient that he never felt it. The blood flowed rapidly. In a few moments the man calmed down, saying "It's not coming any further to-night. Why! it's going out again. The door is closed."

Then for the first time he noticed that he was bled. The doctor explained to him that the cause of his seeing the spectre was the condition of his blood, owing to his bibulous habits and riotous living. He assured him there were two ways in which he might escape seeing bogies—

temperate living, or being bled every month. The man, it is said, chose the latter.

* * * * * * * * *

One night, many years ago, a party of young people were returning from a dance about 2 a.m. The road was dark, being thickly wooded with trees on both sides. The moon cast fitful beams of light across the way, and the clouds rushing across the heavens kept the shadows constantly changing. There had been a funeral along that road not long before, and as the young people in silence passed along, ghostly stories of the fireside came vividly to their minds. One little group in advance of the others suddenly stopped, and a thrill of horror passed through the company, for at this exact spot a ghost had some time before appeared, and just now did they not see a strange sight and hear an inhuman sound resembling a long-drawn snore?

It was in October, and the ditch at the side of the road was filled with leaves that rustled to the movements of the ghost. One lad more venturesome than the rest dared to approach the horrid thing. The leaves rustled, but more closely still he approached, when suddenly what appeared to be a huge living mountain arose from the ditch, and rushed away with great speed and clatter of hoofs. The crowd with ghastly faces were riveted to the spot. Their hair stood on end, as one of them afterwards said, like "quills upon the back of the fretful porcupine." After some time, however, it turned out that the supposed ghost was only Donald Urquhart's horse, which had strayed out of its customary pasture field, and was enjoying a soft warm bed upon the leaves in the ditch.

* * * * * * * * *

Mrs. A. died in Embro, and it was thought necessary to have the burial as early as possible. So the carpenter employed was obliged to work all night in order to have the coffin ready in time. It was the custom of James Mc——, when his day's work was over, to don his best suit, and go courting a pretty girl who lived on the other side of the common, as it was called. The night in question was a dark one, and a feeling of timidity crept over him as he passed the carpenter's shop, where a tallow candle but dimly lighted the large place, yet showed the long queer-shaped box on which the man was working. The young man gave a few moments' serious thought to the present state of the intended occupant, but all feeling was quickly dispelled by the smiles with which he was greeted by his sweetheart. The hours passed all too quickly, and it was very late when he said good-bye for the last time that night, and set out for home. The darkness had deepened. There was that stretch of common between him and the point he had to reach. The stroke of the carpenter's hammer was the only sound that broke the stillness, and it recalled the train of thought which occupied him on his way out. He walked cautiously, the greater part of the way being marshy, and there was a pond which must be avoided. Suddenly there was a fizz, followed by a flash of light, which revealed to him a tall object robed in white. Had there been time for thought, it would have only confirmed the belief which he held that it was the ghost of the woman whose coffin was being prepared in the shop. He screamed and fell, but

CHAPTER XV

PIONEER SCHOOLS AND SCHOOLMASTERS

"A man severe he was and stern to view,
I knew him well, and every truant knew."
—GOLDSMITH.

THE people of Scotland have always been noted for their love of learning. As early as A.D. 563, St. Columba, hailing from the island of Iona, established a Christian college, from which many missionary educators went forth. John Knox instituted the parish schools of Scotland, and thus originated the system of popular education now prevailing throughout the English-speaking world. Dr. Norman McLeod tells us that when public schools were introduced into the Highlands, such was the eagerness of the people for knowledge that it was no uncommon thing to see the grandsire and grandson competing for the head of the same class. This being a national characteristic, we are not surprised at the large number of Scotchmen who occupy and have occupied positions as clergymen, statesmen, presidents, premiers, and educators in the United States and Canada.

This thirst for knowledge characterized the pioneers of Zorra, and though they were poor, and the district sparsely settled, from the very beginning provision of some kind was made for the education of the young.

The pioneer school-house was a very humble affair. A log shanty, thirty feet by twenty-two, cornered but not hewed, with chinks between the logs, then moss, all plastered over with clay. The roof consisted of rafters with poles laid across, and for shingles, pieces of elm bark three feet by four. The chimney was made of lath covered with plaster, and served for heating, ventilating, and lighting the little house. Of course it frequently caught fire, but the boys, by the free use of snow, were equal to the occasion. There was but one small window in each side. The furniture was in keeping with the rest of the building. About four feet above

THE PIONEER SCHOOL-HOUSE

the floor holes were bored into the logs of the wall and pins driven in. Upon these were laid rough basswood planks, three inches thick, and the desk was complete. The teacher's desk was somewhat more pretentious, being built on four upright wooden pillars, and furnished with a small drawer in which the dominie kept his taws, switch, ruler, and other official equipments. The grey goose furnished the pens, and the ink was made from a solution of soft maple bark, diluted with copperas. Sometimes this ink would freeze, resulting in bursted bottles. To prevent this it was not unusual to mix a little whiskey with the ink; for the whiskey of Zorra in those days, though cheap, would not freeze like that alleged to have been used by some politicans in Muskoka a few winters ago.

The paper used was coarse foolscap, unruled. Each pupil had to do his own ruling; and for this purpose took with him to school, a ruler and a piece of lead hammered out into the shape of a pencil. Our first attempt at writing was making "pot-hooks" and "trammels," which mean the up and down strokes of the pen.

After practising this for several weeks, we began to write from "copy" set by the teacher. The sentiment of the "copy" was always some counsel, warning, or moral precept for the young; and as we had to write it carefully in every line of the page, it could not fail to impress itself upon the memory and to influence the life. I ascribe no little importance to this factor in early education. The duty of being on our guard against evil companionship, and making the most of life by every-day diligence, was constantly inculcated by these head-lines set by the teacher. Here are a few in illustration. I give them alphabetically as they used to be given to us:—

"Avoid bad company or you will learn their ways."
"Be careful in the choice of companions."
"Choose your friends from among the wise and good."
"Do not tell a lie to hide a fault."
"Emulate the good and virtuous."
"Fame may be too dearly bought."
"Honor your father and mother."
"Let all your amusements be innocent."
"Omit no opportunity of acquiring knowledge."
"Perseverance overcomes difficulties."
"Truth is mighty and will prevail."
"Wisdom is more to be desired than riches."

SCHOOL RHYMES

Being thus early taught by our teachers, we naturally took to the scribbling of moral rhymes on our books. Here are two or three:

"Steal not this book for fear of shame,
For here you see the owner's name;
And God will say on that great day,
This is the book you stole away."

Or another version was this:

"Steal not this book, my honest friend,
For fear the gallows will be your end."

Here is very wise advice from an old school song:

"Work while you work,
Play while you play,
That is the way
To be happy and gay."

While talking of writing in school, I may give the following note which the boys and girls in early years used to pass back and forth. Let the reader try to make sense of it:

"Read see how me.
Down will I love
And you love you
Up and you as."

Here is a favorite school-boy rhyme, the moral of which, however, may be doubtful. On the first page of the book is written in a good round hand, the following:

"If my name you wish to see,
Turn to page sixty-three."

Innocent of any trick being played upon you, you turn as directed, and here is what is written:

"Since you've taken the trouble to look,
Turn to the page at the end of the book."

Your curiosity is now aroused, and again you turn, only to get this rebuff:

"Oh, you goose, you cannot find it,
Shut the book and never mind it."

The following constituted the usual programme of studies:

1. Prayer by the teacher.
2. Reading the Bible.
3. Shorter Catechism questions.
4. The teacher making and mending quill pens, while the scholars were busily occupied with their studies, most of them writing.
4. The junior class reading and spelling such words as b-a, ba; c-a, ca; d-a, da; etc.
6. Reading New Testament.

7. Class in English Reader.

8. Class in grammar; the text-books being Lennie or Murray.

9. Mavor's Spelling Book.

10. Arithmetic, the text-books being Daboll or Gray.

In the very early days, there was really no school system, that is, no provision made by Government for the education of the young. A few settlers clubbed together, raised money enough to buy sufficient nails and a few panes of glass; then by means of "bees" the building was erected. The teacher boarded round, staying a week or two with each family. No certificate of qualification was asked, and for his services he received six or eight dollars a month, which was raised by voluntary subscription among those who had children to send to school. The amount each man subscribed was, of course, supposed to be in proportion to the number of children he would send. As some families were large and the parents poor, the children would be sent to school week about, so that all would learn a little. Usually there would be in the school during the winter months quite a few young men and women about twenty years of age, trying to pick up the knowledge denied them in earlier years. In some localities, for lack of funds, the school was kept open only for six months of the year.

By and bye something more systematic was attempted. The township was divided into school sections and provision made for the salary of the teachers by levying a certain rate-fee on each pupil. This did not work well as it discouraged attendance. At length Egerton Ryerson introduced the "Free School" system. This system, where adopted, did away with the fee formerly charged, and provided for the expenses of the schools by levying a tax on every acre of land, occupied or unoccupied, within the section. The adoption of this system was not compulsory, but was left to be decided by a majority of the electors regularly assembled at the annual meeting. Long and loud was the controversy between what was called the "Rate Bill" and the "Free School" system. But truth is mighty, and it prevailed in this case. Gradually, in spite of all opposition, the schools of Zorra all became " Free ; " and the blessing can scarcely be overestimated. It recognized the value of education, and put it within the reach of the poorest, and, as a result, all the children received a good public school education.

Times change and we change with them, but all changes are not improvements. Petty criticisms of our present educational system are cheap, and, of course, always possible, for nothing human is perfect. We should appreciate the good, but at the same time, not captiously but faithfully, point out the weaknesses of the system. To-day we have many more subjects on our curriculum than our fathers had, we have better organization, keener competition, and a multitude of examinations. But does all this prove the superiority of the present over the past? Not necessarily. Studying for a prize, or to pass an examination, while very trying on the nerves, is very doubtful education. Organization is only machinery.

A man is not educated in proportion to the

number of facts crammed into his memory, but in proportion to the discipline he has received. Real education, as the word implies, is "a drawing out" of all man's faculties—physical, mental, moral, and spiritual. It develops the whole man, and builds up his character by broadening, deepening, and bringing out in symmetry, harmony, and beauty, all his God-given faculties. Such education depends, not so much upon system, as upon a competent, careful, conscientious teacher. The true test of education is not the number of books a man has read, nor the number of rules, dates, and facts with which his memory may be loaded, but the quality of character wrought out by the discipline. Any system of education which simply recognizes the "here," and ignores the "hereafter" is not good, either for the "here" or the "hereafter." The development of the intellect alone will never produce a high type of manhood. Nay, more; the training which ignores the moral and spiritual, is not only defective, but dangerous: it puts more power into the hands of those who know not how to use it. The ignorant thief will steal a pig or a chicken, the educated thief will steal a bank or a railroad. Lord Bacon was, at once, the greatest and the meanest of mankind. Aaron Burr had a greater intellect than George Washington. The one was a cultured libertine, the other a Christian hero. The memory of the one brings a blush to the cheek of purity and virtue, the memory of the other is the richest heritage of a great nation.

The reader has already seen the prominence given to the development of the religious and moral as well as the intellectual faculties in the pioneer schools. Are all the faculties of the child so well developed in the schools to-day? Is the Bible read and studied now as it was then, and are those great moral principles which lie at the very foundation of civilized society as faithfully inculcated? We fear not; and the result may be seen in the irreverence, the disobedience, and general lawlessness which we see in modern society. Is there no reason to fear that the church itself is becoming superficial rather than serious, sensational rather than spiritual?

The teachers of those early days were for the most part middle-aged men, earnest and faithful, but "severe and stern," and knew little of the theory of teaching as understood to-day. In the main they erred in applying themselves to the repression of the evil in the pupil, rather than to the development of the good. It is said of that great teacher, Dr. Arnold, of Rugby, that his aim in teaching was not so much to impart knowledge, as to impress upon his pupils a sense of the value of knowledge, with a view of stimulating them to seek it. The pioneer teachers were far from being Arnolds, and yet their motives and aims were undoubtedly good. They certainly did not in their ideals rise above their environment; and, like all others of that generation, they had strong faith in the efficacy of corporal punishment.

The language not unfrequently used would not be tolerated in any school to-day. It is related of a certain parent that when he threatened to make his boy "smart" if the wrong-doing was repeated, the youngster promptly retorted, "You can't do it, papa. Teacher says I was born stupid, and no power on earth can make me smart. He says I came of a stupid family." The father afterwards settled it with that teacher.

The method of teaching was exceedingly mechanical. The pupil was taught to parse a word, not by studying its relation to other words, but simply by committing to memory a list of "prepositions," "adverbs," "interjections," etc. He knew that a certain word was a preposition because he had committed to memory a list of prepositions, in which that word occurred; and so on with the other parts of speech. The list of prepositions was of course very long, and was a terror to young grammarians. It was arranged alphabetically; first, the prepositions beginning with "a," then those with "b," etc. Here, for instance, is the list under "a":— "about, above, according to, across, after, against, along, amidst, among, amongst, around, at, athwart." Then came the "b" words—" bating, before, behind, below, beneath, between, betwixt, beyond, by," and so on with the c's, etc.

The list of adverbs was not even arranged

alphabetically, but proceeded in this fashion :—
" So, no, not, nay, yea, yes, too, well, up, very, forth, how, why, far, now, then, etc."

After this the interjections claimed their right to be memorized; but och! och! I forbear. We used to think the long, dagger-like mark after each one of them was put there to indicate some murderous design.

The "taws" was a great institution in those days. It was thought that the knowledge which could not be crammed into the memory, or reasoned into the head, could be whipped into the fingers or the backbone. Pupils, girls as well as boys, were flogged for being late, although some of them came two miles through the woods, climbing over logs, and wading through streams to get to the school. They were flogged for whispering in school, or for making pictures on the slate, or not being able to recite correctly such barbarous lists of the parts of speech as above indicated. And worse than all, they were flogged if they failed to recite correctly the Shorter Catechism. Oh! how the Presbyterians envied the other denominations for their privilege of exemption from the Catechism. It was a premium put upon Methodism, and had it been left to "us boys," all Zorra would be Methodist to-day.

In preserving order the teacher watched all the scholars with the eye of a detective, and soon found out any scholar or scholars guilty of the crime of whispering or talking. Instead of coming down and remonstrating with the offender, as the teacher of the present day would do, he doubled up the "taws" into a ball, and sent it flying with unerring aim, carrying consternation to the delinquents. Those to whom this "fiery cross" came had immediately to come up to the master's desk, each of them holding on to some portion of the detested "taws," and there receive the castigation due to their fault. A friend writes assuring me that the hardening of the scholars' hands in this way was one of the means of making the tug-of-war team of Zorra so invincible.

The following amusing incident will perhaps be remembered by some Zorra readers: A teacher was accustomed to bring with him to the school every morning two or three birches; but if these were not used up in the forenoon they were invariably hidden by the boys during the noon hour. There was a hole in the ceiling right over the master's desk, and here the switches were thrown. But the best of friends must part; and so the day came when the teacher must say farewell to his scholars. Notwithstanding his severity the teacher was a man of warm feelings. So the boys, anticipating a "scene" during the delivery of the farewell address, had one of their number at noon go up the hole, with the instruction that he was to collect all the switches—the accumulation of years—and at the proper time let them down. Late in the afternoon the time arrived; the address began, and the teacher, amid tears, was assuring the scholars how much he loved them, when, lo, and behold! all of a sudden a whole avalanche of switches came from above—tokens of affections. The teacher was nonplussed, the scholars were convulsed, and the school was dismissed without hearing the peroration of the dominie's farewell.

There was no play ground attached to any of

these school-houses; and so, frequently, the bigger boys and girls would get into an adjoining pasture field to play baseball. (O yes, dear reader, the girls of those primitive times would play baseball and be none the worse of it.) Going into the field to play was not prohibited, but it was a strict rule that the scholars must watch for the teacher's return at 1 p.m., and be in before him. This time, however, the young people, some twenty-five in number, were so interested in the game that they did not observe the coming of the teacher. There was, of course, no bell or signal of any kind, and it was some five or ten minutes before the baseballers realized that "school was in." They rushed in as quickly as possible, but only to receive fifteen strokes each from a heavy leather strap. When the flogging was over, the teacher panted, but his pride was assuaged, the majesty of law upheld, and good (?) supposed to have been done. The writer has a very feeling recollection of the occasion.

A visitor to this school, examining a class of little boys, asked the question: "How is leather made?" The answer came promptly, "By tanning." Question 2—"How is tanning done?" Little lad's prompt answer—"You put it in a hole and wallop it with a stick." He had learned this method of tanning by observation and experience.

I have spoken of the faithfulness of the pioneer teachers; their efficiency, however, in teaching good English pronunciation was not so evident. Think of a Scotch teacher who had never heard a word of French in his life, requiring a class to repeat from memory the names of the counties of Quebec Province! Let the reader who knows something of French, imagine such names as the following pronounced in the most approved Gaelic fashion, with a flogging as the penalty of failure: Charlevoix, Chicoutimi, Bellechasse, Berthier, Portneuf, Nicolet, etc. Such pronunciation reminds us of the mother who boasted that her daughter made her "*debut* with great *eclat*," putting a strong English accent on the last syllable of the French words. Some of the pupils of those early days have found a long life too short to unlearn the innumerable mispronunciations acquired in school.

Let us not, however, be too severe on the pioneer teachers. They were not, as a class, cruel or vindictive. They were simply imbued with the spirit of their times. Parents thought that the future welfare of their boys demanded that they be from time to time in a judicious manner laid across the parent's knee. Corporal punishment was inflicted in the army for the most trifling breaches of discipline; and in England a boy was hung for stealing a handkerchief worth five shillings.

After all, are there not boys to-day who would rather suffer the strap and be done with it, than endure all the modern substitutes for the old flogging? "We don't get licked," said a little boy contemptuously, "but we get kep' in, and stood up in corners, and locked out, and locked in, and made to write one word a thousand times, and scowled at, and jawed at, and that's worse."

CHAPTER XVI

REV. DONALD MACKENZIE, THE PIONEER PREACHER OF ZORRA

" Remote from towns he ran his godly race,
Nor e'er had changed, nor wished to change his place ;
Unskilful he to fawn, or seek for power
By doctrines fashioned to the varying hour."
—GOLDSMITH.

"HIS memory will long be cherished." Such are the closing words of the Presbyterian General Assembly's obituary notice of the Rev. Donald Mackenzie. And we may add that so long as life continues his memory will never cease to emit a sweet fragrance in the hearts of those whom, for so long a time, he counselled and led. The pioneer character of his ministry, its long duration, and its powerful influence over a large section of country, all combine to make it particularly interesting. The present sketch

REV. DONALD MACKENZIE
THE PIONEER PREACHER OF ZORRA

must not be looked upon as even an attempt at a biographical survey, but only as an imperfect outline of the life of this good man.

Rev. Donald Mackenzie was born at Dores, Inverness, Scotland, on the 28th of August, 1798, just about one hundred years ago. Very early in life he manifested a clear intellect, and when only thirteen years of age he began to teach a public school. Afterwards he completed a thorough course of study at King's College, Aberdeen. He studied also one session in Edinburgh under the famous Dr. Chalmers; and often has the writer been thrilled as, along with two or three others, seated in the quiet parlor, he has listened to Mr. Mackenzie relating sayings, incidents, and experiences connected with the great disruption leader. We repeat a single incident: "On one occasion," said Mr. Mackenzie, "the students behaved rudely in the class-room, and Dr. Chalmers administered a sharp reproof. This we endured unmoved, but when next day the Doctor humbly apologized to the class for having, as he said, lost his temper the day before, we were all overcome with shame.

The thought of the great man apologizing to us boys was harder to bear than any punishment that could have been inflicted." The incident reveals not merely the character of a noble Christian, but the secret of success in a famous teacher.

On the 23rd of December, 1833, at the request of the Synod of Ross, and after much prayer and serious consideration, he determined to come to Canada as a missionary to his expatriated countrymen. On April 16th, 1834, he was ordained by the Presbytery of Dingwall in the presence of the Synod of Ross. On this occasion the famous Dr. MacDonald, known as "the Apostle of the North," presided, and preached from Acts xxii. 21, "Depart, for I will send thee far hence unto the Gentiles."

On August 18th, 1834, he came to Zorra by stage, and remained the first night at the house of the late Squire Gordon. On Wednesday he conducted the usual prayer meeting, and on Sabbath he preached two sermons, one in Gaelic and the other in English. The hearts of the people were greatly drawn to him, and they earnestly pressed him to remain with them, but wishing to do more missionary work, he proceeded westward by way of London, St. Thomas, Strathroy, Lobo, and Gwillimbury. Here he met lonely but devoted little bands of Highlanders, and preached to them in their native tongue the gospel they loved so dearly. To him more than to any other man, Presbyterianism owes its strength in this western section of Ontario.

In June, 1835, he was inducted into the pastoral charge of Zorra congregation. Prior to this he had anew, and in the most solemn and formal manner, dedicated himself to his God and Saviour. Here are the words of this consecration—words which for simplicity and solemn power have seldom been equalled, and perhaps never surpassed:

"I hang on Thee, O Thou Preserver of men for every breath I draw, and for every thought I think, for every purpose that rises in my breast, and every action of my life. Therefore in my own name and strength I disclaim entering into the covenant with so holy and great a

God as Thou art, but do bring with me a glorious Surety, acknowledged by Thine own sacred authority; and in His strength I promise at this date to be Thy servant in all time to come, to obey Thy will so far as understood, to declare it to others simply, faithfully, and unmixed, so far as knowledge and strength enable me to do. And do Thou, by Thy good Spirit and grace, instruct, lead, sanctify, and preserve me for every duty, trial, and event whatsoever in life, and prepare me for death, so that whether living or dying I may be Thine in soul, body, and spirit.

"In the name of the Father and the Son and the Spirit, this first day of the year 1835.

"D. MACKENZIE."

For thirty-eight years he was pastor, counsellor, and friend to every individual in a larger congregation than has ever fallen to the lot of any other minister in the County of Oxford. He was a man of splendid personal appearance, tall, erect, and with kingly brow. His majesty of manner and weight of bearing, as well as his elevated tone of thought, were such that persons who had no special reasons for approaching him, never thought of doing so. Yet to those who knew him well he was affable and social, and could tell a story and join in a laugh equal to any. His grave step and thoughtful air as he walked to the pulpit, as well as his manner of reading the Psalms and chapters and engaging in prayer, was profoundly impressive. He left no doubt on the minds of the worshippers that he was fully alive to the realities with which he was dealing.

He usually began his sermon with hesitancy, and in a very low and feeble voice. As he proceeded his manner became more animated, his matter intensely practical, and towards the close of his discourse his voice not infrequently swelled into a volume of the most touching and impressive melody. Every faculty was kindled, his countenance glowed, his eyes gleamed with fire, the veins in his forehead and neck stood out like whipcords, and his power was simply overwhelming. I have on occasions observed a breathless stillness pervading the assembly;

each hearer bent forward in the posture of rapt attention.

Who can ever forget the solemn appeals he frequently made to the consciences of his hearers, declaring that he had set life and death before them; that not a drop of their blood would be found in his skirts on the "Great Day"; and that he took heaven and earth to witness against despisers of "the truth as it is in Jesus?" As might be expected of one who so went forth "bearing precious seed," he returned "bringing sheaves with him." Mr. Mackenzie had many seals given him of his ministry. It is said we have two immortalities. One immortality we carry to heaven, the other we leave behind us on earth. Our deeds can never perish even on earth. They shall live in the lives of others for all time to come. And so though this reverend father is here no more, he is not dead; he still lives. He lives in the lives and in the work of thirty-eight ministers who, largely through his instrumentality, were led to consecrate themselves to the preaching of the everlasting gospel. And he lives in the lives of hundreds of men and women whose Christian character he did so much to mould, and many of whom occupy, or have occupied, positions of influence in the various professions—medical, legal, and educational.

Zorra has been highly favored in her ministers. Mr. Mackenzie's successors in the sacred office were Rev. Gustavus Munro, M.A., now of Ridgetown, who for eighteen years carried forward the work assigned him; and Rev. G. C. Patterson, M.A., the present pastor. Both these men have proved themselves faithful and efficient; but none would be more ready than they to testify that their success has been in no small measure owing to the pioneer labors of Rev. D. Mackenzie. He sowed and they have reaped, and the day will come when both sower and reaper shall rejoice together.

Once he observed to the writer, "When I begin my sermon, I begin by preaching the law, and then I bring in the gospel afterwards; for," he said, "it is like a woman who is sewing—she cannot sew with thread alone; she first sticks a sharp needle through, and then draws the thread afterwards; so," he observed, "does the Lord with us; He sends the sharp needle of conviction, the needle of the law, into our hearts, and pricks us in the heart, and He draws through the long silken thread of consolation afterwards."

Mr. Mackenzie would scarcely be ranked by the schools as an orator, but he seldom failed to clothe his thoughts in both Gaelic and English, in keen, ringing, vigorous language. Warning against bitterness and strife in the home, he characterized the unchristian language sometimes used with the following Gaelic adjectives: "Their words are," said he, "biorach, gobach, loisg, toinnte, tarcuiseach, tarsuinn, teumach, aig a bhord, air an teallaich, aig an dorus"; which may be translated as follows: "Their words are piercing, scolding, scorching, twisted, contemptuous, cross, and stinging at the table, on the hearth, and at the door." The Gaelic alliteration cannot be brought out in English, and this greatly weakens the force of the words to the English reader.

Some traits of Mr. Mackenzie's character

have already appeared in this book. In his social intercourse with his people, while characterized by dignified reserve, he always manifested sturdy, practical common sense, and never failed, even in trivial affairs, to make a point for his Master.

Often was he called upon to act as arbiter in some matter of dispute between two of his parishioners, and seldom did he fail to bring matters to a satisfactory conclusion. After frank conversation, and then prayer, first by Mr. Mackenzie, followed by each of the disputants, the latter usually shook hands and went home the best of friends.

A few illustrations may be given. One of his parishioners happened to be greatly annoyed with his neighbor's pigs breaking into his potato patch. Time and again he had driven the pigs out, but as often they returned, for pigs have proverbially short memories when potatoes are in question. At last he lost all patience, and instead of driving the hogs out as he had been accustomed to do, he went straight to the owner of the hogs and belabored him most unmercifully. He was not, however, a bad man, and his conscience was ill at ease for what he had done. So, to put himself right, he went to his minister and laid the whole case before him. "Noo," said Donald, "this is what she pe did; and what will my minister pe thinkin' apout it?" "Well, Donald," replied Mr. Mackenzie, "your conduct was good enough for a Hielan'man, but very bad for a Christian." It is needless to say there was no ambiguity in this reproof to the keen religious perception of Donald.

Another story may be given as a type of the many humorous experiences of this eminent pastor, arising from the defective knowledge of English possessed by the majority of his parishioners. In those days a "bank'd barn" was a great rarity, and the farmer who possessed one was usually quite elated over the fact. Sandy M—— had just completed such an elegant structure. One day he saw his pastor driving by, and asked him if he would not come in and see his grand new barn. "Certainly," was the prompt response. So Mr. Mackenzie was shown through the barn, while all its conveniences and excellences were pointed out and explained in detail. When taking leave, the minister expressed his sincere admiration of the barn, and his satisfaction at seeing his friend getting along so well in the world. "But," added he, in a a tone of warning, "Sandy, don't lean on your barn." "Lean on her!" cried Sandy, in amazement, "if all ta Hielan'mans in Zorra pe leanin' on her she will not pe hurt." The reader will observe how completely Sandy failed to grasp the force of the English metaphor in the word "lean."

Another well-known incident, illustrating a similar defective English vocabulary, may here be given. A young Highlander, known as Sheumais dearg (Red James), while driving along the rough road, just to the south of Embro, had the misfortune to break his cart. Soon a number of the village gentry gathered around, when the following dialogue took place: Highland driver in despair—"Coot some of ta shentlemans gif her a nail?" Wag in the crowd—"Cha 'n eil." (Gaelic for "no"). Driver—

"Aye, aye, you wass fery coot in ta joke, but if she wass a braw shentlemans in a shiny hat, an' an you wass an olt proken caart like hersel', she'll not pe said, 'cha 'n eil,' she'll pe gif you one whateffer."

Very early in his ministry, Mr. Mackenzie was impressed with the evils of intemperance and the duty of total abstinence for the sake of others. This duty he rigorously practised himself, and earnestly sought, in the pulpit and out of it, to persuade his people to do the same. While frequently only partially successful, his efforts in promoting sobriety among the people were untiring. A few out of many cases are here given in illustration:

Uisgebeatha (whiskey) was abundant in those days. There were no less than three distilleries in Embro, and consequently much drinking, as we have already observed. Big John was on his way home with a small barrel of whiskey in his sleigh. To his great discomfiture, Mr. Mackenzie met him, and seeing the barrel, at once began to upbraid John for the evil he was doing himself and others. Quite oblivious to the per-

A TRICK UPON THE MINISTER

suasions of his pastor, Big John replied, "Na, na, minister, she pe coot whiskey. We hef not much in ta house, and we pe gif her to ta chiltren wi' ta potatoes."

Not so guileless was another parishioner who was accustomed to carry his whiskey home in a small tin pail. Often had he been reproved. This day he knew he would meet the minister, and he formed a plan to get the better of him. He filled his pail with milk, and marched forward looking for his pastor. Sure enough they soon met, and the Highlander at once assumed an air of guilty fear. Of course Mr. Mackenzie gave him a long and faithful lecture on the evils of strong drink. To it all Donald listened, cap in hand, and without a word of interruption to the close, when he replied as follows: "Weel, minister, you was aye suspecting hersel' and she pe no guilty. This is gude drink," and with this he removed the lid of his pail, exhibiting to the minister, not the fiery liquid suspected, but beautiful white milk. The minister felt somewhat taken aback, but Donald looked innocent, and for a long time chuckled over the uccess of his trick.

John McPhee was an industrious, honest man, and very devoted to his church. Usually he was kind to his wife and family, and was a good provider. But occasionally he would give way to his enemy, the drink. On these occasions he would for a time completely desert his home, and spend his whole time in and around the village bar-room. It happened that at one time there was in the hotel a very sick man confined to his room. Mr. Mackenzie made daily visits to the sick-room, spending an hour or more there on each occasion. Day after day the good man noticed John loafing around the hotel; so one day he called him aside to give him a word of remonstrance. "John," said the minister, "I am very sorry to see you here and in this condition. Do you not know that you are injuring yourself and neglecting your family? Now go home like a Christian man, and attend to your duties." Thus far John McPhee listened attentively, head uncovered and cap in hand. But now it came his turn to speak. "Aye, minister," said he, " I confess I ha'e been taking a drap too much;

but I have a sair heart, and it's to droon my trouble that I drink. It amaist braks m' heart to see my ain minister, wham I respekit and lovit, every day for a week or more, come to this hoose, and spending his time drinking in a bed-room. I have been trying to droon my sorrow with a drappie now and then, but oh, it's hard to bear! To see my beloved pastor coming under the inflooence of the drink! But gin ye'll say naething aboot it I shall haud my tongue, and we'll baith do better in the future." In after years Mr. Mackenzie told this story with much glee.

Let it not be inferred from these few instances that drunkenness prevailed to an unusual degree among the pioneer fathers. Such an inference would be unjust. The fathers were, as a class, industrious, sober, self-respecting. Total abstinence did not, perhaps, prevail to the same extent as to-day, but the bar-room treating and the bar-room loafing of to-day, were almost unknown; and intemperance was regarded as dishonoring to God, degrading to character, and destructive to both body and soul.

The incidents we have given will indicate the various duties Mr. Mackenzie was called upon to discharge for his parishioners in those early times, and the extraordinary influence he wielded over them. Perhaps no chieftain possessed such a mastery over the clans in the days when the fiery cross or the wild pibroch summoned to the field, as did this humble minister of Christ for many years over the devoted Celts of Zorra. His work at the yearly Communions, when the people assembled in great multitudes from far and near to celebrate the sacred ordinance, has been spoken of in previous chapters. His sermons, in both Gaelic and English, were plain, earnest, practical discourses, dealing with the hearts and consciences of his hearers ; and in his household visits and catechising, he was indefatigable in his care and instruction of the young.

No one could be long acquainted with Mr. Mackenzie without being struck with his profound experience of the Spirit's work, his clear views of the doctrines of grace, and his life of holy watchfulness and prayer. His religion was of a most healthy, practical type. Perhaps never was he heard parading his assurance of salvation, and never, so far as I remember, have I heard him moaning and groaning over his own corruptions. Frames and feelings formed no part of the foundation of his faith. His thoughts were with his Saviour and his Saviour's work, and about these he loved much to converse.

He died at Ingersoll on the 8th April, 1884, in the 86th year of his age.

The stars shine brightest in the darkest night, and the gold looks brighter for scouring. So it was with this revered father. The time of conflict was a time of conquest, and the time of trial a time of triumph. Patiently he bore his heavy affliction. And when the end came and he was within sight of the celestial city, he felt the pressure of the loving arms of Jesus about him, and he triumphed gloriously. Being asked for his dying testimony he whispered his last utterance on earth, "Neither death nor life * * * * can separate me from the love of God which is in Christ Jesus our Lord."

CHAPTER XVII

REV. LACHLAN McPHERSON OF WILLIAMS

" Brother thou wast mild and lovely,
Gentle as the summer breeze ;
Pleasant as the air of evening
When it floats among the trees."

AWAY back in the thirties, three young men, all in the prime of life, started from the township of Williams to attend the Communion in Zorra, a distance of forty miles. For some time they travelled by themselves, but, like Israel of old going up to Jerusalem to attend the yearly feasts, these young men went from strength to strength, their number being constantly increased until when they reached Zorra, the Jerusalem of their day and country, there was a goodly company of them. The Communion services were greatly enjoyed by all the three, and now they were on their return journey—quite a com-

REV. LACHLAN McPHERSON OF WILLIAMS

pany at first, but they soon began to separate, each going his own way, until the original three were left to pursue their journey alone as they had begun it. Conversation was kept up at first, but at length was dropped, and the three walked in perfect silence for some time, until they came to a resting place. This was a spring of water by the roadside, bubbling up from a white pebbly bottom, and gushing out from between the roots of a great oak tree that had probably sheltered it for many centuries. It was a lovely spot, bestrewed with maguerites, dandelions, blue flags, yellow daisies, white lilies, and the wild roses delicately fair with their faint evanescent odor. Here on a rough stone they all sat down and slaked their thirst, while they satisfied their hunger with bannock bread, butter, and crowdy, with which their hospitable Zorra entertainers had furnished them on parting. Still not a word was spoken; all were silent. At last one of them broke the spell by asking the others:

"What are you thinking about?"

"I was thinking," replied one, "that I would

sell my property in Williams and go to Zorra, where I can get the gospel."

"And what are you thinking about?" was the return question.

"My thought was different from yours; I was thinking how we could get the gospel to Williams."

While sitting there under the shadow of the great oak, and by the spring of water, they held a counsel and the decision was that they would begin by holding a prayer meeting, each in his house by turns. One of them who was soon to return to Zorra to teach school, was to be on the lookout for some minister or probationer who could be persuaded to come to Williams, for as yet there was no settled minister there. This latter was Lachlan McPherson, and the result of the conference was that, when Rev. Duncan McMillan came to visit his friend, Rev. D. Mackenzie of Zorra, Mr. McPherson, who was now teaching school in Embro, prevailed upon him to visit Williams. Soon after he was ordained and inducted as their first minister; and in this way the gospel was brought to this important section of country. The other two who took part in the conference were J. McIntosh and D. Fraser. After teaching in Embro for a few years, and studying Latin and Greek with the Rev. Mr. Mackenzie, Mr. McPherson took a full course of theology in Knox College, Toronto. In 1849 he was settled as minister of Williams, his first and only charge. Here he labored with fidelity and success for thirty-four years, when, owing to ill-health, he resigned, and took a trip to Scotland, hoping to regain his health; but in vain. In July, 1885, he wrote from Inverness to his old and esteemed elder, Mr. William Menzies, of Ailsa Craig, to come to Scotland and take him and his wife back to Canada, if only (as he said) "to die among his dearest friends." He was too weak to undertake the journey alone. Mr. Menzies says: "I gladly responded to his most pathetic request, and aided by a kind Providence, removed Mr. and Mrs. McPherson, as they desired, to Ailsa Craig." But health returned not. The cistern was broken and the waters were too surely ebbing away. He died in March, 1886, in the seventy-second year of his age. Mrs. McPherson returned to Scotland in July following.

Mr. McPherson deserves a place in this volume because of his intimate association with the minister and people of Zorra, especially on their Communion occasions.

In stature he was rather under the average height; in disposition he was grave and serious, but very pleasant and never morose. His portrait appears at the beginning of this chapter, and the artist, as if by an unconscious inspiration, has wonderfully succeeded in giving expression to the kind, benignant countenance of Mr. McPherson, strikingly reminding one of the well-known pictures of the sainted McCheyne. There was nothing trifling or frivolous about him, and yet he was perfectly free from everything like affectation in his manners. He had that dignity that so befits the servant of Christ, and yet he answered to a remarkable degree Paul's description of a Christian minister, "gentle, apt to teach, patient, meek."

In the pulpit his manner of address was rather slow, but earnest and solemn. His subject was always well studied out, and very orderly, everything being in its proper place. Indeed, orderliness was one of his characteristics in every department of life; his very penmanship was model, every letter being perfectly formed. What a contrast to the hieroglyphic penmanship of some ministers! He was a patient, conscientious student; and every week wrote out in full two long sermons, one in Gaelic and the other in English, but the manuscript was never brought into the pulpit.

He was a man of much prayer, and this gave mellowness and sweetness to his home life.

> "When one who holds communion with the skies
> Has filled his urn where those pure waters rise,
> And once more mingles with us meaner things,
> 'Tis e'en as if an angel shook his wings;
> Immortal fragrance fills the circuit wide,
> That tell us whence these treasures are supplied."

From the ivory palaces of meditation and prayer he came forth to unfold the glory of the Saviour, and to woo sinners for Him whom his soul loved. The great leading doctrines of the scriptures were expounded with singular clearness, fidelity, and zeal. The atonement of the

Lord Jesus Christ; the infinite merit of His righteousness; the necessity for the Spirit of God to enlighten, convict, and save; justification by faith the only way of salvation; the crown rights of Immanuel, King of Zion and King of Kings;—these great doctrines, not "thundered" but "poured out in gentle streams" by Lachlan McPherson, were blessed by the powerful demonstration of God the Spirit to the souls of men, putting life into dry bones, and clothing them with power and beauty. He had many souls for his hire; some in Zorra, but more in Williams. And the unflinching maintenance, and vigorous defence of these doctrines are urgently demanded in our day when there is such a strong tendency to formalism and worldliness.

On the doctrine of the Headship of Christ over the Church and over the Nations, he was peculiarly sensitive lest the scripture standard might be lowered. And when the Free Church and the United Presbyterian Church were united in 1861, Lachlan McPherson and his devoted people testified against the union, and refused to enter it. This is scarcely the place to discuss the great practical importance of this doctrine; but just as its importance is appreciated and maintained will the Church of Christ be free from human excrescences in its polity and doctrines, and Christ be recognized in our politics, from which at present He seems to be excluded. Afterwards, however, Mr. McPherson and his people came into the united church, only to leave it forever, along with his life-long friend, John Ross of Brucefield, and their two elders, when the larger union of 1875 was consummated. The reasons will appear more fully in our next chapter.

Strange that a man of such a mild and gentle spirit should yet, Athanasius-like, stand out alone against the action of all the ministers of his church. But such a man was Lachlan McPherson. He combined the lion and the lamb. To him conscience was supreme, and its behests he always obeyed at whatever cost. Perhaps few men ever possessed at the same time so much of the "*suaviter*" and the "*fortiter.*"

"Nor number, nor example, with him wrought
To swerve from truth, or change his constant mind,
Though single."

The following are a few specimens of Mr. McPherson's pulpit utterances, for which I am indebted to a correspondent who was, for many years, intimately associated with him in church work. This correspondent writes: "The first time I saw or heard Mr. McPherson was in the summer of 1852, at the Communion in Brucefield. His text was Isaiah 50: 10, 'Who is among you that feareth the Lord, obeyeth the voice of his servant, that walketh in darkness, and hath no light? Let him trust in the name of the Lord, and stay upon his God.' He raised the question, Is it so that one who is trusting in the name of the Lord, and obeying the voice of His servant, can, nevertheless, be walking in darkness and without light? Yes, even such a one can be in darkness; but here is the remedy, 'Let him trust in the Lord and stay upon his God.'"

On one occasion in the same place, his text was 1 Pet. 2: 11, "Dearly beloved, I beseech you, as strangers and pilgrims, abstain from fleshly lusts which war against the soul." He said, "War supposes killing; and if you do not kill your lusts, your lusts will kill you—they will kill your soul."

At another time, preaching from Malachi 3: 17, "And they shall be mine, saith the Lord of hosts, in that day when I make up my jewels," he said, "Some of them are not much like jewels now; they are jewels, but they are diamonds in the rough."

At another time, preaching from 2 Cor. 6: 17-18, "Wherefore come out from among them, and be ye separate saith the Lord," etc., he said, "You cannot coax the world to heaven, it will not go with you one foot; the best thing that you can do for the world is to come out and testify against it."

On Gal. 2: 20, "Christ liveth in me," he remarked, "Let Christ speak through your mouth, and weep through your eyes, and smile through your face; let Him work with your hands, and walk with your feet, and be tender with your heart."

At times his illustrations possessed great force and beauty. Speaking of the believer's peace, and its independence of external circumstances, he compared it to the still, mysterious depths of ocean, that are beyond the reach of winds and waves.

Describing the natural blindness and folly of the unrepentant sinner, he said, " Be not like the foolish drunkard, who, staggering home one night, saw his candle lit for him, and exclaimed, ' two candles,' for his drunkenness made him see double. ' I will blow out one,' and as he blew it out, in a moment he was in the dark. Many a man," said the preacher, " sees double through the drunkenness of sin—he thinks he has one life to sow his wild oats in, and then the last part of life in which to turn to God ; so, like a fool, he blows out the only candle that he has, and in the dark he will have to lie down forever. Haste thee, O traveller to eternity ! thou hast but one sun, and if that sets, thou wilt never reach thy home."

For Mr. McPherson we do not claim any extraordinary gifts of intellect, but we do claim for him a rich endowment of that goodness which only the Divine Spirit can impart. We may not be able to say, " Tread lightly on his ashes, ye men of genius, for he was your kinsman ;" but we can say what is far better, " Weed his grave clean, ye men of goodness, for he was your brother."

CHAPTER XVIII

JOHN ROSS OF BRUCEFIELD

"Erect before man, on his knees before God."

THE line which we have quoted above as the motto of this chapter, describes as briefly and clearly as words can do, the character of Rev. John Ross of Brucefield. Such reverence towards God, and such manliness towards man have characterized few since the days of John Knox. His devoted and scholarly widow has published in brief form a memoir; and while excessive modesty has prevented her putting some things so strongly as they might be put, and constrained her to omit many things well worth publishing, yet the history of "The Man With the Book," may be read with profit by all true Canadians; and it can scarcely fail to inspire the

REV. JOHN ROSS OF BRUCEFIELD

reader to more earnest devotion, and a nobler purpose in life. We trust it may prove one element in developing in our land, and especially among Mr. Ross's Highland kinsmen, a robust, God-fearing character.

The life of John Ross was distinguished, not by striking events or by wonderful achievements, but by a holy, humble, consistent walk with God; and no Zorra minister has left so deep and lasting an impression on all with whom he came in contact.

John Ross was born in the famous little village of Dornoch, Sutherlandshire, Scotland, on the 11th of November, 1821. When eight years of age he came along with his father's family to Zorra. The experiences and adventures of his boyhood are well told by Mrs. Ross.

"He was," she tells us, "full of life and fun and ambition, and very fond of athletic sports. Whether it was a hard mathematical problem or a school fight, a game of shinny or a tough debate, he was always ready, and entered into it with all his might. He who in manhood's prime began to be known as "The Man With the Book," was not, in his earlier days, one of those quiet and thoughtful lads, whose story makes other boys feel that they were made of different stuff from themselves. He was felt by his companions to be a boy every inch of him, and one with real and serious faults besides."

One who has passed the allotted span of years, but who is still an enthusiastic curler, being recently asked by the writer, "Did you know John Ross as a sport?"

"I did to my cost. Look at that," said he, pointing to his mouth, which was minus a front tooth, "John Ross did that with his shinny stick—of course accidentally. And strange to say, he, a few minutes afterwards, had the corresponding incisor knocked out in the same way. At the Embro Re-union in '83," continued the Woodstock man, "that is nearly fifty years after this incident, I met Mr. Ross and pointing to the vacancy in my jaw, I said, 'Do you remember that?' In an instant he pointed to a corresponding vacancy in his own mouth, saying 'Do you remember that?'"

HIS CONVERSION

But in his love of sport he did not forget that he had a mind, a soul to care for. Even in his boyhood he was a great student of the Bible and a lover of Shakespeare.

His first teacher was Lachlan McPherson, the subject of our last chapter. Mr. McPherson was not only a faithful teacher, but an earnest Christian, and his personal character and conversation were a powerful means in leading Mr. Ross into the way of life. The preaching of Mr. Mackenzie, and more especially the gospel proclaimed by Mr. Allan, were also instrumental in leading him into a clear knowledge of the way of salvation. How thorough his conversion, and how clear his apprehension of salvation through free grace, he himself tells us. In a private letter written only a few years before his death, he says:

"If I am born again, my spiritual birth took the most pronounced anti-Roman form. I first fled from God and from the gospel to which my heart refused to bow, though I was still believing it. I fled on down to dark despair, and for years refused to leave that loathsome dungeon. At last, in my loathsome dungeon or den, God gave me a sight of myself which made me feel that there was not an eye among all God's creatures that could endure to turn one look upon such a man. With this sense of overwhelming shame at its height, I sprang over at one bound to God for covering, saying, 'If thou wilt not look on me no creature can.' That one leap changed my relation and attitude towards the universe. I fled from all God's creatures to Himself as my hiding-place. Freedom from human — say rather creature—authority in all matters concerning God and my soul is one characteristic of my spiritual liberty to this day; and it had its birth in that leap."

Soon after experiencing the wonderful change he stood up for Jesus. A man with his deep conviction and strong personality, could not long remain hidden. Very beautiful, as well as strong and lasting, was the affection that at this time sprang up between the young recruit and an esteemed elder of the church— Mr. Alexander Murray. After the lapse of nearly half a century, when the old elder was on his death bed, Mr. Ross came from Brucefield to visit the friend and counsellor of his youth, and the meeting was worthy of both men.

The year 1844 was memorable for the disruption in the Church of Scotland. The following year John Ross entered Knox College, having studied Latin and Greek for some time with Rev. Mr. Mackenzie. He soon became the most conspicious figure in his class. His intellectuality as well as his spirituality could not fail to impress his fellow-students.

One of these, who now occupies the chair of Systematic Theology in Knox College, thus writes of him at that time : " He did not parade his religion ; he spoke comparatively little of his religious feelings and experiences; but no one could come into close contact with him without learning something of his deep spirituality and profound earnestness. * * * His religion was not a garment put on, but a life which manifested itself; and his character was so transparent, and the currents of his religious nature so strong that the spirit which reigned in him was visible to all around him."

The writer has heard him repeat from memory with fluency, one Psalm after another in Hebrew. On the occasion of his death all the Professors and students of Knox College assembled for the purpose of bearing testimony to his intellectual and spiritual attainments.

After completing his college course he was ordained to the gospel ministry on the 25th of September, 1851, over the congregation of Brucefield, in the county of Huron. There he continued to labor with great fidelity until the end came on the 8th of March, 1887, in the thirty-sixth year of his pastorate and in the sixty-sixth of his life. And during these thirty-six years he only missed one Sabbath that he did not preach.

It is not easy to describe John Ross as a preacher. Like many men of genius his habits of study were irregular. There were times when he spoke with much hesitation and difficulty; but there were other times when he enjoyed great liberty in the pulpit, and his preaching was always doctrinal, evangelical, earnest. Never was his pulpit a spiritual dormitory where all creeds were equally true, and all forms of worship equally safe and equally sensible.

Who that has ever heard him can forget the faithfulness and thoroughness with which he expounded God's law—its holiness, its spirituality, its requirements; or the fiery earnestness with which he reproved sin and showed men their danger, loss, ruin. But the great subject of his preaching was Christ—Christ the prophet, the priest, the king of his people. He gloried in the Cross, and never wearied of speaking about the precious blood of the Lamb. Perhaps his mind ran chiefly on the kingship of Christ.

" What are the distinguishing characteristics of the three Reformations?" said he. Then answering his own question, he replied:

"In Germany Christ was lifted up as a Priest, in Geneva as a Prophet, and in Scotland as a King. That is the glory of Scotland. She has not only believed in Jesus Christ as the all-sufficient Sacrifice and Advocate for each individual soul, nor rested in him merely as the all-sufficient Instructor, revealing the whole will of God for ecclesiastical, as well as individual guidance; but besides these two she has had a fuller revelation of the glory of Jesus Christ, she has seen him as her King. Germany struck the keynote of the Reformation, and preached faith, faith in the adequate work of the Great High Priest. Geneva added to the faith of Germany the knowledge that comes from careful attention to the instructions of the Prophet like unto Moses. But Scotland added to the faith of one and the knowledge of the other loyalty to a personal and glorious King. Her's was a mighty step in advance." Our young people to-day, in sincerely pledging themselves to "do whatsoever He would have me to do," are honoring this aspect of our Lord's character. "Christian Citizenship," of which we now justly hear so much, is only the development of the truth, Christ our King—our King in the political meeting as well as the prayer meeting.

"You doubt," said John Ross, "if you are Christians. But have you the impression of the King? In some coins the impression is dim, in others bright and clear, but in all it is genuine."

Some of my readers will recall Mr. Ross's appearance in Woodstock, at the great farewell meeting to Dr. MacKay in 1881, on the occasion of the missionary's leaving for Formosa. The meeting was held in the Central Methodist church, it being the largest church in the town. The place was packed from end to end, there being, as was estimated, a congregation of fifteen hundred persons present. The chair was occupied by Rev. J. J. Hill, rector of New St. Paul's church.

There were thirty or forty clergymen, and many prominent laymen from all over the Province, including Sir Oliver Mowat, now Premier of Ontario. A good deal had been said about the heathen, their degradation, and the duty of the Church to them, when it became Mr. Ross's turn to speak. Suddenly springing to his feet, he took the audience completely by surprise. His tall form, his clear, ringing voice, and his strong Doric accent at once arrested the attention of everybody. "What is the matter," he cried, "with Formosa? What is the matter with China? What is the matter with Canada? What is the matter with Oxford? What is the matter with Zorra? What is the matter with Woodstock?" These questions were put with great deliberation and solemnity. At the close of the last, he made a long pause, looked round upon his audience, and then answered his own questions with three short words, expressed with an emphasis that was startling: "IT IS SIN!" The younger and more superficial of his hearers, of course, failed to catch the point, but experienced Christians at once were impressed with the deep theological and practical significance of the answer. Bad as were the heathen, and sad as was their condition, we ourselves were in the same category with them, afflicted with the same malady, and requiring the same physician. A most important truth that cannot too frequently be impressed upon the minds of Christian workers. Much as we may plume ourselves upon our superior knowledge and attainments, it will be more tolerable for Sodom and Gomorrah on a day of judgment than for the people of Zorra, Woodstock, Canada, who reject Christ.

It will here be in place to explain, as briefly as possible, John Ross's action in refusing to enter the union of the Presbyterian Churches in Canada in 1875—an action regretted, profoundly regretted by nearly all his friends, but condemned by none.

Prior to the year 1875 there were four Presbyterian Churches in this country. To the outward observer these differed only in name. The division was the result of importing into Canada from the mother country controversies concerning the proper relationship of Church and State, which were of no practical importance in this country.

In the above year these Churches agreed to unite in one organization, to be called the "Presbyterian Church in Canada." Into this union, John Ross, together with his friend and old teacher, Lachlan McPherson, and their representative elders, four persons in all, declined to enter, on the ground that they could not do so " without betraying the integrity and interests of the truth of God, and the purity of His worship." In particular, they objected to any sanction being given to the use of the organ in public worship, and they characterized the basis of union as "exceedingly defective and unsatisfactory in reference to the Headship of Christ, both as regards His church and the nations of the world." The importance of this latter doctrine will be acknowledged by every intelligent Bible student. This, however, is not the place to discuss the necessity or propriety of Mr. Ross's course. One thing is certain, Mr. Ross, after much prayer and deliberation, was fully convinced that he could not enter the union, " except by such an act as that of Judas." The behests of conscience must be obeyed, cost what it would, and he dared to stand alone.

It was a time of sore trial to John Ross. With his strong social nature, and his unabated loyalty to the Presbyterian Church, it was like rending his heartstrings to be ecclesiastically separated from brethren he loved, and with whom he had so pleasantly associated in Christian work for many years.

But the trial must be endured. And John Ross was both a Christian and a philosopher. He had learned the very important lesson that a man's happiness springs from within and not from without; that it is determined, not by what a man has, but by what a man is. And so even when the strong ties of church relationship were broken, and he stood apparently alone and unbefriended, he was never gloomy or morose, but always bright, cheerful, happy. Once, indeed, we are told, he became discouraged; he feared the effect his attitude toward the union might have on his ministerial brethren, association with whom he prized so highly. But he received encouragement from heaven in a way so peculiar to himself. One bright winter afternoon he came out of his study with his Bible open in his hand. "Look at this," he said to his wife, pointing with his finger to part of the blessing pronounced by Jacob on his son Joseph. "Blessings * * * on the crown of the head of him that was separate from his brethren."

Yes, John Ross's life was a happy one to the end in spite of his loneliness.

John Bunyan "was separate from his brethren," and spent twelve years as an outcast in prison; but he lived in the sweetest peace, and had glorious visions that will never die.

S. Rutherford "was separate from his brethren," and confined a prisoner in Aberdeen Castle, but his letters show us how happy he was, and at the head of each letter he wrote "Christ's Palace, Aberdeen."

David Livingstone "was separate from his brethren." Henry M. Stanley found him in the heart of Africa surrounded by savage tribes, where he had not seen a white face for many years, in the midst of indescribable loneliness. But the blessing of God was upon his head, and the presence of Christ was so apparent in his life, filling it with comfort and gladness, and giving him a victory over outward difficulties, that a few weeks of conversation and association with him, transformed the infidel Stanley into an earnest believer in the Lord Jesus Christ.

To John Ross the Word of God was precious, and he searched it diligently to know God and his Son Jesus Christ. His mind was illumined by the Holy Spirit, and when suddenly a new truth flashed upon his keen vision his whole soul was stirred, his countenance glowed, and his eyes beamed with very joy.

For many years he constantly carried his Bible wherever he went, holding it in his hand or under his arm ; and, after looking to God for direction, he would open it, and as his eye was guided to a text or passage, he would give it to any with whom he conversed, be he stranger or acquaintance. Wonderful indeed, was the appropriateness of the passages furnished him. Many, very many, who never heard him in the pulpit, will have reason to bless God to all eternity for the words spoken to them by John Ross in a stage-coach, or at a railway station, in the shop, on the street, or in the house. This extraordinary method of personal dealing with souls is a work which few have the courage or the qualification to enter upon. But John Ross did it faithfully, and in such a spirit of humility, and self-unconsciousness that seldom was he rebuffed, even by the careless, the profane, the ungodly.

To illustrate his method of work I will quote from a letter written by a Presbyterian minister. He says: "During my college days I had the pleasure of Mr. Ross's company coming from Toronto to Zorra. He was going to his relatives and I to visit my good friend Mr. ——. I felt very much at home in his company. There was nothing stiff or formal about his manner. He conversed freely upon a variety of topics. When we came to the Woodstock station, Mr. Ross met a young man he knew and inquired after his welfare. Then opening his Bible he read a verse or two to the young man, gave a word of advice, and then good-bye. Next we went into a store to inquire if there was any chance of a ride to Embro. The clerk could tell us of none. Mr. Ross opened his Bible, read a verse to the clerk as he stood beside the counter, gave him a word of advice and a good-bye; then we called to see his sister, who, with her family, was living in Woodstock. We stayed only a few minutes. Mr. Ross called the children around him, spoke to them, prayed with them, said good-bye, and we started for Embro on foot."

I have mentioned the wonderful adaptation of the passages frequently given him for those with whom he conversed. A young Presbyterian minister had received a number of " calls " within a comparatively short time, probably not without his seeking them. Meeting him one day on the street, John Ross as usual opened his Bible, and the first passage his eye rested on was Zech. 11 : 17, "Woe to the idol shepherd that leaveth the flock," which he read to the young preacher.

"I am not an idle shepherd, I hope I shall never eat the bread of idleness in the Lord's service," was the somewhat tart reply.

" It is not i-d-l-e," said Mr. Ross, " but i-d-o-l." Then the young and popular brother saw the point.

In company with a brother minister, he was taking his horse out of an hotel stable in Stratford. Parting with the hostler, he handed him his customary fee, read to him Luke 2: 7, kindly adding, "Now John think of Him who was born in a stable."

He visited Zorra a few months before his death, and in company with Mr. Munro, the pastor, called on a number of families. Of course he took his Bible with him and read a verse or passage in each home.

At the close of the day he observed to the pastor, " Did you notice anything peculiar in the passages of scripture the Lord gave me to-day?"

"I did," was the reply, "they all had reference to death, resurrection, and eternity." He at once, in a most earnest way, said, "My brother, depend on it the Lord is speaking to some one to be ready, for He is coming soon. I never had passages of that class recurring in the same way but some of my friends were soon removed by death."

"But can you," said the Zorra pastor, "make the personal application?" "No, I can not," was Mr. Ross's reply; "it may be yourself or myself." He returned home, never again visited

Zorra, but a few months afterwards the Master called him home.

It may also be mentioned that one of the homes visited on this occasion, a few days after the visit and the warning, experienced a very sudden and painful bereavement.

The same minister writes me as follows:—
"Late in October, or about the first of November, 1873, I was assisting at a Communion in Harrington, with the Rev. Daniel Gordon, and Mr. Ross was also present. On one of the Preparatory days, just as we were taking our places at the dinner table, I mentioned that Dr. Candlish of Edinburgh was dead. This was sad news to all present, and Mr. Ross sprang to a bedroom close by, exclaiming as he went, "Is Candlish dead?" He quickly returned with his diary, and called our attention to the fact that about two months previous to this he had written in it that God was soon to take Dr. Candlish to his reward. All present were curious to know how he arrived at this conclusion; and, in his own transparent and child-like way, he explained to us how God had

in His Word revealed this matter to him. Sceptics may sneer, and infidels may deny, but the fact is as above related; and the witnesses are still living, and can be produced any day in court."

Let Zorra stand with head uncovered in presence of John Ross, the ablest scholar, the most profound theologian, and the most Biblical preacher of all her sons. One who knew him well writes, "As a teacher of theology, John Ross would have been as able as Dr. Young was as a teacher of philosophy."

Why then did no college ever officially recognize his gifts? Why did no Presbytery ever mention his name as Moderator of Assembly? Perhaps light may be thrown on these questions by asking another, "Why did England treat Charles Gordon, now of world-wide fame, as she once did?" When a man of thirty Gordon had saved the Chinese Empire from breaking up; but on his return the Secretary of State could only with great difficulty recall his name, and knew absolutely nothing of his work in China.

Both Gordon and Ross were men of great ability and piety. They both were men who gave a high place to the Word of God, and to prayer. They both possessed right kingly hearts and hands. Both were mastered by a great devotion to a noble purpose, and both alike experienced the ingratitude of their fellow-men. The lesson for Britain to learn is, to find out such men as Charles Gordon, and place them. The lesson for the Presbyterian Church to learn is, to find out such men as the late John Ross, and place them.

He died March 8th, 1887, in the thirty-fifth year of his ministry, and in the sixty-fifth of his age. And now

"He wears a truer crown
Than any wreath that we can weave him."

His dying testimony was just such as we might expect from his life. Confidently his faith rested on the Word of God. Two lines from a Psalm formed his death song:

"Surely that which concerneth me
The Lord will perfect make."
—Psalm cxxxviii. 8.

Very tenderly and solemnly he bade farewell to his weeping wife and children and loved ones around his bed. His wife he referred to the passage, "Thy Maker is thy Husband; the Lord of Hosts is His name; and thy Redeemer the Holy One of Israel; the God of the whole earth shall He be called." To his little daughter Bessie, weeping in another room, with her heart like to break, he sent the message, "Blessed be the glory of the Lord from this place," and then added the promise, "I will never leave thee; I will never forsake thee!" Taking Maggie's little hand in his, and looking at her, as one who was there writes, with his heart in his eyes, he said, "O, my little daughter Maggie, seek the Lord Jesus Christ, and remember that He has power to draw your heart right over to Himself." Similar parting words he gave to each member of his family, and then fell asleep like a wearied child in its mother's arms.

The company that gathered to pay the last tribute of respect was unprecedentedly large. Eleven ministers representing Presbyterians,

REV. DANIEL ALLAN OF NORTH EASTHOPE

Baptists, and Methodists were present, and all felt that a prince in Israel had fallen.

"He being dead yet speaketh:" and though we shall hear his faithful words, or enjoy his fervent prayers no longer, his influence will live forever in the hearts of many, and will be a constant inspiration to a higher and nobler life.

> "Sleep on, it is not by the years
> We measure life when all is done—
> Your task was big, your crown well won—
> Sleep on, good-night, we say with tears."

CHAPTER XIX

REV. DANIEL ALLAN OF NORTH EASTHOPE

"Daniel—a man greatly beloved."
—DAN. x. ii.

IN the early forties, and for many years after, no man was more welcome to the Zorra pulpit, and to the Zorra homes, than Rev. Daniel Allan of North Easthope, the intimate friend and neighbor of Rev. D. Mackenzie, the Zorra pastor. Especially on Communion occasions were his services greatly enjoyed by all classes of the people.

Daniel Allan was born 25th Sept., 1805, in Fortrose, Scotland. He completed his education in King's College, Aberdeen. While a very young man he experienced a sudden and remarkable change of heart under the ministry of the Rev. Dr. MacDonald, the famous "Apostle of the North." Before his conversion, he was for some time under deep conviction of sin. The power, the justice, the holiness of God he viewed with alarm. The terrors of the Lord were upon him, but he was not allowed to despair. Every Sabbath he travelled fifteen miles over the hills to hear the great evangelical preacher of the north; and one day listening with all the intensity of his awakened nature, suddenly the light dawned upon him. In a moment he saw that his salvation was through the free grace of God, as manifested in the atonement of Christ. There and then, sitting in the church, he took Jesus Christ as his Saviour, and entered into the full assurance of his acceptance with God. His fears were all gone, and a sweet peace filled his soul. It was like a calm after the storm. The clouds parted and the sun shone out gloriously. Great was his alarm when awakened to a sense of his lost condition as a sinner; correspondingly great was now his joy in the assurance that God was his friend, and Jesus his brother. Speaking of this experience to a friend many years afterwards, he said: "Such was the overflow of my soul's joy on that wonderful Sabbath day, that on my way home from the church, I could scarcely refrain from speaking of it to the stones and the trees on the roadside."

He left Aberdeen, 16th August, 1836, and arrived at Quebec on the 7th of October, following. Coming west he received a joint call from the united congregations of Woodstock and Stratford, which he accepted, and was ordained at Stratford on Thursday, 21st of November, 1838. He was therefore the first Presbyterian minister settled in Woodstock, although Rev. Mr. Mackenzie, of Zorra, and Rev. Mr. Murray, of Blenheim, held occasional services before '38. Mr. Allan's labors were equally divided between Woodstock and Stratford, two weeks being devoted to each field alternately, an arrangement rendered necessary by the distance, and the very bad state of the roads. Owing to his impaired state of health, the resignation of a portion of his charge soon became necessary; and on the 15th of Aug., 1840, he was released from his connection with the Woodstock congregation, and he became the minister of Stratford and vicinity alone. In 1846, North Easthope became a separate charge with Mr. Allan as their pastor; and in spite of many difficulties and discouragements, erected what is supposed to have been the first Presbyterian brick church in Upper Canada, west of Toronto. Here for thirty-eight years, more than a third of a century, among a people devotedly attached to him, he labored faithfully and with great success.

In stature he was perhaps a little below the medium size, with a slight frame, but compactly put together and capable of great endurance. His eyes clear and penetrating, very expressive of the tender emotions of his heart, often filled with tears as he pleaded with sinners. Like many famous preachers, such as Dr. Arnot, Dr. Guthrie, C. H. Spurgeon, and others, nature had endowed him with a rich fund of humor. This, mellowed and sanctified, gave tone and charm to his discourses. In private life and among Christian friends he was exuberantly happy, jovial, and free, and his conversation full of mother-wit and quaint humor.

A minister thus writes of him: "Daniel Allan was a living delight to childhood, youth, and age. His dignity as a gentleman was elevating, his remarkable adaptation enabled him to inspire those of every age with high ideals. His incisive, humorous utterances kept the atmosphere of the home of his host surcharged with pleasant wit from the time of his arrival until his departure.

"Mr. Allan's own home was a little world of cultured minds and tender hearts, of Christian charity and domestic love, of ideal tact and exquisite refinement. The centre round which mother, sons, and daughters moved was the high-minded, pure-spirited, happy-hearted father. Few men attained to such perfection in the domestic virtues. He never lost sight of his high and holy office with its weighty obligations, yet his family circle was his chief care and delight. The sparkling humor that pervaded his conversation never allowed the home to become a dull or dreary place."

The following will illustrate his original and quaint mode of expression. Hearing of a faithful minister of the gospel who was being persecuted by some of his people, Mr. Allan said: "That is nothing strange. The world never permits a man to rebuke her follies without replying with a volley of mud. If she cannot stop the man's mouth, she tries to blacken his character."

One or two instances of his ready wit may here be given. He was fond of his pipe, and on one occasion, when enjoying a smoke in one of the horse sheds standing by the church, a young minister not noted for spirituality, reproached him, "There you are again at your idol."

"Yes," quickly responded the witty Mr. Allan, "I am burning it; have you done so with yours?"

"What," I think I hear some one saying, "Mr. Allan smoking?" Oh, yes, and he snuffed, too. It was a fad of the time; and there are fads still. There are not many perfect men,—or women either. It is related of a noted revivalist, well-known in this country, that he is an inveterate smoker. On one occasion a good Christian lady remonstrated with him as follows :

"Mr. J——, I'm so sorry you are a smoker. If you did not smoke you would be a perfect man."

"I don't want to be a perfect man," was the ready reply.

"Oh, dear, why not?"

"Because," said the witty preacher, "I'd be so lonesome."

Mr. Allan had in his congregation a man whose employment was to gather ashes for the Stratford market. Unfortunately this man was addicted to strong drink. His minister, had repeatedly remonstrated with him, but apparently to little purpose. One day Mr. Allan, in company with a brother minister, was walking from North Easthope to Stratford to attend a meeting of presbytery. Sitting on his load of ashes the ash pedlar overtook the two ministers, and the day being wet, the ashman had thrown a sack or bag round his shoulders to protect him from the rain.

Mr. Allan looked at him, bade him the time of day, and then said :

" I am glad to see you in this condition. You have at last listened to my advice."

" How is that ? " said the ashman.

" I see," was the quick response, " that you are now sitting in sackcloth and ashes."

On another occasion in his presence, one minister accused another of having used undue influence to induce a family to change its church relationship. The matter was referred to Mr. Allan, who gave his judgment in these words, " They used to hang sheep-stealers."

Mr. Allan and Mr. Mackenzie were as David and Jonathan; but on one occasion at least, Mr. Allan displayed his wit and readiness at the expense of his good brother, who seemed to enjoy it no less than Mr. Allan himself. On one of the " Preparatory days," a hot summer day, Mr. Mackenzie entered the vestry shortly before service, poured water into a basin and washed himself. Just as he was in the act of doing so, Mr. Allan entered, and Mr. Mackenzie turning to him said :

Mr. Allan, would it not refresh you to have a wash this hot morning, before commencing service?

"No thank you," responded his friend, "it was the Pharisees who were in the habit of doing that sort of thing."

Mr. Mackenzie simply smiled and silently ruminated over the joke, but, doubtless, waited till his turn would come.

Let no one undervalue the importance of this trait of character. Next to the sunlight of heaven is a buoyant spirit and a bright, cheerful face.

> "Smile once in a while,
>   'Twill make your heart seem lighter,
> Smile once in a while,
>   'Twill make your pathway brighter.
> Life's a mirror; if we smile,
>   Smiles come back to greet us—
> If we're frowning all the while,
>   Frowns forever meet us."

But this was only one aspect, and by no means the most important aspect of Mr. Allan's character. There was no frivolity or levity about him. "It is only with God's children," said he, "that I make merry. How could I jest with the world, or sport with men on the brink of a precipice?" He was profoundly reverent. The search-light in which he first saw his sin and his Saviour never left him, but kept him humble and adoring all his life.

Here is how a minister's wife writes of him: "It was decidedly toward the sunset of his life. He was with us during a Communion. He was too frail in body to attend all the services, and during the evening meetings he stayed at home, lying for the most part on his back on the sofa, his eyes closed. He was evidently thinking very actively and intensely, a stage beyond meditating. He was in the dining-room where household duties called me back and forth, but he seemed to be oblivious of my presence or absence, pursuing his own thoughts, sometimes audibly. At last I heard him going over it somewhat in this way: "What an undertaking to remove from me every stain of sin; to restore the image of God in me that had become the image of Satan; to work out in me the likeness of the Lord Jesus Christ, so that I shall yet be known by the resemblance as a young brother of the Lord of Glory! What an undertaking! But God has laid the task upon one who is mighty, and He will do it,—yes, He will do it gloriously before He is done with me."

Another sweet and characteristic word of his may here be given. He was from home assisting at Communion. It was the month of May. There was on the dinner-table a magnificent bouquet of lilacs. After all had sat down at the table, Mr. Allan reached out his hand, and almost reverently touched one of the outmost clusters, saying with real reverence in his tone: "Verily He (the Creator) hath taste." As Hugh Millar said once, there was worship in both words and manner. There was so much more in it than simply the apprehending of the beauty—it was "the holy and reverent use of God's works."

He was a diligent student, and a classical scholar beyond the ordinary. The writer has seen his diary wholly written in Latin; and he could write letters to his ministerial brethren in Latin, Greek, French, or Hebrew. He studied

Gaelic after coming to Canada, and he could preach in it with fluency. In those pioneer days grammar schools were few, and not many parents could afford to send their children to them. The work of preparing young men for the colleges had to be done by the minister; and next to the late Rev. Mr. Robertson, of Chesterfield, no minister in Oxford ever did so much of this good work as the Rev. Daniel Allan. But for all this work he never would accept fee or reward.

Those who knew him most intimately speak to this day with enthusiasm of the vigor of his intellect, the force of his will, the brightness of his wit, the honesty of his purpose, the warmth of his friendship, the generosity of his heart, and integrity and purity of his private life.

His preaching was clear and scriptural, fervent, heart-searching, and instinct with life. It exhibited characteristics that are not often found in combination—it was both doctrinal and practical, courageous and tender. The writer has seen him overcome with emotion, and bursting into tears even in his introduction; and then before the sermon was over he was roused to highest pitch, and thundered forth in fiery sentences the most scathing denunciation against the sins and shams of the day. Sometimes he plead like a mother tenderly pleading with her children; at other times his sentences fell like the blows of a warrior; never did Highlander wield broadsword with greater force than did this clansman of Christ wield "the sword of the Spirit, which is the Word of God."

No doubt his remarkable conversion at an early age both moulded his character and gave clearness and force to his pulpit ministrations. It is hard, perhaps impossible, to communicate through the printed page the electric effect upon a large congregation, when Mr. Allan related from Bunyan's "Holy War," the capture of Mansoul by Prince Immanuel. "Diabolus from within the city," said he, "strove hard to keep him out, and it was a hard time for Mansoul. But at last the place was taken, and the Prince rode down the city streets in triumph, and the liberated citizens welcomed him with all their hearts, and the silver trumpets were sounding, and the flags were flying, and the bells of the church towers rang out merry peals, for the King of Glory had come. Up to the castle he rode in triumph, and sat upon his throne, to be henceforth the sole Lord and King of the city."

"That," said Mr. Allan, "is Christ entering the soul of man; Christ in your heart, swaying His sceptre from the very centre of your being, over every power and faculty, desire and resolve, and bringing every thought into captivity to Himself." It was, at any rate, a true type of the preacher's own conversion and after-life.

"Many a night you kept me awake," said Rev. Mr. Ross, the subject of our last sketch to Mr. Allan years afterward. "The arrows from your bow went right home, and they were so barbed that it was impossible to draw them out again. Once after service, as I was watching you coming down from the pulpit, and one after another speaking and shaking hands with you, my own internal comment was, 'I would as soon shake hands with the lightning.'"

But, perhaps, the most striking part of his pulpit ministrations was his prayers. "I have heard," says one who sat under him for many years, "others who could preach as well or better, but I never heard one like Mr. Allan in prayer. He spoke to God as a man speaks to his friend. Such holy familiarity! such simplicity! such fervor! From the beginning to the close you felt you were in the divine presence."

Being accused of using too great familiarity in prayer, he made reply, " May not a child be familiar with his father?" Just then the little child of his reprover had clambered on her father's knee, thrown her arms around his neck, and was raining kisses on his cheek.

"Do you call that presumption?" said Mr. Allan. "And does not the Spirit teach the Lord's children to say, Abba Father?'"

He was an active worker in the temperance cause, and did perhaps more than any one else in bringing about in that district, the new and better era when liquor ceased to be used at raisings and "bees," and in the homes of the people.

Mackenzie, McPherson, Ross, Allan—we have now briefly looked at each. How different!

Yet how like one another! Different in personal appearance, in temperament, in talent, in habit, and in manner of address; but all agreed in rendering supreme, absolute authority to the scriptures, and in rejecting every doctrine and practice for which there could not in their judgment be pointed out a "Thus saith the Lord." They were all manly men who kept back nothing that was profitable but each regarded himself

"A messenger of grace to guilty man."

Accuse them not, gentle reader, of bigotry or intolerance, because they courageously opposed some things that are now practised in the church. They feared God rather than man; and though in judgment, they were like ourselves, human, yet their heart was always right, and their purpose true. According to their light and ability they endeavored "to keep pure and entire all such religious worship and ordinances as God hath appointed in his Word."

Daniel Allan died at Goderich, December 10th, 1884. For some time he longed for the hour of his departure, and when the Master came, he found his servant not merely resigned but triumphant.

"Do you not hear the heavenly music?" said he to his wife at his bedside.

"Do you not see the Lord Jesus coming with his chariot to take me home?" These were his last words. His remains, accompanied by a number of friends, including his life-long friend, John Ross, were taken to Guelph, where they were interred to await the resurrection of the just. His spirit is with God.

His name is as ointment poured forth. May the consideration of his life inspire each reader to a greater hatred of sin, a stronger faith in God, a wider sympathy with our fellow-men, and a more earnest desire to advance the Redeemer's Kingdom.

REV. JOHN FRASER, M.A., OF THAMESFORD

CHAPTER XX

REV. JOHN FRASER, M.A., OF THAMESFORD

"We thank thee for the quiet rest thy servant taketh now,
We thank thee for his blessedness and for his crowned brow;
For every patient step he trod in faithful following thee,
And for the good fight foughten well and won right valiantly."

REV. JOHN FRASER'S connection with Zorra dates from a time much more modern than that of the other ministers we have mentioned; but forty years ago he was a frequent visitor to the district Communion occasions, and he was an important factor in the upbuilding of the sturdy Presbyterianism of that day. His commanding figure, his stately bearing, his powerful voice, his unctuous tone, his vigorous delivery, and his impressive discourse will long be remembered.

He was a son of Mr. John Fraser, banker, of

Inverness, Scotland. His mother was a daughter of Major Alpin Grant, of the Glenmoriston Grants. He was born in Farintosh and was baptized by the famous Doctor MacDonald, "the Apostle of the North," for whose memory he had great veneration. Mr. Fraser studied in Aberdeen, where he won high repute as a classical scholar, and graduated from King's College there. His tastes were scholarly, and he had a wide acquaintance with English and classical literature. At that time the writer was a pupil in the Woodstock Grammar School, taught by Mr. Strauchon. Mr. Fraser visited the school, and found some of us trying to translate a very difficult Latin sentence in Horace. He took up the book, at once cleared the difficulty, leaving us with this sound advice : "Gentlemen, study thoroughly the Latin Grammar, and you can go through such a passage as this like a horse galloping." Here is a pointer for our young students to-day ; study well your grammar, and in every department of life remember how important that the foundation be well laid.

His special subject of study, however, was the

Word of God ; and so proficient did he become in that department of sacred learning that he not only seemed able to repeat most of the scriptures, but he had studied critically nearly every portion of the Old and New Testaments. It was a rare treat to hear him discourse in private regarding the contents of one of the books of the Bible, especially Paul's epistles.

Mr. Fraser came to this country in 1845 as one of the pioneer missionaries of the Free Church. His first charge was Melbourne, Que., from which he passed successively to the following charges in Ontario: Cornwall, St. Thomas, Thamesford, Kincardine, and Indian Lands.

His induction into Thamesford was on April 4th, 1859, and his resignation in July 1866. Prior to his settlement here, he taught for some time the St. Thomas Grammar School, at the same time supplying neighboring pulpits. For two years he thus preached at Wallacetown, travelling each week, for the most part on horseback, a distance of 36 miles, and receiving for his work the little "copper" collection, which was frequently less than he had to pay for his horse.

In the home, his life was very tender and affectionate. "He was dearer to me," writes a member of his family, "than ever I made known. I have read McCheyne, Paton, and Drummond, but in the memory of my father I find more to impress upon me the grand worth of character and godliness than books could ever teach."

Concerning Mr. Fraser's social qualities, I will quote at length from a letter by one of his most intimate ministerial friends:

"We knew Mr. Fraser in both his public capacity, and private conversation; and much as we appreciated his public ministrations in pulpit, we enjoyed his private conversation still more. For my part I do not expect again to meet one whose practical knowledge of the whole system of revealed truth was so complete. His natural endowments, early religious training, culture, scholarship, and still higher, the illumination of the Spirit enlightening and guiding him into all truth,—all combined, qualified him for the glorious work in which he spent his life and exhausted his strength, although not unwillingly, above the most, even of his fellow laborers in the Master's vineyard. His simplicity and gentleness were traits of character rarely to be met with. The Christian manner in which he always spoke of those who opposed him, or did him an injury, or caused him trouble, was of the highest order. I have more than once said to my wife, I wonder will we see a minister like Mr. Fraser any more? The last time we had the privilege of entertaining him, he was as interesting as ever, although in delicate health. His interest in the Bible, in the Church, in theology, and in all pertaining to the salvation of of souls, and the glory of God, and the honor of his Master was unabated. Well do we remember how his pleasant face would beam with celestial radiance, when a fresh religious idea, or a new scripture view occupied his mind."

Mr. Fraser was a good platform speaker, and frequently gave addresses on astronomy, botany, etc., and while his subject may not always have been studied with scientific accuracy, his fine appearance, beautiful diction, and remarkable fluency never failed to command admiration.

But the pulpit was his throne. As observed, his personal appearance was striking; he was somewhat above the ordinary height, a florid complexion, strong features, and a bearing peculiarly solemn and dignified. As he entered the pulpit and took his seat there could sometimes be discerned on his countenance, gloom and sadness as if the shadow of Sinai were upon him; at other times his countenance was radiant with joy, indicating that the Great King was giving him a royal message to the people. "*Am fac thusa mar a thog e shuilean?*" (Did you see how he raised his eyes?) was an expression not unfrequently heard from some of the older portion of his hearers on their way home from the church.

His preaching power did not by any means show itself on all occasions. His wonderful facility of speech was a powerful temptation to neglect that special preparation so necessary to the gospel minister to-day. But when he was at his best, and his theme the great central truth of our religion, few could speak with such eloquence and power.

"In the cross of Christ," said he, "justice and mercy and all the attributes of the God of glory met and kissed each other; justice raised the flaming sword but the Mighty Shepherd bore the stroke and paid the ransom price and mercy triumphed."

Preaching on John 12: 32, "And I, if I be lifted up from the earth, will draw all men unto me," he said: "As the lifeboat will attract the sailor battling for his life amid the waves, so long will the preaching of a crucified Saviour draw men from their sins, to a high, pure, and noble life. Other things may tickle the ear and amuse the imagination, but only the preaching of the cross brought home by the Spirit of God, can change the heart, purify the life, relieve the troubled conscience, and save the soul. This is the only lever that will turn the world upside down."

He knew the Highland heart as a musician

knows his instrument, and could move his hearers as the leaves are moved in a storm. On Communion occasions what crowds flocked to his ministrations! The fact needed only to be known that John Fraser was to preach, and all classes, old and young, English and Gaelic, would hasten to the place of meeting; and all would be stirred into enthusiasm or melted into sadness by the mighty power of his eloquence.

He was equally at home in both languages. Professor Blackie tells us that Gaelic is a language which "few can speak and nobody can spell." Mr. Fraser could both speak and spell it well, and write it in penmanship of such clearness and beauty, that the dullest *Sassenach* could not mistake the letters.

Who that heard him will ever forget that wonderful Communion Sabbath, when on the hill-side in Dent's woods south of Embro, he preached to an immense congregation, his subject being "The last Judgment?" Suddenly the clouds gathered, there was a flash of lightning, and then the roll of the distant thunder. The preacher, with the tact and readiness of the true orator, took the alarming commotions of nature around him to illustrate the thunders and lightnings of an angry God against his enemies on that "Great Day." As he depicted with a full, rich voice, and in solemn sentences, the terrors of the judgment day, and called upon the stones and trees to witness that he had set life and death before his hearers, the impression was simply overwhelming. Sighs and sobs and groans were heard throughout the great congregation and many trembled as if the judgment had actually come.

"Did you ever hear anything more powerful than that, even from Dr. MacDonald himself?" was the question put afterwards by an aged and intelligent elder.

"That sermon will be for the fall or rising of many in Zorra," said one.

"It will meet us again," said another.

In the church courts he seldom spoke, but when he did speak, few men were listened to with more respect. His anti-organ speech before the Synod in Montreal, on June 12th, 1868, during the debate on instrumental music, is universally acknowledged to be one of the finest dialectic efforts ever witnessed in any of the church courts. The address as published in pamphlet form is a classic worthy of preservation.

I give some extracts from it here for two reasons: First, because of the intrinsic merit of these extracts; and secondly, because they will help to relieve the memory of John Fraser and those ministers associated with him in opposition to the organ, from the unjust charge of ignorance, narrowness or bigotry. None of these men, so far as I know, took the ground that the use of the organ in public worship was unscriptural. Mr. Fraser, I know, repudiated such an argument. But they did take the ground that neither the demands of God's Word, nor the necessities of the church called for the use of the organ in public worship, and that its introduction was an innovation likely to disturb the peace of the church, and do much harm. And who will say that such an argument was not tenable—that it was not consistent with breadth of thought, spirituality of mind, and thorough loyalty to the church.

But let us hear Mr. Fraser. In seconding the motion against the introduction of organs and hymns, he began as follows: "Nothing is more out of place than the reflections which are cast on Gaelic adherents of our church. Dislike of these innovations is not a peculiarity of the Highlanders; and even if it were, is there a heart in the Free Church of Scotland that does not beat in unison with their feelings? They feel strongly. It would be a wonder—perhaps an unhappy indication—if they did not. It would be, to me at least, the sign of an altered, a declining loyalty to the church of their fathers —of a declining piety. They love their church; they love her with an intense, a chivalrous affection. The very rocks and water-falls of their native glens are holy for her sake. Cradled in their northern hills, where Presbyterianism has had for ages the whole field to itself, they know no church but one; and sad and untimely is the legislation that would sorely aggrieve and alienate the hearts of that faithful and ardent people by the engraftment, in the face of their conscientious protests, of a foreign element on the service of our sanctuaries, against which the Presbyterian sentiment of Scotland is so strong as to be proverbial." . . . .

"Call it ignorance, if you will—or obstinacy, or bigotry, or rustic prejudice, that our people love their church with a devotion so deep, so true, as that you are not able to bend it to an acquiescence in changes which violate the simplicity of a service enshrined by holy memories in their fondest veneration. Is that a thing to be deplored, to be treated with indignation, to be held up for satire, for the taunts and acerbity of an oratorical invective?"

Fear having been expressed that if the organ was not introduced our young people would in large numbers leave the church, Mr. Fraser, with great warmth and power, replied as follows: " It is argued that without the magic power of instrumental music the great body of our young people will fall away from the communion of the church, attracted by the popular and splendid entertainments of other denominations. This, sir, if true, would be a dark prospect. But I do not believe it. What! do they mean to assure us that the pulpits of our church are so deficient in the great attributes of power and attractiveness as that we must be driven to the fantastic expedient of an organ and orchestra in order to keep our young people in steady adherence to our cause? Does Brownlow North need the echoing harmonies of a pipe or chord when he draws out to heaths and mountain hollows, the tens of thousands that hang on the gospel simplicity of his ministration? Was it an organ that filled the aisles of St. Peter's Church in Dundee; or was it the glowing earnestness of Robert Murray McCheyne.

If we would have a devoted people—a happy, living, vigorous church we must depend on an influence of another character than the fine music, or the flashing oratory that regales the fancy, and wakes up the thrill of fleeting emotional transport; we must rely on the purity of her doctrines, the efficiency of her ordinances, and the apostolic fervor of her pastors; on the descent of a "power," and a "glory" that would make her tabernacles the birth-place of souls. It is then that our people would love our Zion as "the perfection of beauty," "their chiefest joy," their "resting place," their "home."

One more extract must suffice.

Mr. Fraser closed his address as follows: "Sir, I would pour out my prayer for the peace of the church, that God would be gracious to us, and quell the agitation that afflicts us. We are called to do a great work, to lay the foundation in this vast country of the Christianity of future ages; and we cannot do it but in the power, the quiescence of fraternal unity. Our church is feeble, it is the period of her infancy; why shatter her strength with questions that gender strife rather than godly edifying? The sound of an iron tool was not heard when Solomon's builders were busy on the temple; it rose amid silent and harmonious activity, a dwelling place on earth for the God of peace."

In 1886 he retired from the active service of the ministry; but still, though physically infirm, he continued to preach the gospel he loved so well, travelling extensively east and west, visiting his old congregations and friends; and everywhere, in public and in private, holding forth the word of life.

For some time Mr. Fraser had been in feeble health, and was seized with paralysis in the house of Mr. Donald Morrison, Thamesford. He was tenderly cared for, and Mr. Morrison accompanied him to his home in Montreal, where he lingered in much weakness for a short time, and then departed this life on the early morning of Sabbath, September 24th, 1893.

Where the angels veil their faces, where the elders cast their crowns, where the weary are at rest, where the everlasting song is sung—there reposes the freed spirit of John Fraser.

CHAPTER XXI

REV. WILLIAM MELDRUM OF HARRINGTON

"I would express him simple, grave, sincere;
In doctrines uncorrupt; in language plain;
And plain in manner; decent, solemn, chaste."
—Cowper.

Rev. William Meldrum's connection with Zorra dates from the year 1857, when he was inducted into the pastoral charge of Harrington congregation. He belonged to an intensely conservative school of thought, and few of the pioneer ministers exhibited more distinctive characteristics. The present brief sketch can give these only in a brief outline.

He was born in the parish of Abernethy, Morayshire, Scotland, in the year 1806, and was educated at Aberdeen College. On being licensed as a minister of the gospel, he at once received a call from a church near the home of

REV. WILLIAM MELDRUM OF HARRINGTON

his childhood; but he felt that America was to be the field of his labors, and so he set his face westward. Arriving in this country in 1839, he was soon after ordained and inducted as pastor of the congregations of Puslinch and Nassagaweya, Ontario.

Here he labored for fifteen years ministering the gospel, not only to his own people, but to many others in the regions round about, especially to the north and west. On these journeys he was frequently accompanied by Dr. Smellie, of Fergus, Dr. Gale, of Hamilton, and Dr. Bayne, of Galt. From Puslinch he went to Vaughan, in the county of York, where he labored for four years. From Vaughan he came, as we have observed, to the large and important congregation of Harrington in Zorra.

Shortly before leaving Vaughan he met with an accident in which his horse fell on him, breaking three ribs, and severely bruising his whole body. He was badly injured, although with the persistance of the typical pioneer, he preached regularly and attended to his pastoral duties. At times the bruised blood would run from his legs to his feet, until he was forced to preach sitting down, and the people placed a high chair in the pulpit, with a rest for his feet. He was often heard to say, with great delight, that during all his ministry he had never missed a Sabbath. Harrington was his last charge, although he preached in vacant congregations and mission fields until 1876, when he retired from the active work of the ministry.

As a preacher, Mr. Meldrum spoke with a strong Doric accent, and in his matter he was deep, rather than broad. He knew nothing of that liberality which makes no difference between truth and error; and although in private life affable and genial, in his pulpit ministrations he was stern and decided. On one occasion, hearing a student preaching loose, incorrect doctrines, he rose at the close of the sermon, and to the consternation of the congregation, unsparingly denounced the utterances of the young orator.

His style was exegetical, without any pretence to being homiletical. On one occasion he consulted some of his prominent members as to their preference for texts chosen in the ordinary way, or for a continuous course from some book of the Bible. Preference was expressed for the latter; and so Mr. Meldrum went to work, and continuously preached from Isaiah for several years, without giving any signs of completing the book. Hearing that some murmured he wondered how any one could take exception to the course they had preferred, and to which he had so faithfully adhered; but when a change was suggested he willingly returned to preaching from texts chosen in the usual way.

His illustrations were in accord with the genius of the Gaelic rather than the English language; and while considered chaste and appropriate in the former, would occasionally be condemned by the more exacting taste of modern society.

He was remarkably specific and powerful in prayer, and had great discernment in the selection of words to suit the occasion and circumstances, entering sympathetically into the interests concerned. There were some rich scripture passages which he seldom failed to repeat in his public prayers. Few of his hearers can ever forget the solemnity with which he slowly pronounced, in the most approved Gaelic fashion, "Thou magnifiest thyself above all that is written. Thou art a terror to evil doers and a praise to them that do well." In asking the blessing at the table, often there would be a reference to some remark just made by a member of the family or visitor.

His observance of the Sabbath would have pleased the strictest of the Puritans. It is related of a rural Scotchman that, when he returned home after a visit to Edinburgh, he said, "It was an awful sicht to see the people sae happy on the Lord's day." It may be that Mr. Meldrum would not have objected to his children being happy on the Sabbath; but beyond contradiction, his ideas of happiness were very different from theirs. There was a fine spring of water about one hundred yards from his house at Puslinch, and even in the hottest weather in summer, only one pitcher of water could be brought from it on the Lord's day.

In his family he was kind and tender, and his memory is lovingly cherished by his surviving wife and children. And yet, according to our more modern ideas, the discipline of that home was somewhat severe. On the Sabbath, after public services in both Gaelic and English, the family returned to the manse and partook of dinner. Then the table was cleared, and family worship was observed, — making three times each Sabbath. After this the Shorter Catechism was repeated. The older ones had to go all the way through, and the younger as far as they had learned. Mr. Meldrum would sometimes close his eyes and seem to be asleep; but the mistake of a single preposition or a transposition of words would wake him up with a suddenness that alarmed the erring one. At other times he would walk the floor while the recital was going on, carrying in his hand a red cane with an iron head; and quite often a rap on the head of the one who made the mistake was a painful reminder that contributed to accuracy. The family knew that the iron head was harder and heavier than he supposed. The children had to repeat all the Psalms in metre, Paraphrases, and Hymns bound with them. Very faithfully he attended to the catechising and pastoral work of the congregation.

Most of his travelling he did on horse-back, dressed in white moleskin overalls, buttoned along the sides from top to bottom, with about twenty-five buttons on each side. These overalls were removed when the formalities of a service were required. He always had a good horse, and was allowed to be a superior judge of horses. Although never guilty of horse-racing, it was almost a passion with him to show the young "Jehus" that a minister could take delight in having a horse as speedy as any on the road.

He was wonderfully methodical in his habits, and kept an accurate account of every cent received and expended. He carried the silver in one pocket, and the coppers in another. He always washed his face before his hands, as he preferred the clean water for his face. At family worship the Old and New Testament were read alternately night and morning. The Psalms were sung from beginning to end, about three verses at a time; no Paraphrase or Hymn was allowed. For private reading Mr. Meldrum had the whole Bible marked so as to include so much for every day of the year, and to read the whole every year. This regularity he observed for many years.

When about forty years of age, he married Miss Anna McLean, who was several years his junior, and the most popular young lady member of his church. Shortly before his marriage a prominent gentleman from a neighboring city, whose heart had been affected in the usual way by meeting Miss McLean a few times, but whose Scotch prudence counselled extreme caution, referred the matter to Mr. Meldrum, lest any mistake should be made in choosing a life partner. Mr. Meldrum in unmistakable language declared from his personal acquaintance he had every confidence that the young lady would make an excellent wife. The gentleman ever believed Mr. Meldrum sincere in the words he then spoke.

Mrs. Meldrum by her characteristic wisdom, prudence, and executive powers was a true helpmeet in congregational, financial, and family cares. Their large family, distinguished for their piety, as well as for intellectual and social qualities, bear evidence to the strong powers they inherited, and the vigorous discipline through which they were nurtured.

He was an advanced temperance man, and as far back as 1852, the church records show how faithfully he and his elders administered the discipline of the Church in the matter of intemperance, as well as in sins against the fourth commandment.

Mr. Meldrum was a man of high social qualities, and nothing could be more delightful than Christian fellowship between him and neighboring ministers. Indeed, it may be observed of all the pioneer preachers of Zorra that they lived in unbroken Christian love and unity. These ministers exhibited great variety of gifts and graces, and differed widely in their manner of presenting truth. Occasions occurred that might have given rise to petty jealousy and unseemly rivalry, but grace prevented any appearance of unbrotherliness. Dr. Kennedy, in his book, "The Days of the Fathers in Ross-shire," tells us of two Highland ministers. The name of the one was Fraser, and that of the other Porteous. Fraser preached largely the law, seeking the awakening and conversion of sinners, while Porteous excelled in preaching the consoling doctrines of the gospel, directing his remarks to the comforting of the broken-hearted and the building up of God's people. Each was faithful according to the gifts bestowed upon him; but Mr. Fraser's people complained that their minister preached the law so exclusively, that those who sought the bread of life must starve under his ministry, and they began in considerable numbers to forsake their own church and to attend the ministry of Mr. Porteous. But Mr. Porteous, being a Christian man and knowing Mr. Fraser to be on the whole an excellent minister, spoke to him about it. Meeting Mr. Fraser at a funeral, he said to him, "It gives me, my dear brother, grief of heart, to see some of your people in my church every Sabbath. My elders tell me that those who come to us complain that you preach almost entirely to the unconverted, and that the 'poor in spirit' can get no food for their souls. "Now, my dear brother, if the Lord gives it to you, I pray you not to withhold their portion from the people of the Lord, which you could dispense to them as I never could."

"My dear brother," was Mr. Fraser's striking reply, "when my Master sent me forth to my work, He gave me a quiver full of arrows, and He ordered me to cast these arrows at the hearts of His enemies till the quiver was empty. I have been endeavoring to do so, but the quiver is not empty yet. When the Lord sent you forth, He gave you a cruise of oil, and His orders to you were to pour the oil on the wounds of the broken-hearted sinners till the cruise was empty. Your cruise is no more empty than is my quiver. Let us both then continue to act on our respective orders, and as the blessing from on high shall rest on our labors, I will be sending my hearers with wounded hearts to you, and you will be sending them back to me rejoicing in the Lord."

This spirit of mutual confidence and kindness strikingly characterized the pioneer preachers of Zorra, and it is worthy of being recorded as an example to the ministers and people of to-day.

After leaving Harrington, Mr. Meldrum moved back to his old home in Puslinch. Here he lived till his Master took him on the 19th day of November, 1889, in the eighty-fourth year of his age. The night before, he worshipped with his family around his bed, he leading in prayer, and one of his sons conducting the reading and singing. He is buried at Puslinch, and a prominent monument near the entrance of the cemetery, reminds us of the enduring monument which the Christian life and work of this pioneer minister have reared, not only in Puslinch, but in Zorra and other places throughout Ontario.

CHAPTER XXII

REV. DANIEL GORDON

" War a good warfare, holding faith and a good conscience."
—1 Tim. i. 18, 19.

Our series of pen sketches would be incomplete without a chapter on Rev. Daniel Gordon, of Harrington. For though the period of his labors scarcely dates back to what is commonly known as pioneer days, yet in character and work he formed the last but not the least of that noble band of seven, who did so much to build up a sturdy Presbyterianism, and to mould the religious character of the people in this district.

Rev. Daniel Gordon was born at Tummelside, Perthshire, Scotland, on March 22nd, 1822. On both sides of the house he was, as the Scotch would say, " weel connec'it." On the mother's side the lineal descent can be traced to the

MRS. GORDON

REV. DANIEL GORDON OF HARRINGTON

celebrated Stuarts of Fincastle, and through them to Mary Queen of Scots.

In the sixteenth year of his age, and while a student at the Perth Academy, he was brought to a saving knowledge of Christ through the preaching of Rev. W. C. Burns, afterwards the famous missionary to China. Burns was at this time occupying, in Dundee, the pulpit of Robert Murray McCheyne, who was sent by the church on a mission of inquiry to the Jews in Palestine. It was a time of mighty out-pouring of the Spirit upon the people. At Kilsyth, Dundee, Perth, and the regions round about, great meetings were held from night to night, and many souls were saved. "It pleased God," says McCheyne (Memoir, p. 282), "to bring an awfully solemn sense of divine things over the minds of men. It was, indeed, the day of our merciful visitation."

Mr. Gordon, the subject of our sketch, entered fully into the spirit of the revival, and travelled for a time, from place to place, with Mr. Burns; and although only sixteen years of age, assisted in the good work. May we not in large measure trace the strong evangelical views of doctrine and the fervor of delivery which have ever characterized Mr. Gordon's ministry, to the powerful spiritual impluse his nature received at the time of his awakening?

A letter he received at this time from Mr. Burns is full of interest. It is dated, Dowally, June 16th, 1841. In glowing language Mr. Burns refers to the work of grace in which he was engaged. After mentioning a number of students he had met the Sabbath before, he adds, "May Jehovah keep them and you and me in the hollow of His nail-pierced hand, and then we shall be safe, and shall shine as the stars forever and ever. Oh, Daniel, keep near to Christ! Be like him whose name you bear. The decree of a king could not keep him from entering into his chamber, and with his window open toward Jerusalem praying three times a day! Surely he had found his noonday season of prayer precious, when he would not give up even it to save himself from the jaws of the lions! May you find Jesus as sweet and as near as he did, and be made fit through divine grace to serve Him even in the days of desolating trials." What a prophetic significance it imparts to these last words, when we remember that within two years from the time they were penned, the disruption of the Church of Scotland took place. And was not the prayer of Burns for Daniel Gordon wonderfully answered? Who that knows the character and work of Gordon but will testify that even " the decree of a king" could not prevent him worshipping and serving his God?

In 1840 Gordon entered Marshall College, Aberdeen, and here completed his Arts course in 1844. In 1845 he entered the Free Church Assembly Hall, Aberdeen, where he studied theology for three years. Then going to Edinburgh he studied for two years longer under such professors as Buchanan, Cunningham, Duncan, Candlish, and Fleming.

On July 12th, 1849, he was licensed by the Presbytery of Dunkeld, and in the following month he set sail for Canada. He came here under the auspices of the Colonial Committee of the Free Church of Scotland.

Arriving in Montreal on September 27th, he was, without delay, ordained by the Montreal Presbytery to the work of the ministry.

For four years he labored as an ordained missionary over all the eastern townships, his centre of operations being Lingwick, Que. Like many of of the pioneer missionaries, Mr. Gordon abounded in labors and privations. Long journeys, scanty fare, preaching twice every day for weeks at a time, marrying, baptizing, burying, settling disputes, healing divisions, organizing congregations, counselling and cheering, and attending to the temporal as well as spiritual wants of immigrants—these were among the things that demanded his constant care.

In 1853, Mr. Gordon received a call to Indian Lands, Glengarry, Ont., which he accepted. Besides looking after the spiritual interests of Indian Lands, he had the pastoral oversight of the large district of country now represented by the congregations of Maxville, Roxborough, Kenyon, and Apple Hill. The country was in a very primitive condition, and the story is told of how, on one occasion, a bear entered Mr. Gordon's log manse at Indian Lands, and ate up a large share of the family's provisions.

The first part of his ministry here was greatly hindered by disputes between the Free Church people and the adherents of the Old Kirk, concerning the ownership of the church property. Mr. Gordon, as representing the Free Church party, was taken before the Court of Queen's Bench. The trial took place before Judge Day, and the the late Sandfield Macdonald was Mr. Gordon's lawyer. Like a chieftain in the old feudal days, our friend marched to Cornwall at the head of fifty stalwart Highlandmen. He was charged with housebreaking, because, contrary to the wishes of half a dozen kirkmen, he had taken forcible possession of the manse. To lose his case meant imprisonment. But he and his friends were triumphantly vindicated, and returned home to engage in more congenial work than going to law with brethren.

About this time also our friend was greatly

annoyed by a preacher of the Plymouth persuasion. This man had already succeeded in breaking up the congregations at Lochabber, Lochiel, and Lachute; and he was now travelling Glengarry, like Pat at Donnybrook Fair, challenging anyone to fight him. The people were disturbed, and the faith of some was being shaken. Mr. Gordon was no lover of controversy, but he could not remain indifferent while the armies of the living God were thus daily defied.

He accepted the challenge. It was decided to meet each evening for ten nights and discuss the disputed question under the ordinary rules of debate. The first night came. At least twelve hundred persons were present to hear the combatants. We cannot go into particulars. Suffice it to say that Mr. Gordon, surrounded by his Glengarry Highlanders, swept everything before him like a Western tornado. The debate came to an end the first evening, for the opponent never showed up again.

After this, Mr. Gordon led the people in the

erection of a large and beautiful church at Indian Lands. His own people were liberal but poor; and to raise the necessary funds he went home to Scotland. His mission was cordially commended to the sympathy and liberality of the Scotch people, by such eminent men as Dr. Guthrie, Dr. Duff, Dr. Candlish, Dr. Thomson and others. So commended, it was, as might be expected, highly successful.

The opening of the new church was made the occasion for earnest and persevering prayer for an outpouring of the Spirit. These prayers were heard; and from 20th July, 1864, till August, 1865, "no twenty-four hours of the whole year passed away that the walls of that sacred house did not resound with the voice of praise and prayer." Night after night the place was packed. There were many enquirers. Mr. Gordon took charge of the young men, Mrs. Gordon looked after the young women, and the elders talked with the old people. Many were born again, and upwards of one hundred were added to the church. Among them were not a few who afterwards studied for the ministry and most of whom are still living. The following names may be given: Rev. Colon McKeracher, Rev. D. McKeracher, Rev. D. McRae, of British Columbia; Rev. D. B. McRae, of Collingwood; Rev. Mr. Bennett, of Montreal, Rev Mr. McGregor, and Rev. James Stewart.

Mr. Gordon was inducted into the charge of the Harrington congregation on July 4th, 1871. Here for nineteen years he labored earnestly and effectively, preaching three times each Sabbath—first a Gaelic service, then immediately after, an English service, and then English service in the evening. For the first eight years, the evening service was held one Sabbath in the church, the next in Mr. McLean's bush, east of the village, and the next in Mr. Murray's orchard, to the west. These outdoor meetings were largely attended, and greatly enjoyed by preacher and people. Many will long remember the powerful voice borne on the still evening air, warning, pleading, exhorting with all fidelity and affection.

In stature, Mr. Gordon lacked less than an

inch of six feet, straight as a needle, and military in his bearing. His eyes, usually of a soft, melting blue, sometimes in the pulpit fairly blazed with excitement.

As a preacher he was *sui generis* and paid little attention to the ordinary rules of homiletics. He was a thorough Calvinist, seldom preaching without keeping the distinctive Calvinistic doctrines prominently in the front. His oratory was not the gentle, flowing stream, but the rushing, roaring torrent. He frequently took his manuscript or notes into the pulpit, but after the first few minutes, he forgot all about them. He was not what is usually called a textual preacher, but he said many good things and expressed many grand evangelical truths in his sermon, and was regarded by his own people as a good preacher.

He was practical to a fault. Once, preaching on "Wheat and Chaff," he observed some of his congregation listless. Suddenly he stopped and shouted, "Wheat! Wheat, $1.75 per bushel in Stratford! Instantly every eye was open and every head raised. "Ah," said the preacher, I don't know what wheat is in Stratford, but I see you all wake up when you hear about money; but when I offer you first class wheat out of God's own granary, you are indifferent, and go to sleep." Needless to say there were no more sleepers that day.

In one of his congregations before coming to Harrington, some of the people allowed their dogs to accompany them to the church. This was a great nuisance, and one morning when the canines were present in great numbers, Mr. Gordon, after announcing the text, said in a calm, dispassionate, but firm tone, "In dealing with this text we will first and foremost put out the dogs." The thing was done as speedily as possible, and a wholesome lesson taught Mr. Gordon's Highlanders.

At another place some of the people were in the habit of coming late to church, and what was still more annoying to the preacher, the whole congregation would turn round to see the late comer. On one of these occasions Mr. Gordon exclaimed, " Brethren, never mind turning round; it's J. B—— and his new wife; I married them last Wednesday."

Preaching on Zacchæus he described him as a " *duine beag bronach cosmhuil ri Ian so* " pointing to his light-weight precentor, (a weak little man like John here).

Nature was to him an open book which he loved to read. Once when attending the General Assembly at Winnepeg, he went with others across the prairies. One day looking out of the car window across the vast expanse, he exclaimed, " It's all mine " (stretching out his hand). When every eye in the car was upon him, he said, " All things are yours," etc.

He held strong views on the temperance question, and was not afraid to announce them. When, in 1884, the Canadian Temperance Act was being submitted in Oxford, Mr. Gordon was among its foremost advocates. One night the meeting was in Kintore church. Both sides were announced to speak. E. King Dodds appeared on behalf of the liquor men, to oppose the measure. The church was packed full. Many clergymen of different denominations were present. It was arranged that a number of ministers would speak, then King Dodds would reply, after which Mr. Gordon would give the closing speech. He did, and the scene will never be forgotten. He dealt with the whiskey champion's pleas for licensed bar-rooms, and as he went on depicting the domestic brutality and destruction, temporal and eternal, of the liquor traffic, he warmed up to his subject, his eyes glared like a tiger's, his voice roared like a lion's, his hands gesticulated like a madman's. He fairly danced with excitement.

"My soul," exclaimed he, "abhors this traffic in the bodies and souls of men; God could not be God if He didn't hate it, and there can be no devil who doesn't love it. And shall we continue to license and protect it? In behalf of childhood and womanhood and manhood; in behalf of the gospel of Christ I appeal to you my friends against this enemy of our race, this demon of hell."

Under this terrific fire the liquor champion cowered, and left the platform, and took his seat near the door. But Mr. Gordon, still pouring forth a torrent of denunciation, soon followed him. The crowd cheered vociferously, and King Dodds, concluding that under the circumstances absence of body was better than presence of mind, quickly seized his hat and fled from the building. But the excitement was too great for Mr. Gordon, who suffered for weeks after with nervous prostration.

Mr. Gordon has been described in one of our church papers as "one of the manliest men that ever served the Presbyterian Church in Canada." "He could, and often did," continues the same writer, "stand up alone for his convictions."

He was often called to contend earnestly for the faith, but to a wonderful degree he was able to eliminate offensive personalities from the discussion, and never did he emerge from the contest with besmirched garments.

The late Samuel Wilberforce, Lord Bishop of Oxford, was a very learned ecclesiastic, and quite a polemic. He was, however, a man of polished manners, and very courtly address. Indeed, many regarded him as too disposed to say pleasant things, and so he came to be dubbed "Soapy Sam." One day he was the guest in some great house, when a child, noways awed by his greatness, ran up to him, and asked, "Why do people call you 'Soapy Sam?'"

He took the question good-naturedly, and placing the child on his knee, said, "I will tell you, my darling. It is because I very often get into hot water, but always come out clean!" So our friend, Mr. Gordon was frequently in hot water, but we have never heard of an instance when he did not come out clean.

Mr. Gordon, while faithful, was kind and generous in dealing with offenders. John G., an adherent of his congregation, was a victim of strong drink. One day Mr. Gordon found him lying drunk in the ditch. He took him up, shook him well, asking him, " What brought you here John? The drunken man made prompt and correct answer, "Hic-hic—sin, Mr. Gordon, sin."

On another occasion he found the same man paralyzed with drink. He took him to the manse, put him to bed, and next morning the drunkard woke up amazed to find that he had slept all night in his minister's house.

A poor girl, a member of his church, had been betrayed; but her betrayer made what reparation was in his power by marrying her. However, both had to appear before the session. There were a number of "Lachlan Campbells" in that session. Many severe things were said, and it was proposed to expel the guilty couple. Mr. Gordon, for a time, listened in silence to all the hard speeches; but he could stand it no longer, and with tears streaming down his cheeks he sprang to his feet, stood by the poor weeping woman, and shaking his fist defiantly at his elders, exclaimed, " Let him that is without sin cast the first stone at her."

In private life he was extremely warm-hearted and loveable. A few weeks ago the writer interviewed him at his present home in London, Ont. I found him recovering from severe illness, but bright and cheerful, rejoicing in the Lord. He talked of Dr. Willis, the keenest logician the Canadian Church has ever had; of Dr. Chalmers, the great Free Church leader in Scotland; and of W. C. Burns, the famous missionary, to whom under God he owed his conversion. He spoke hopefully of the Canadian Church to-day. Then he took down his bagpipes, the gift to his father from the late Duke of Gordon, and played with spirit that pibroch that never fails to stir the Highland heart—"Mackintosh's Lament." It was a fine scene, not readily to be forgotten, the old man approaching his four score years, buoyant as a boy, and happy as if already by anticipation in heaven. Before separating, we, on our knees, commended each other to God and to the Word of His grace.

In the portrait, at the beginning of this chapter, Mrs. Gordon appears with her husband. She is well entitled to this place for in the highest sense she was his "better half." She was a woman of excellent education and lofty piety. Her quiet and pleasant manner, and the kindly interest she took in the concerns of the congregation endeared her very much to the hearts of the people. The existence of "Gordon Mission Bands" in the Presbyteries of Stratford,

Paris, and other places will continue as monuments to her memory. She belonged to a highly intellectual family, including the late Robertson Smith, Professor of Hebrew in Cambridge College; Rev. Andrew Murray, the author of so many well-known works on the Christian life; Miss Robertson, a well-known author; and her own son Charles, an able minister and a brilliant writer.

Mr. and Mrs. Gordon were married at Sherbrooke in 1851, and until her death, in 1890, she wrought to the limit of her strength, yea, and beyond it, in doing the Lord's service—teaching a Bible class that often had more than 100 members in it, visiting the sick, relieving the poor. She organized all the Presbyterian Auxiliaries of the Women's Foreign Missionary Society in the Stratford Presbytery, and many other auxiliaries and mission bands throughout the country. She will long be remembered.

CHAPTER XXIII

PIONEER METHODISM IN ZORRA

"Give me one hundred preachers who fear nothing but sin and desire nothing but God, and I care not a straw whether they be clergymen or laymen; they alone will shake the gates of hell, and set up the kingdom of heaven upon earth." —JOHN WESLEY.

IT was in the year 1823, early in the spring, before the trees had burst into bud, or the song of birds heard in the silent forest, that a Methodist first set foot in Zorra. Not long after came those brave pioneers, Robert Ford, Wm. Land, Peter Alyea, Henry Larue, Barnabas Ford, David Ford, Isaac Burdick, Alexander Sweet, John Gordon, Thomas Piper, Grout, and Jacobs. A few years later Christopher Williams, Ira Day, Benjamin Thornton, Eldridge Gee, with their families, entered; and about the year 1830, George H. Harris, Thomas

Couke, John Couke, John Wilkerson, Joshua Youngs, Ralph Kent, Levi Warren, Horace Dean, and John McDonald. They had come, some from the land of heather, and some from the United States, but all set bravely to work to hew out for themselves homes in the wilds of Zorra.

Their religion they brought with them, and morning and night the Bible was read and the Wesleyan Hymns were sung with as much fervor as in the days, when, in the old land, John Wesley held sway over the multitude.

Once in two weeks, the circuit minister arrived, and service was held in school-houses, dwelling-houses, or even in barns, where logs cut and rolled there for the purpose, made substantial, if not very comfortable seats. Besides these fortnightly meetings the scattered Methodist families would, on stated Sunday afternoons, join in a "love feast," followed by a class meeting, at which one of the class leaders presided.

On one of these occasions, a young man, a stranger to the ways of Methodism, was present. The good woman who sat next to him at the head of the class, was of an emotional temperament. When addressed by the leader she burst into tears and answered his kindly questioning only with sobs. The young man, expecting that his turn would come next, and fearful lest he might be expected to follow his neighbor's example, became visibly embarrassed. His confusion increased when the leader, turning to him, gravely enquired of him how he felt. Blushing violently, the youth stammered forth, "Very well, thank you, sir; how are you?"

The difficulties under which the minister labored few now can realize. The circuit embraced a district extending from Ingersoll to St. Marys—towns which were then in size scarcely worthy of a name, and the only approaches to which were by Indian trails. A circuit of about forty miles, he covered in two weeks, preaching usually in two places in one day. In his saddle-bags he carried Bibles, Testaments, hymn books, and such other books as "The Memoirs of Dr. Adam Clarke" and "Guide to Truth," which he sold or gave to people along the way. His was a life of hardship and self-denial. His salary of twelve dollars a month admitted of few luxuries, and neither man nor horse fared sumptuously on such food as the settler could provide. During the cold weather the minister slept rolled in a home-spun blanket in front of the log fire of his cabin; the one room of which served as parlor, kitchen, and bedroom for the entire family; but during the summer months his nights were spent in the hay mow in the barn, where, with the stars gleaming through chinks in the roof, and often with the four-footed beasts of the field for company, he slept the sleep which only the toilers of earth can know.

Rev. Mr. Corson was the pioneer Methodist preacher of Zorra. A man of Pauline type, he counted it no hardship to journey from dawn till dark in the bitter cold of a Canadian winter, making his way through unbroken country, often with no path but a forest "blaze," that he might speak a few words of cheer to the handful of people eagerly awaiting him at his next appointment.

Following Mr. Corson, came Rev. Edmund Stoney, a faithful preacher, in whose earnest nature ran a quaint vein of humor. "What do you think," he enquired once of one of his hearers, "of that old prophet in Bethel, right where the wicked king Jeroboam had established the worship of the golden calf, and never opened his mouth against it. He was an old backslider. But the death of the good prophet from Judah, caused by the old Bethel prophet lying to him, may have brought him to repentance." It was an attractive way of telling the story.

Rev. Mr. Armstrong, the third regular minister, was of a deeply spiritual mind. Often the congregation waited within, while he, outside on his knees, pleaded for the Spirit's presence, without which he could never preach. Then when his prayer was answered and he re-entered the building, it is said that none could listen unmoved as, with his heart burning with love to God and man, and his face all aglow with the very light of heaven, he told the story of Jesus and His love.

He was succeeded by Rev. Mr. Pettit, and later Rev. Mr. Holtby, Rev. Mr. Gray, Rev. Mr. Wakefield, Rev. Mr. Kennedy, had in turn charge of the circuit.

Zealously as these devoted Christians worked, so large was the field and so scattered the people that little could have been accomplished had it not been for the help given by the local preachers, or class leaders as they were more familiarly called. Prominent among these was Thomas Brown, of East Nissouri. His was a peculiarly joyful nature, ever living on Pisgah's height, and commonly known as "Great Heart." At the love-feast, it is said, his voice was always raised in thanksgiving. He was a universal favorite, and so successful was he as a preacher that at length he was ordained. After his death a memoir of his life was published in book form.

Another highly esteemed class leader was George H. Harris. He was specially gifted with the Spirit, and this appeared in his prayers. It is said by one who can recall his teaching that "at prayer meeting he seemed to be in the immediate presence of the Holy One and to lift others with him."

Frequently on the Sabbath, Mr. Harris preached on the 16th line, East Zorra, riding in one day the entire distance there and back to his home, a distance of about forty miles. Once when asked by a friend if he did not feel the journey wearisome, "Long!" he exclaimed, "I never find it so; I spend the time in prayer and meditation, and the distance seems as nothing."

Other local preachers were Isaac Burdick, John Symons, Horace Dean (who afterwards entered the ministry), Alexander Nasmyth. The latter while serving his country as one of the Edinburgh militia in England during the Napoleonic war, owed his conversion, under God's grace, to the preaching of a Methodist layman, who was the sergeant-major of another regiment. An extract from a biographical sketch of Mr. Nasmyth, written by Rev. Matthew Holtby, which appeared at the time of his death in the *Christian Guardian* of December, 1846, gives some conception of the spirit of Methodism as evinced in its early followers:

"About fourteen years ago, he emigrated from Scotland to this country and settled at Embro. He invited the Methodist people to his place. A small class was formed of which he was the leader; every Sabbath he held a meeting among the society and others, and read, sang, and prayed, and made such remarks as he thought likely to be useful; and these services were rendered a blessing to his hearers. He had remarkably clear views of truth, a ready utterance and a concise, pointed manner of expression. Few, indeed, could remain unmoved while, with a heart flaming with love to God and man, he would pray them "in Christ's stead, be ye reconciled to God." Influenced by this great principle, love, he was a stranger to sectarian bigotry; he was constant in his attendance on the means of grace in the Presbyterian Church, of which he was a member to the day of his death. He was a man of much prayer, and his stated times of private retirement were indeed times of refreshing."

His house was a home for the preachers who travelled the circuit.

There were other influences at work at the same time, moulding the character of the rising generation. One of the first, if not the first school teacher in Zorra, Miss Nancy Brink, was an earnest, active young Christian, a member of the Methodist Church, who, in the year 1824, taught in a log school-house on the side-line south of where Embro now stands. She would at times, after school hours, plead with tears for her pupils to come to the Saviour. A hoary-headed man of God, still living says: "My first religious convictions were through her influence.

During a religious revival which was due chiefly to the labors of Horace Dean, the girls and young women who had been converted and who were attending the day school south of Embro, where the meetings were held, would go at the noon recess down the hill to the edge of the woods, and there hold a prayer meeting.

With rare exceptions, the Methodists were on terms of only cool friendship with their Presbyterian brethren. Between the two denominations there existed a certain rivalry which often made itself apparent at unexpected times, and sometimes under rather amusing circumstances.

Among the Lowland Scotch who came to Zorra in the early thirties was a pious, liberal-minded Wesleyan, who, in order that he and his family might enjoy regular church privileges, united with the Presbyterians, and became a zealous worker in that church, although at the same time actively employed, as opportunity offered, in supporting Methodism. The Presbyterians viewed this course of action with silent disapprobation for some time. Finally one of the elders, also a Lowland Scotchman, decided to put an end to this state of affairs. Cautiously he approached the subject, "We've been thinkin', sir, a good time back o' makin' you an elder, Mr.——, but," with an ominous shake of the head, "if so be that you become one, it'll na do to be encouragin' they Methody folk aroun'. Maun, maun," in a sudden burst of indignation, "they're na fit for the like o' you!"

A Methodist minister found occasion once to reprove his people for their irregular attendance at divine service. Unconsciously he paid a tribute to Presbyterianism. "You want the gospel peddled to your firesides," he said, "while the Presbyterians, who don't claim to have half of your religion, will walk ten miles to listen to their dry preachers."

Dating from the visit of Rev. W. C. Burns to Zorra, this feeling of rivalry gradually disappeared, until now perfect friendship and harmony exist between the two denominations.

Slowly the little band of Methodists increased in numbers. Other names, such as Father Allan, John Adams, John F. Matheson, John McCombs, the Rusts, Hallacks, and Dixons were added to the roll.

For many years the old school-house at Cody's Corners was used as a meeting-place. Three services, Episcopal Methodist, Wesleyan, and Baptist, were held each Sunday.

There was one of these early preachers who, although not a Methodist, but a Baptist, must not be overlooked here. This was "Father Beardsall," as he was commonly called. He was a man of strong personality, and great devotedness to his work. His home was south of Ingersoll, but for twenty years he drove regularly to Cody's Corners, and preached, with no reward but the consciousness of doing his duty and seeing the Lord's blessing upon his labors.

On one memorable occasion, Rev. Mr. Callamore, an Episcopal Methodist, was drawn into a controversy with Elder Wilson of the Baptist denomination. For three days the subject of infant or adult baptism was debated in the meeting-house, while people of all denominations flocked to hear the disputants, many travelling considerable distances.

The Wesleyans were the first to enter Embro, meeting in the school-house which was situated very near the site of the present building; afterwards meeting in the Temperance Hall, the upper storey of a frame building, situated on the corner of Commissioner and Argyle Streets.

In 1854 the Episcopal Methodists erected the first Methodist chapel in the township. It stood on the summit of the hill south of Embro, a little frame building capable of holding not more than two hundred people, but it represented the loving toil of many days. Twenty years later a comfortable brick church was erected in the village, and the old building was removed. The cemetery which surrounded the little frame chapel is still occasionally used for the interment of some aged member of a family, whose desire it was to be placed beside the honored dead of long ago. The hillock with its many marble slabs with quaint inscriptions, sometimes overgrown with moss or hidden by the roses which have clambered over them, is a place of interest to visitors to the village.

In the month of February, 1856, Rev. Mr. Huntsburgher, who had come to Embro during the previous year, began a series of revival services in the Youngsville school-house. The whole township became interested, and it was soon found necessary to change the place of meeting to Embro, where for six weeks services were held. A number of the Presbyterian elders joined heartily in the work, and many people of all denominations experienced a change of heart.

Among these were the late Joseph Laycock and wife, parents of the Rev. John Laycock, now actively engaged in Christian work as a minister of the Methodist Church in the North-west Territories.

The above short and necessarily imperfect sketch of "Pioneer Methodism in Zorra" will show that while this Church was not, for evident reasons, the strongest numerically, yet she was the first to enter the field; and to-day she can point with laudable pride to her brave men and women who "loved God and feared sin, and set up the kingdom of heaven" in Zorra.

CHAPTER XXIV

ZORRA'S FAMOUS MISSIONARY

(Rev. George Leslie Mackay, D. D.)

" In these deserts let me labor,
On these mountains let me tell,
How He died—the blessed Saviour,
To redeem a world from hell."

ONE of Zorra's sons effected a revolution in the Presbyterian Church of Canada. In the year 1854, Dr. Alex. Duff visited this continent, and the result of his burning eloquence was the appointment of a committee for the establishment of an independent Canadian foreign mission, in connection with the western section of the Presbyterian Church. In the eastern section they had already been aroused to action by Dr. Geddie, and had begun work in the New Hebrides. But a foreign mission committee and a foreign mission are not identical. Sixteen years had passed

REV. G. L. MACKAY, D.D.

(ZORRA'S FAMOUS MISSIONARY)

OFFERS TO BE A MISSIONARY

before they found the first foreign missionary. Several attempts were made without success. On three occasions calls were extended to ministers whose Presbyteries refused to release them from their congregations.

In 1871 the Church had just one ordained missionary, the Rev. James Nisbet, laboring amongst the Indians at Prince Albert. It is not surprising that the Foreign Mission Committee felt somewhat depressed, and so expressed themselves to the Synod.

But the turning point came. In June, 1855, the members of the Committee had agreed to hold a concert of prayer every Saturday evening, and through the *Record* to invite the co-operation of others, in seeking a blessing upon their work. These prayers were about to be answered.

George Leslie Mackay, son of God-fearing parents in Zorra, who had just completed his theological course in Princeton Seminary, N. J., offered his services to the Committee. His mind was made up that his life should be spent among the heathen; but before applyng elsewhere, he felt it to be his duty to seek the patronage of his own Canadian Church, and, if possible, lead the Canadian Church into more aggressive work. The offer was accepted, and it was agreed, after a good deal of correspondence, that he should go to labor amongst the Chinese in Formosa.

The English Presbyterian Church had begun work in southern Formosa in 1863, and they cordially invited the Canadian Church to co-operate with them in that island. The proposal was favorably entertained, but the Committee wisely left the final decision to the missionary when he arrived in the field. Strong inducements were offered to settle at Swatow, but Mr. Mackay resolved first to see Formosa. He visited the Southern Mission and then, accompanied by two of the missionaries, Dr. Dickson and the Rev. Hugh Ritchie, he visited Tamsui in the north, and there, on the 9th March, 1872, decided, with the full consent of his companions, to plant the standard of the Cross. Thus began the first foreign mission of the western section of the Presbyterian Church; with it began a revival of foreign mission interest, resulting in steadily increasing contributions, enlargement of the staff, and expansion of the work.

Dr. Mackay is below the average height, broad-shouldered, deep-chested, without superfluous flesh, of swarthy complexion, and has an eye that never falls in the presence of danger. Highland blood without alloy flows through his veins. Under excitement his Celtic fire leaps into flame, and his intensity is contagious. Audiences are swayed and mastered by his fervid eloquence, and sometimes angered by his fearless and direct denunciation of selfish disobedience to his Master's last command.

Immediately after his appointment he spent some months visiting congregations in the interests of his work. The reception was not inspiring. He afterwards spoke of that period as the glacial age of the Presbyterian Church. Ten years after he returned, and his reception was enthusiastic. Immense audiences thronged to hear him. The Church had somewhat awakened to the importance of the work and to her new responsibility. This was largely due to the story he had to tell. His mission was remarkably successful. His thrilling letters had been read with intense interest. The narrative of his work had been read and repeated and commented upon in the pulpit and by the fireside. The Church only knew him by name and longed to hear and see the man whom God had so signally honored. Fears were sometimes expressed lest the bodily presence might not sustain the enchantment of distance. All such fears were disappointed. He came and conquered, and returned to Formosa a greater hero than when he had arrived.

One of the surprises to his friends on this visit was that he had been able to keep himself abreast of the times in literature and science. He had collected what is regarded as one of the best museums in the orient, and is himself accounted an authority on the geological and ethnological history of the island. Attention was given to these subjects both to keep his own mind in health and as a part of the educational equipment of his students. It was on the occasion of this visit, and in recognition of his work and attainments in scholarship, that the Senate of Queen's College conferred upon him the degree of Doctor of Divinity. Not always is that distinction so worthily bestowed.

Not primarily, however, in temperament or health, or scholarship does his success lie. He was born and reared in a home in which the Bible was reverently read as a message from God to man, and Mackay has ever regarded it as such. What is written there is to him the Word of God. "Go ye into all the world" was a direct command to him from the Lord Jesus Christ, and as such he obeyed. With as much confidence did he accept the assurance that in going forth the Lord would go with him and would supply all his need. The simplicity of that faith appeared when travelling across the continent of America in his first outward journey. There were no through tickets with such other facilities for travel as are common now. He had to deal with different railway companies and seek as he could to secure such special privileges as were granted. But when asked for his credentials he had none, and naturally turned to his Bible, on the fly-leaf of which was an inscription indicating that he was a missionary on his way to China. That was accepted and the privilege granted. In hours of loneliness by sea and by land, or in the midst of a Chinese mob, he turned with the same composure and simplicity of faith to the promise. "God is our refuge and strength." He had gone forth at the Lord's command, how could the promise fail? It seemed as impossible as that the sun should fail to rise. His Highland loyalty to the Word of God had never been shaken in either cottage or church or college by any of the doubtful and doubt producing discussions of recent scholarship.

To the faithful discipline of the humble Christian home in Zorra, may in no small measure be traced the human side of the wonderful work which God hath wrought in Formosa.

The island is liable to be visited at certain seasons of the year with a deadly malarial fever, and the natives often succumb in a few hours. Dr. Mackay has suffered much from it, and has, indeed, been frequently at death's door; but his iron constitution, along with indomitable strength of will, has enabled him thus far to withstand this implacable foe.

The story of Dr. Mackay acquiring a knowledge of a difficult foreign language is very interesting. After several vain attempts, he one day saw a dozen boys herding water-buffalo and made advances to them. They at first fled. The second approach was more successful. On the third day they stood their ground, examined his watch, clothes, and hands, and were ever after friends. He spent with them four or five hours a day, and learned from them more of the language than in any other way. In five months he attempted his first sermon in Chinese, from the text, "What must I do to be saved?" Several of these boys were afterwards converted, and one became a student and preacher.

The only house available had been intended for a stable. It was on the side of a hill, and through it streams of water flowed when the rains fell. Here he slept and studied, dined and received callers, who were uncomfortably numerous. The haughty literati who, in China as sometimes elsewhere, imagine they have exhausted the stores of knowledge, would strut into his room, look around with a curl on the lip, take up the Bible or other book, look at it, cast it on the ground with a grunt of contempt, and strut out again. Pride comes before a fall. Soon these same men ventured into a discussion, and bye-and-bye discovered that there were some things after all they did not know.

Amongst the many visitors came a young man of more than ordinary intelligence who asked many questions. He returned bringing others with him for discussion, and finally acknowledged himself a believer in the new doctrine. Dr. Mackay, anticipating the advantage to himself and his mission of securing the allegiance of a young man of character and ability, had prayed, and in A Hoa the prayer was answered.

The second Sabbath of February, 1873, is a day of tender memory. It was but a year after he had landed in Tamsui, yet five men boldly declared themselves in the face of an angry mob, and were received by baptism into the Christian Church. The following Sabbath, for the first time, the Lord's Table was spread in north Formosa. It was also the first time the missionary presided at such a service; and to the new converts it was a solemn and mysterious performance. When the warrant for the ordinance was read, after the Scottish fashion, one of the converts broke down completely, sobbing out, "I am unworthy, I am unworthy." He retired for a season, and after some time alone, he returned and partook of the sacred emblems.

With the blessing of God upon the faithful labors of the missionary, and those associated with him, the churches multiplied, until there were over sixty in all, with a native pastor in charge of each. "The taking of Bang-Kah," as related in "From Far Formosa," is one of the most thrilling missionary stories on record.

In 1884 trouble arose between the French and Chinese in Tonquin. The result was that Formosa was attacked, and Tamsui and Kelung bombarded. It was a time of great anxiety on the part of the missionaries. Every foreigner was suspected of being in league with the French. All Christians were, of course, supposed to be allied with the missionary. Torture and death were threatened against all converts. Chinese soldiers ground their long knives in the presence of Christians, and sometimes brandished them over the heads of the children, and swore that they would all be cut to pieces when the first barbarian shot was fired. The first shot was fired, and destruction of chapels, torture of Christians, and looting of property began. At Sin-tiam the mob entered the chapel, found the Communion roll, and marked every member as a victim. Thirty-six families at that once prosperous station were left homeless and penniless.

At Tamsui, during the bombardment, Dr. Mackay was asked to go aboard a British man-of-war which had sailed into the harbour for the protection of British subjects. This he declined to do, preferring, if need be, to suffer with his students and converts. After the war, representations were made to the Chinese Commander-in-chief as to the losses of mission property, and without delay or investigation an indemnity of ten thousand Mexican dollars was paid. At Sin-tiam and elsewhere better churches were erected than those destroyed, and the people said, "What fools we were to destroy the old chapels. Look, now the chapel towers above our temple. It is larger than the one we destroyed. If we touch this one, he will build a bigger one. We cannot stop the barbarian missionary."

The policy of the mission from the beginning has been to train a native minister. The greatest work in a mission is not the conversion of a few souls. It is rather the organization of a church, an agency that will go on converting souls long after the missionary has ceased his labors.

At Tamsui a college was built with funds contributed by friends in Oxford, his native county, and is for that reason called "Oxford College." Alongside of it is another building of the same dimensions for the education of women.

Dr. Mackay never visited stations alone. He was always accompanied by a number of students, who were taught by the way; and thus long before college buildings were erected, academic work was done. Theory and practice went hand in hand. They cultivated in the chapels the art of communicating the truths learned in their peripatetic classes.

In the girls' school women of all ages were taught, some becoming Bible women, others workers at home, and others the wives of elders and preachers, each in her own way making a contribution to the cause.

The experiences of the French invasion were repeated in the recent Japanese war. The enemy took advantage of the opportunity for persecution and plunder. Many Christians fled and many were slain, and the mission was greatly reduced in numbers. The rebels not only harassed the Japanese, but, as heartless robbers, captured defenceless Formosans, who had to be ransomed by friends or were tortured to death. The stations where mission work was not disturbed, were few indeed. In the year 1897, there were 436 deaths and 227 removals elewhere.

These trying times were succeeded by the

bubonic plague, which appeared for the first time in Formosa. Locusts also appeared for the first time, aud what is nearly as uncommon, a drought that threatened starvation to many. In 1898 much loss and hardship were sustained by typhoons which completely carried away two chapels; three were utterly ruined, and sixteen greatly damaged. There was much loss of life through these various causes. The mission has been tried as by fire during nearly the whole of its history, but the missionary does not retain the word "discouragement" in his vocabulary.

This is amongst the most interesting and noticeable of modern missions, and the name of George Leslie Mackay will be enrolled as a devoted and successful missionary, who has completely identified himself with his work and with the people for whose salvation he labors. His wife is a Chinese lady who has proved a true helpmeet. His two daughters are married to two Chinese preachers. All his interests are centred in Formosa and there will he end his days. "He that loseth his life, saveth it," is for such the amplest reward.

CHAPTER XXV

WHAT SHALL THE HARVEST BE?

"Men, my brothers, men the workers, ever reaping
  something new :
That which they have done but earnest of the things
  that they shall do." —TENNYSON.

THE task I undertook is now nearly accomplished. I lay down the pen with mingled feelings of disappointment and gratitude,—disappointment because of the many imperfections of my work, and gratitude that I have been enabled, during fragments of time snatched from a busy pastorate, to speak some kind words concerning good men and women to whom we owe very much. The work has been to me a very delightful one, causing me, in a sense, to live over again the days

"When hearts were light as ony feather,
Free frae sorrow, care and strife ;
Before the clouds began to gather
That dim the noon-tide sky of life."

The memory of the pioneers of Zorra is worthy of being cherished; the reader of the foregoing chapters, will, I think, agree with me that these humble toilers of the forest, though possessed of little wealth or learning, yet knew their Bible, cherished true love to God and a genuine sympathy for one another; and in laying the foundations of society in this new land, showed marvellous industry, patience, perseverance. They have bequeathed to us sound minds and healthy bodies, a rich country, and a good hope through grace.

But we must not live in the past. Our eyes were not put in the back of our heads, that we might be always looking backwards. Last summer's sunshine will not paint the flowers of this summer. We cannot live on memories. The nobility of our fathers will not necessarily make us noble. Changing Longfellow a little I would say :—

> " Lives of good men all remind us
> We can make our lives sublime."

And this is especially true when the good are united to us by nature and by grace, and we have their example and their prayers to encourage us. Shall we prove ourselves the worthy sons of noble sires? They died in the hope that we would fill their places: shall not their hope be realized in fact?

What shall the harvest be? What will be the record of the next seventy or eighty years? Will the future be worthy of the past? As a new country we have great opportunities and great responsibilities. We are laying the foundation of what will yet be a magnificent edifice? Shall we not do our work well? To change the figure:—We stand almost at the fountain-head, and can direct the stream. That stream shall one day be a mighty river. Shall it be foul or clear? To drop all figure:—Canada will develop; and the question that should concern us most is, shall she develop along moral lines? Will the Home, the Church, the School, the Sabbath, continue to have the same warm place in the affections of the generations yet to come that they had in the hearts of our pioneer fathers? If so we fear not the future. Happy is the people whose God is the Lord.

CPSIA information can be obtained at www.ICGtesting.com
Printed in the USA
LVOW08s2202110913

352011LV00001B/28/P